EDDIE'S DESERT ROSE

ಆಆಆಆಆಆಆಆಆಆಆಆಆಆ

A NOVEL

VINCENT MEIS

Enjoy the book.
Vincent
9/29/11

The characters and events in this book are fictitious. Any similarity to real persons, living or dead, is coincidental and not intended by the author.

Printed in The United States of America
Cover design by Martin Salazar
Cover photo by Martin Salazar and Gilberto Leon
Interior design by Rose Rock

FIRST EDITION

ISBN-13: 978 1463746810

EDDIE'S DESERT ROSE

for my father
William A. Meis, Sr.

ACKNOWLEDGMENTS

I would like to thank all my family members, friends, and colleagues for their encouragement and suggestions after reading early drafts, listening to podcasts of chapters, and reading the ebook version.

I would particularly like to thank Donna Hanelin for her careful reading and comments; my book club, especially Gilberto Leon for choosing the book as one of our monthly selections; and Martin Salazar for his help with the cover design. I should also mention Jerry Day, who came up with some last minute corrections.

I would like to express a heartfelt gratitude to my brothers and sisters, their spouses, nieces and nephews for their continuing support, but especially my brother, Bill, who read a very early draft and is always the first to give encouragement. I particularly cherish the comments made on an early version by my parents—my mother, an avid reader for as long as I can remember, and my father, who was a prolific writer of rhyming verse social commentaries.

1

IN THE NAVY

The digital clock cast a sickly green light on his wife's face. Dave leaned over and planted a kiss on her forehead. She didn't react with her usual "Umm" and he wondered if she was really asleep. The numbers on the clock changed to 5:31. It was a day like any other, but something felt different.

The dark hallway closed around him with the smell of new paint. His fingers played over the wall by the front door until he found the switch to the porch light. He flipped it, giving him enough light to turn the deadbolt and find the handle to the door, and then stepped out under the harsh bare bulb. With a steady hand he attempted to close the door without a sound, but the tiny click seemed to echo throughout the house.

The porch was a slab of concrete with a few struggling plants and an aluminum patio chair. It always reminded him of the ranch style house back in Illinois where he had grown up. But Dave Bates and his brother, Eddie, were eight thousand miles from home. For several months they had been working at the Royal Saudi Navy Academy in Dammam, Saudi Arabia.

Winter reigned in the desert, and the air was heavy with a bouquet of just watered lawn and toxic stench from the chemical plant down the road, the wind always seeming to blow in their direction. Along the path to the street was the oleander bush he kept forgetting to trim. He brushed against it and drops of water sprayed onto his black loafers. He felt a chill and zipped up the company issue nylon jacket, tugged on the collar to bring it up around his neck. He reached the sidewalk and looked up at the buttery yellow streetlamp wrapped in a misty halo.

From the building across the street, a pair of shadowy figures emerged. Dave nodded to them, and they mumbled the usual gruff, "Mornin'." The two men always hung close together and spoke in low muscular voices, ignoring Dave as they walked in the same direction but on their side of the street. The other houses along the way, identical to Dave's, gave up more men in company jackets and gray pants. It was the daily march toward the break in the fence that would funnel them from the residential compound, where the Americans lived, into the Saudi part of the base.

Outside the brightly lit training center, Dave looked up at the eastern sky where a hopeful band of pale white emerged along the horizon. He lifted his arm and popped his finger at the minaret of the mosque next door. Taking his cue, the speakers began to crackle and the woeful sound of prayer call began. Mike Sims came up beside him. "Hey, pretty good trick," he joked. He pulled the door open for Dave and said, "Quick! Let's get inside."

While the students prayed at the mosque, the teachers gathered in the lounge and plied themselves with coffee, prepared lessons, or sat dumbfounded in their cubicles staring at pictures of their families back home. The two-minute bell sounded. Dave got up and started down the hall. Through the wall of east-facing windows, he watched the sun make a final push and inch above the murky haze that hung over the Arabian Gulf. Then the clang of the second bell drove the last of the uniformed young men into their classrooms with military precision. In the empty hall he took the customary minute of silence before he had to face the students, stopping in a patch of warm sunshine.

While he soaked up the sun, he plotted how he was going to keep the students under control today. The first hour was the worst. But more on his mind was his brother and the talk he had been meaning to have with him. He wouldn't see Eddie until the mid morning break. Eddie, with a chronic case of morning phobia, had convinced the administration to give him a later starting time.

Dave took a deep breath and set his feet in motion toward his classroom down the hall. Everything was just like normal. But when he put his hand on the polished steel of the door handle, a jolt rushed down his spine and passed through his extremities. His Aunt Hazel used to say someone was walking over your grave when that happened. He shook it off and opened the door.

On the other side was the usual bedlam of uniformed young men, in every shade of skin color from tan to black, squabbling over pencils. Dave and Eddie had signed one-year contracts to teach English to Saudi naval cadets. It was their job to raise the competency of the students to a level where they could follow the naval training courses provided by retired military men from the United States. The Tanley Corporation had the contract to train the newly formed Royal Saudi Navy, a pet project of one of the King's brothers, Prince Sultan.

A green soft-cover English workbook sailed across the room and landed on the P-coat-covered head of a student trying to steal a few more moments of sleep from the confusion. A pencil, which had been snugly cradled in the book's center, fell to the floor and was quickly snatched up.

Dave sat down at the desk and opened the worn teaching manual. The class was out of lock step with the other classes in their company, so they were on a rushed schedule to catch up. He went directly to the exercises at the end of the chapter.

"Abdullah, please begin—"

"Teacher, no pencil," Fahd said in a whiney voice, his jaw dropping to accentuate his painful circumstance. His neighbor, Saleh, had a smirk on his face.

"Saleh, do you know where Fahd's pencil is?" Dave asked.

"Who me?"

"Saleh," Dave said in a raised voice. "Where is Fahd's pencil?"

"I don't know."

Since Dave had singled out Saleh, Fahd's nemesis in the class, it prompted an argument. Saleh and Fahd jumped up and faced off, posturing and lashing out at each other with the guttural thrusts of their language. The flying of fists appeared imminent.

"Muhammad, go get the chief," Dave said. He didn't like to call the chiefs, but teachers were prohibited from breaking up fights. The rules were posted on the wall.

With the threat of an officer coming, the atmosphere calmed slightly and Fahd attempted to retake his seat, mumbling something under his breath. The only word Dave understood with his limited Arabic was *ukht*, sister. Saleh snarled and, defending the honor of his sister, pushed Fahd into the desk behind him. Fahd, regaining his balance, responded with a harder shove, which sent Saleh falling back over his desk and onto the floor. The student closest to the door warned that a chief was coming, and within seconds all the cadets were seated at their desks.

A short, droopy-eyed sergeant with a paunch shuffled into the room, and all the young men snapped their knees together and sat up straight at attention. "What's problem?" he said.

"Two students were fighting," Dave answered.

"Who's fighting?" The sergeant's voice boomed over the heads of the boys sitting like robots. Their eyes, so normally full of expression, were as cold as stone. The officer glanced at Dave, and then barked something in Arabic. Saleh and Fahd began to speak at the same time. He questioned them briefly before turning back to face Dave, looking past him as if he really didn't exist.

"Small problem. Is nothing."

"But a few minutes ago—"

"Where's problem?" the officer said, sweeping his chubby arm over the rows of students sitting stiffly in their seats.

Dave knew it was pointless to argue with a chief. "I was just following the rules."

"No problem," the sergeant said. He gave a quick order to the students, who then relaxed, and he walked out.

The cadets were a blur of dark uniforms before Dave's eyes as he told himself to forget it. "Don't let them get to you. It isn't worth it. Six months to a year, and you'll be out of here."

"Don't be angry, Teacher," Saleh said.

"I'm not angry."

"The chief is Bedouin from the desert," Abdullah said. They all laughed at the modern-day insult.

"His mother is camel," said another. More laughter.

Fahd came up to Dave's desk and put his hand on Dave's shoulder. "You angry me, Teacher?"

"No, Fahd. Sit down."

Dave felt a smile emerging and starting to work its way up to the corners of his mouth despite his effort to control it. The students took notice and smiling faces spread around the classroom. It seemed they didn't want him to be unhappy.

The sea of smiles in front of Dave made him feel guilty that he often blamed the students for his less than joyful time in the Kingdom. He shouldn't have let the chief get under his skin. Eddie was constantly telling him that he needed to relax. For Eddie, the students were difficult, but at the same time endearing. He reminded Dave to look at them as individuals rather than a class of students acting out. "Sure they fight sometimes," Eddie pointed out. "But remember all the times they are sweet and friendly. Think of the times they hold hands or put a supporting arm on the shoulder of a classmate who is feeling down. Think of the times they beg for your attention and then light up when you praise them for a right answer. It's just their collective unhappiness that makes them so difficult as a group. They don't want to be here, and they've got a hell of a lot more reasons to feel frustrated than we do. They have been pulled from their families, sent to a faraway province and thrown into a regimented life. They don't know what the hell they're doing here. How would you feel?"

Dave knew Eddie was right. His brother was always open to the good in people. It was one of the things Dave most admired about him. He wished he could more like Eddie.

"You okay, teacher?" Fahd said.

"Yes, thanks. All right, everybody, open your books to page 53. Muhammad, where is the stern of the ship?"

"Who me?"

"Yes, you." All the students laughed and Dave joined in.

At the end of the second period, Dave went to the teacher's room while the cadets went out on the parade ground for marching practice and the raising of the flag to the playing of the national anthem written by an Egyptian and performed by a Pakistani band. As Dave entered the smoke-filled room, he heard just outside the window the band starting up "Anchors Aweigh," a prelude to the anthem. He didn't see Eddie, but Jerry Whitman, the English program coordinator, looked up and made a sign that he wanted to talk to him. Jerry had been standing off to one side with arms folded across his chest, head down, listening to one of the teachers complaining about a disruptive student. He had a silly smile on his face, a nearly permanent fixture there. He was a slight man with thinning brown hair and wore the blue shirt and gray slacks a couple of sizes too large. He looked like a kid in hand-me-downs.

Jerry approached Dave, still with the smile on his face. "Eddie hasn't signed it yet. Have you seen him?"

"No. I was looking for him myself."

"Tell him to come and talk to me. He's supposed to start a Company 9 class today and I need to fill him in on the procedure."

Dave was worried that Eddie had overslept again. In the last few minutes of the break he ran over to the building where single men were housed. He knocked loudly on his door. There was no answer. "Eddie, are you in there? Wake up. Eddie, open the damn door." When he still didn't answer, Dave pounded the door with his fist and walked away.

Dave hadn't spoken to Eddie since he called the night before to say he wasn't coming for dinner, the dinner that his wife, Maura, had gone to a lot of trouble fixing. The get together was to be a reconciliation of sorts. Last week's dinner hadn't gone well. Things had never been easy between Maura and Eddie. Lately things seemed worse. So when the phone the night before had produced the long ring indicating a call from outside the base, he had a suspicion it was Eddie calling to cancel.

"Hey, bro," Eddie said.

"Can't stand it when you start with 'Hey, bro.' I know something is coming I'm not going to like."

"I'm out on the road to Hofuf. The desert is so beautiful this time of day."

"You're going to be late for dinner."

"I've been on a dig."

"For what?"

"Desert roses."

"Desert what?"

"You know, those sandstone rocks that look like the petals of a rose. Khalil tells me they are formed from camel piss seeping down into the sand and petrifying."

"Who's Khalil?"

"This guy I met. He brought me out here to dig for the roses. It's magical when you find one. You touch it and feel the age of the desert, but you're afraid to pick it up, like there's a curse on it or something."

"Of course you picked it up."

"It would have been a waste of time otherwise, to come all the way out here."

"What about dinner?"

"Don't think I'm going to make it." A horn honked and Eddie muffled the phone, shouting to someone at a distance, "Be right there."

"I could come and get you."

"No, he's cool. He's Lebanese and drives a really neat green Chevy pick-up."

"That makes him okay, I guess."

"He's a nice guy. He wants to take me to meet a prince."

"A Saudi prince?"

"What other kind of princes are there around here?"

"Eddie," Dave said like a warning.

"Would you relax? This is an opportunity that doesn't happen every day. A Saudi prince in his palace. I'm not going to pass that up."

"How do you know the guy isn't bullshitting you?"

"You're so Midwestern. You sound like Albert." Albert was their stepfather and Dave bristled at being compared to him.

"You're the one that's a hick, wowing over princes and palaces."

"I'm sorry I'm not coming to dinner. I'm a shit. I know it."

"I worry about you."

"Don't do this."

"Somebody has to."

"I'll be all right. Tell Maura I'm sorry." There was another honk in the background. "Got to go. Khalil's waiting."

If Eddie had stayed out all night, he was in big trouble. Dave had spent a good part of his life covering for Eddie when he screwed up. Sometimes when they were teenagers, Eddie would stay out past their curfew and Dave had to go out and find him. He couldn't count the number of times he had lied to protect him from their parents. When was Eddie going to grow up?

At noon Dave's classes ended for the day. He stopped by Jerry's office to see if Eddie had shown up. The door was closed, but he could hear voices on the other side. He knocked. Jerry opened the door and waved him in, the silly grin replaced by a pale, haggard look.

"Dave, we were just going to look for you," said Jerry. Mike Sims, one of the lead teachers, and Bud Connors from administration stared at the floor.

"All right, what did Eddie do now?"

"Have a seat, Dave," said Jerry in a barely audible voice.

"Not if you all are going to stand up." The three sat down simultaneously. There was a creaking of office chairs and then silence.

"I know he's probably done something stupid, but you're going to give him another chance, right?"

Bud looked at Jerry. Jerry nodded.

"What's going on? Is he in jail or something?"

Jerry cleared his throat, but his voice was still barely above a whisper. "We have received word that Eddie was in an accident. It was...uh...fatal. I'm so sorry."

Dave shook his head and laughed absurdly. "You guys are kidding, right? Is this some kind of a joke?" His eyes held onto hope and his mouth twisted into a false grin. The others continued to examine the floor while the marching band started up outside within an absurdly jaunty tune and the air conditioner rumbled into compressor mode, sending out a wisp of ozone.

"Eddie died in the accident," Mike said in a quiet, slightly bewildered voice.

The words fell on him like meaningless sounds. "What?" Dave shot out of his chair and picked up a stapler off of Jerry's desk. The movement startled Jerry and his chair rolled back hitting the wall. Dave squeezed the stapler and a staple fell to the floor. He slumped back down in his chair and continued punching staples, watching them fall one by one to the ground. "No," Dave said, shaking his head. "Eddie...it must be a mistake." His voice sounded loud and hollow inside his head.

"We just got word about a half hour ago. They found his Tanley ID at the crash."

Dave focused on a yellow happy face sticker someone had stuck on the front of Jerry's desk, probably during a meeting without Jerry being aware of it. ID? Crash? What were they talking about?

"We don't have any details. A pickup truck. The accident occurred some time during the night. That's all we know." The words came from one of them, but he couldn't be sure which. He looked around the room in a daze. Everything and everyone in the place had become props in a tragic play. His mind thrashed about, looking for something to grab onto. Then the first twitch of reality appeared in one eye. He felt a ripping inside him. It spread across his face and jerked his body up out of the chair. He threw the door open and walked out.

Mike followed him into the hall. "Can I walk you home?" he said.

Dave shook his head and started to run.

"Dave, wait. I'm sorry." Mike's voice trailed off as he hurried after him. But Dave was already out the main entrance.

He walked along the navy base side of the fence that separated it from the American compound. It couldn't be true. Eddie gone? He had just talked to him the night before. He felt dizzy. Nothing made any sense. He looked over and saw activity in the lot that yesterday had been a sandy soccer field for the navy boys. Now the field was half green, transformed by Yemeni hands sticking plugs of grass into the fertilized sand. The whole world was changing. Six small, wiry Arabs worked with their baggy pants rolled up to their knees and colorful cloths tied around their heads. They moved with the grace of people comfortable with the land. Dave watched them, mesmerized by their weaving back and forth across the reclaimed earth in the ancient art of planting, singing a soulful chant as they changed the surface of the desert for their Saudi masters. He, too, was part of this greening and modernizing of Saudi Arabia, another worker bought for a price, a price about ten times what the Yemenis were being paid. Yet, when he had awakened that morning, there had been a purpose to it all—Eddie's plan. The three of them, Eddie, Maura and Dave, had left behind the ruts their lives were in. They were in Saudi Arabia to make enough money to buy a piece of land back home in California and build on it. Dave and Maura would have their dream house, Maura her studio. Eddie would build a cottage and have a garden. Though Dave and Maura had been hesitant at first, Eddie's excitement had won them over.

Dave stumbled and grabbed his stomach. The ground slipped out from under him, his legs seeming to have lost their bone. He reached for the chain-link fence, but missed, and slid to the ground. The Yemenis stopped their song and stared at him.

When Dave didn't get up from his crumpled heap below the Cyclone fence, two of the Yemeni workers ran over to him, and with muddy hands lifted him to his feet. They half-carried him to the gate that lead to the American side, but they weren't allowed to go any farther. Dave held on to the fence for a minute, and then stood up straight. He touched his heart in thanks and nodded to the two men. He took one step. Then another. He passed through the gate and dragged himself toward the imitation of suburban America where his Honda Accord sat under the carport and his wife awaited his return for lunch.

2

THE COMPOUND

Maura Haggerty Bates lay in the bath like a log in a still pond, not causing the slightest ripple in the now tepid water. Her head was uncomfortably wedged in the space where the tile wall met the edge of the tub. When they were packing she had discarded the bath pillow in an attempt to show how practical she was. Dave had urged her to pack the minimum in case they wanted to make a quick getaway. It was their first experience living overseas and Saudi Arabia wasn't known as an easy place to live.

She thrust her arm up out of the water, and from the rack, grabbed a hand towel. She folded it in quarters and stuck it behind her. Now, with her head cushioned against the hard surface of the tub, she closed her eyes.

Through the window came the spin-chirp-spin of the water sprinklers, and she could hear the quartz clock above the toilet ticking off jerky seconds. These were the sounds that signified Saudi Arabia to her, the sprinklers keeping up the facade of suburbia in this desert land and the clock ticking off the seconds until they could leave. Nowhere was it more obvious that time equaled money.

She was sorry that Eddie hadn't shown up for the dinner because she had wanted to mend fences after the last disastrous get-together.

She had brought up the story of a Saudi woman who was raped in Jeddah. Everybody in the ex-pat community was talking about it. "Can you believe it?" Maura had said. "She was sentenced to a hundred lashes and the man got off Scott free. The man's testimony was taken as fact. Women aren't believed. Too emotional, they say. They accused her of breaking the law of segregation of sexes because her husband forgot to pick her up at the market. It's outrageous. You guys have no idea what it's like to be a woman in this country."

"Hey, being gay here isn't exactly a cakewalk, never knowing if you are going to end up in jail for flirting with the wrong guy," said Eddie.

"How can you compare? You shouldn't be flirting in public anyway. God, be a little discreet." It had turned into a shouting match and Dave had to jump in to play the referee, his designated role.

Maura had thought she was prepared to live in an Islamic country. But it was much tougher than she had imagined. The lack of nightlife, alcohol, and normal social interactions between men and women weren't easy for any of them. But she was certain that women suffered more, not being allowed to drive cars or eat in restaurants except when accompanied by their husbands, and then only in special screened-off family dining areas. If she dared to go into town alone on public transportation, she had to sit in the "protected" compartment in the back of the bus with its own entrance. There was only room for six women in them, and she ran the risk of being jammed in amongst a chorus of women draped in black cloth, flapping away in a language that sounded harsh to her, and smelling of spice and digested lamb. And when she went into town with Dave, there was the chance he might be cited by the religious police, who found her dress or conduct inappropriate.

A couple months back she had been cited by the *mutawain,* the Organization for the Encouragement of Virtue and Elimination of Vice. Virtue wasn't on Maura's mind that night when she went out with Dave and Eddie. They were still new in the Kingdom, and despite all the literature they had been given to read, she wasn't sure how strict she had to be.

They had been watching a video and wanted ice cream. The three of them hopped in the car to go to the Baskin-Robbins near the Safeway in Al-Khobar. Maura hadn't thought of changing her shorts—Bermuda shorts down to her knees—or her extra-large T-shirt. They came out of the ice cream place and were approached by three men in traditional Saudi dress and a policeman in uniform. Since the men carried canes, she knew that they had fallen into the hands of the *mutawain.* The oldest of the men rapped Maura on her bare calves with the bamboo pole and said, "Who is husband?"

Maura stepped back. "Stop that."

The man, looking only at Dave and Eddie, brought the cane down much harder against her calf and asked again in a louder voice, "Who is husband?"

Maura winced and dropped her pistachio ice cream cone on the pavement. "Damn you," she screamed, trembling with rage. Dave rushed toward the man with the cane, but the policeman with a hand on his rifle moved in front of him.

"I'm the husband," Dave said in a strong voice, Eddie by his side. "What's this all about?"

One of the other men with a clipboard ripped off a sheet of paper and stuck it in Dave's face. It read, "Guidelines to Our Brothers in Humanity About Proper Dress and Behavior in Saudi Arabia." Dave took the paper and stared at it while the ice cream in his other hand began to melt down over his fingers. He stopped reading to lick it up.

A crowd had gathered, and the *mutawa* asked for Dave's *igama*—his identity papers and permit to be in Saudi Arabia. Maura, now ignored, stood off to the side, still fuming. Just as she was at the point of jumping in and saying something, an Arab in Western clothes moved in behind her right shoulder and said in a low voice, "It is better you say nothing." She whipped her head around, thinking of telling him to mind his own business, but he stared straight ahead. Still without looking at her, he said, "Believe me." He was very good-looking and the concern on his face made her hold her tongue. When she looked back at the *mutawain,* the youngest of the three, peering over the shoulders of the other two like a trainee, caught Maura's gaze and a smile almost formed on his lips.

The man with the clipboard wrote down the information from Dave's *igama* on a pad of triplicate forms that looked like parking tickets. He tore off a copy of the citation and handed it to Dave. It was in Arabic.

"What do I do with this?" He shook the paper in the air. "I can't read it."

The men stared at him blankly and then walked away.

A number of times Maura had thought about the handsome Arab who stood next to her that night. While shopping at the Al-Khobar Safeway one morning, she saw him again. He met her stare with a casual smile before proceeding down the aisle. But when she saw him later at the checkout counter, he looked past her, seeming not to recognize her. She wanted to thank him for helping calm her down that night, but since the incident with the *mutawain,* she knew she had to be careful about talking to strangers in public. She followed him out the door and saw him enter a women's clothes store in the same shopping center.

Maura stood outside the store window and gazed at the elegant dresses, gowns that she would never have the occasion to wear, nor were they her taste. She entered the store and saw him behind the counter. He greeted her coolly, making her feel the great gulf between them. With her face becoming prickly hot under his stare, she couldn't bring herself to remind him who she was. Perhaps he, too, had disapproved of the way she was dressed that night. "I have to go," she said. "The bus." She ran out the door, leaving him looking bewildered. On the trip home she couldn't stop herself from thinking about the Arab, wondering what she would have done if he had pulled her into the back room and put his hands on her. She loved her husband, but life so far from home was taking its toll. She must have been crazy to agree to the Saudi plan. When Dave wasn't working, he was off playing pool with Eddie and the other guys, or participating in another pastime not permitted to women. The culture was set up so that women were stuck at home in their cloistered sections of the house, and she couldn't believe that Dave was falling into the habits of the local machismo.

With her head still cushioned against the washcloth and her eyes closed, she saw a message on the back of her eyelids. She had to change. The culture wouldn't. Sitting in a bathtub feeling sorry for herself wasn't doing anybody any good. She had to get back to painting. No one could tell her she couldn't do that. She would paint a desert and then throw splashes of vibrant color on it, gigantic flowers and people swathed in multicolored veils. She laughed at the thought. Within seconds she had conceived a whole series of canvases.

The rhythm of the sprinklers and the ticking clock was broken by a sound inside the house, the movement of steps down the hallway. Her body remained motionless in the lukewarm water while her heart began to run. The bathroom door opened slowly revealing a tall dark figure standing in the shadows of the hallway. A scream began in her throat though it could not be pushed from her lips. An impulse to modesty made her want to cover her body. She was paralyzed. He stepped into the room, focusing his emotionless brown eyes on her nakedness, and moving his thick pouty lips under a heavy moustache, he mumbled something. Although she couldn't hear what it was, she recognized the man, the salesman from the clothes store. Her mind skipped over the details of how he had gotten into her house, accepting that it was destiny that brought them together, that desire had cut through a thousand years of cultural and religious taboos, not to mention compound security. All fear was gone; instead, she began to worry about how horrible she must look with her hair unwashed and unbrushed. Her insecurities quickly passed as she felt his rugged good looks riveted on her fair features and she could already taste the exotic aroma of his lips. He seemed to drink in every part of her, her auburn hair, her green eyes, and even her freckles.

His eyes knew all her secrets. He began unbuttoning the rest of his half-open silk shirt. Inside was a gold medallion in the shape of a book resting in the thick hair of his wide chest. Letting the shirt fall carelessly to the floor, he reached down into the water. Maura watched the hair of his arm become plastered to his shiny dark skin as his gentle hand inched toward her breast.

Then the house shook with the rumble of a large truck hitting the rough spots out on the Gulf Road. She opened her eyes and there was Dave standing in the doorway.

"Dave!" Maura yelled. She jumped up out of the water and grabbed her white terrycloth robe, feeling the color in her cheeks, as if he had caught her making love with another man. "You're back. Where did the time go?"

His silence made her stop and really look at him. His face was white and his arms hung like two lead pipes at his sides.

"Is something the matter?" As soon as she said it, the question seemed ludicrous. He was on the verge of collapsing on the bathroom rug. "Dave, where's Eddie?" Ever since Eddie had called the previous evening to say he wasn't coming to dinner, Dave had been preoccupied, a worried expression putting lines on his face. She now watched his head bobbing in agony. "What is it?"

"Eddie's...Eddie's..." he struggled with the words. "Eddie's gone," he said in little more than a whisper.

"What are you talking about? What happened? Dave, tell me."

His knees gave out and he collapsed on the floor. Maura, too, felt weak and sat down on the toilet cover. She took his head in her lap and he buried his face in her wet thighs where the robe had parted. He began to cry, soft at first, unable to let it out. The pain quickly became a primal moan. It touched the mother inside her and jolted her into a bedrock of strength.

"Dave, please. Talk to me."

"An accident, a fucking accident." His words came out soggy as if drowning in his tears. "I told him to come home. He wouldn't listen."

"Dave, look at me. Eddie was killed in an accident?"

He raised his head, and in his eyes she saw a last desperate plea that it wasn't true. He dropped his head again, his whole body drained. She held him tightly, rocking him and whispering, "I'm sorry, baby, so sorry."

When his shaking stilled, she got him into the bedroom and sat him on the edge of the bed. Then she went for a glass of water and something from the medicine cabinet.

"Here take one of these." He looked at the pills in her hand as if they were poison. "It's just Valium. There you go. Now lie down. I'm right here with you." After a few minutes, she braved a question.

"What happened?"

He shook his head.

"You don't know?"

"I can't. . .I can't talk. . .about it."

"I know. But you need to. . .soon." She lay down beside him and hugged his limp body.

He began in a low voice. "They didn't have much information. An accident out on the highway."

"On is bike?"

"No, a truck. Riding in someone's truck."

"Whose truck?"

"I don't know."

She held him a long time, until his breathing became heavy and regular, then slipped her arm out from under him and went into the bathroom. In front of the mirror she picked up a brush and began working on the tangles of her wild hair. It helped her concentrate as she pieced together the jumbled fragments her life had just become. When Maura married Dave five years ago, she knew she was getting a package deal. Dave and Eddie were a team. In the trio, Eddie had provided a childlike enthusiasm, a vitality, and a solution, rational or not, for every hopeless mess. When there was a need for a plodding determination to carry things through, Dave had that. Maura had to walk a thin line between Dave and Eddie. There were times when she had to step in to save Dave from the more outrageous of Eddie's schemes—Dave agreed to most everything he proposed—causing friction between her and Eddie. She had often wondered if Eddie would ever embrace her as Dave's wife. But on the Saudi Arabia plan, Maura had sided with Eddie. It made sense to earn some money, far more than they were getting at home, money that could change their lives for the better. As much as she regretted the decision at times, she knew that in the end they would have something to show for it.

With the news of Eddie's death they had entered a new world. Maura had a much more difficult task than trying to make Eddie accept her. She would have to help her husband mend. Dave and Eddie were as close as twins, showing a brotherly bond that was far beyond anything she had experienced with her siblings. It was just the two of them now, but she knew the ghost of Eddie would always be nearby.

In the mirror, she saw movement in the bedroom and went in to find Dave standing by the bed. The only parts of him that seemed affected by the Valium were his eyes; the rest of his body appeared to be going in several directions at once.

"I've got to. . .got to go."

"Where?"

"I have to see Eddie." He started out the door.

"Wait. I'll get dressed and go with you."

He looked at her sadly, shook his head, and then continued through the door. She dressed hurriedly, but by the time she caught up with him, he was passing through the gate to the navy base, a barrier she could not cross because of the compound rules.

"Dave," she screamed. "Wait"

"I'm okay," he shouted back. "I'm okay."

Jerry wasn't in his office, so Dave went in to see Bud. Bud was what a lot of the guys referred to as a good old boy from Virginia, a short, stocky man who always looked impeccably neat. He had settled in as Tanley Project Manager, though Dave didn't know what he really did except have meetings every so often and spend a considerable amount of time composing the "Message from the PM" for the weekly newsletter.

Bud sat back in his chair with his hands behind his head. The white permanent press shirt looked as if he might burst out of it and he appeared to be composing something for the next newsletter, something very thoughtful and profound about Eddie's death. Dave by contrast looked less than the model employee with his curly brown hair tousled and heavy eyelids hanging down over his gray eyes. The shirt of his uniform, bearing the distinctive patch of the Tanley Company over the left breast pocket, was untucked. His pants were wrinkled and too short for his long legs.

Bud shook his head and let his sad eyes try to show what he hadn't yet been able to put into words. "Dave, Dave, Dave," he said, shaking his head. "This is a hell of a thing. Tell me. What can I do for ya?" He spoke in a soothing Southern drawl.

"I want to see Eddie."

"I just made reservations for you and Maura to fly back tomorrow night with the casket. Someone will take over your classes."

"I mean now. I want to see him now."

"I'm afraid that'll be difficult. After he was identified—"

"Identified?"

"Tom took care of it. I guess they don't do things the same over here. Just needed someone to say it was Eddie." Tom was Bud's administrative assistant. No one knew what he did either. When he wasn't jetting back and forth to the States, his main function seemed to be captain of the company softball team. If you weren't on the team, he didn't have the slightest idea who you were. Eddie wasn't on the team.

"I'm supposed to do that. I'm his brother."

"I understand how you feel, but Tom's taken care of it and anyway, I don't know if you'd want to see it. . .him. They said it was pretty bad, the accident, and—"

"You don't understand. I want to see Eddie." His voice was in low gear, slow and deliberate.

"Take it easy, Dave. I don't think it's possible. We've ordered one of those traveling caskets and they seal the thing right up."

"Where's Tom? Can I talk to Tom?"

"Tom's not here," came a voice from the doorway. Dave turned around to see Jerry. An alert must have gone out.

"He's on his way to the States," Bud said. "That's why he made the identification. He had to go to the airport anyway, which is by the consulate. . .that's where Eddie is, at the consulate. . .and so it seemed logical for him to do it."

"Does he even know what Eddie looks like?"

"Of course he does. He knows all the employees, excepting maybe those ones that came in last week who he hasn't had a chance to meet with yet. Anyway, here are a few of Eddie's things the driver brought back." Bud picked up a manila envelope off his desk and handed it to Dave.

"Can I see a report of what happened? I'd like to know who was in the car. Was anyone else hurt? Some details."

"Tom said the Saudi police have a full report. All he knew was that Eddie died in a truck that went off the road," Jerry said. "Listen, Dave. We'll have y'all back to the States as soon as we can. And. . ." He looked at Bud for confirmation. ". . .if you want to pack up most of your stuff, you know, in case you didn't feel like coming back, well, we understand. Don't worry about the contract. We'll give you a nice severance."

"Yeah, thanks," Dave said. They were treating him like a nuisance, not a solid employee who had just lost his brother. Realizing he only had a little over twenty-four hours to find the answers to his questions, he didn't want to waste any more of it with them. He turned around and walked out.

Maura was sitting at the kitchen table having a cup of coffee when Dave burst through the front door. "Come on. Let's go," he said. "Is there any gas in the car?" He had a wild look in his eyes.

"I can't drive here, remember?"

"Right. Okay. Right. The keys?"

"What's going on?"

"I can't find out anything. Jerry and Bud know their usual half of nothing, or at least that's all they're saying. Something about a truck going off the road. No details. Nothing. I can't even see my own bother. He's already been identified. I can't see Eddie."

He paced around the room and talked very fast until he got tripped up by the saying of Eddie's name and his voice cracked.

"Dave, slow down. Who identified him?"

"Tom. Isn't that a laugh? He did it on the way to the airport. He's halfway to the States by now for some meeting, so I can't talk to him. We'll be leaving tomorrow night. They're getting Eddie ready now, so I guess that's why I can't see him. I just wish I could see him. I don't care what he looks like." Dave started to cry, but shook it off. "I want some answers before we go. They didn't seem the least bit concerned how it happened. We give up our lives to come over here and work for them.

Look how they treat us, like we're parts in a big machine. Wouldn't you think Tanley would want to know more details about the death of one of their employees?"

"Yeah, I guess." Maura didn't know what to say to Dave's flood of words. She felt dumb and happy, happy that he was kicking and that's all she could concern herself with at the moment.

"I want to see the police report. I want to know what happened."

"You want me to go, too?"

"Yes. I want you with me."

"Dave, I love you." She threw her arms around him and hugged him tightly. He accepted her embrace, but couldn't find a way to return it.

"Let's go," he said

3

Dead-end Streets of Al-Khobar

The police station in Al-Khobar at the end of the town's main thoroughfare was functional and drab, a structure of 1960's minimalist architecture surrounded by a chain link fence and a fleet of green and white squad cars. Inside, the furnishings were sparse and the only decorations on the pale green walls were three large, framed portraits—former Kings Faisal and Khalid, and the present King Fahd.

The diminutive young man who greeted Dave and Maura with suspicious eyes looked like he should have been in school, yet had a rapid-fire submachine gun strapped to his shoulder. Many of the national police were recruited from a desert tribe who were hereditarily very small, and very loyal to the Al-Saud family.

"Do you speak English?" asked Dave.

The boy shook his head and disappeared into the office behind him. He came out with a portly, middle-aged man nearly twice his size.

"May I help you?"

"I hope so. My name is David Bates. My brother Eddie, Edward, was killed in a car accident sometime last night or this morning. I would like to see the police report."

"I'm sorry to hear about your brother. I can get you the report, but can you read Arabic?" The man picked at a stain on the front of his shirt and tried to loosen his collar. A table fan droned on the counter nearby.

"No, but if you gave me a copy, I could have it translated."

"I'm afraid I couldn't give you a copy, but I translate it for you now and tell you what you want to know." He acted pleased, as if he was doing them a great favor.

"I would appreciate that."

When the officer left to go get the report, Dave and Maura turned around to look for a place to sit down. The only bench was occupied by a young Saudi woman, at least they guessed that she was young from her small, delicate hands, which were the only parts of her they could see. She was covered from head to toe in the black robe-like dress called an *abaya.* She rocked back and forth while two small children groveled on the floor at her feet, dressed in outfits that looked like they came from K-mart. The little girl, wearing tiny pink overalls with a duck embroidered on the bib, looked up at Maura with big brown eyes. Maura waved at her and smiled. The little girl stared back, and then, after a lengthy consideration, attempted to mimic the wave with her small chubby hand. The mother continued to rock, ignoring her children.

"Mr. Bates. Here it is. What did you want to know?"

"Where did it happen?" Dave was in control of himself now, calm and focused.

"Let's see. On the road to Aziziyah."

"Aziziyah? And what time did it occur?"

"I'm afraid it doesn't say exactly. Just 'night.' The officer has not made a very complete report, I'm sorry to say." Dave wasn't surprised. The country wasn't known for concise records and documents, things that hadn't been necessary before the country was thrust into the modern world.

"What kind of vehicle was it?"

"Truck. Yes, green. . .how you say. . .pickup."

"Chevy?"

"Yes. Your brother's truck?"

"No. He didn't have a truck. What about the driver?"

"Driver? Your brother was alone."

"But he was with someone, the guy who owned the truck."

"It says nothing here. Only your brother was in the truck. The truck went off the road and turned over." Dave pictured Eddie trapped in the overturned truck, his body twisted and blood running down from his battered blond head. His stomach knotted up and he felt his face going blank-white, but he had to go on with it.

"The driver must have walked away. Were there any witnesses?"

The officer shook his head.

"What was his name? Khalil! That's it. Khalil."

"There is nothing in the report."

"What about the registration? The truck must be registered."

"No registration. We thought it was your brother's."

"I'm telling you, the truck belonged to a Lebanese man named Khalil. My brother didn't have a truck." The policeman stared at them expressionless. Maura took hold of Dave's arm. The officer looked at her disapprovingly and she remembered that physical contact between a man and a woman in public was frowned upon. The man saw her pull her arm away and the corner of his mouth twitched as if he were about to smile.

There was a long uncomfortable silence as they all stared at each other, and then Dave said, "Well, thank you very much for your help."

"I'm sorry," said the man sincerely. He leaned closer to them and said quietly, "You see that woman on the bench? Her husband was also killed in an accident. She doesn't know. We're waiting for her family to come and tell her."

Maura was shaken by the news. When they passed the little girl on the way out, Maura felt her eyes well up with tears. But once out the door, she focused her attention on Dave, who was quiet, beginning to have a beaten down look again. He went in and out of sanity, one minute on a mission, and the next lost, trudging along as if he didn't know where he was going.

"You're not giving up, are you, Dave?"

"I need to go home and think a while. We've still got all day tomorrow."

About an hour after they had gone to bed that night, Maura rolled over and found Dave on his back, eyes focused on the ceiling.

"I can't sleep either," she said. "You want a valium?"

"I want to be awake. I want to think about Eddie, not let him go."

"What's on your mind?"

"The last conversation I had with him. I wasn't very nice. I should have insisted he come for dinner. I should have gotten in the car and gone to get him."

"You didn't tell me about the truck and the Lebanese guy last night when you said he wasn't coming to dinner. You just said he had other plans. How come?"

"I guess I was embarrassed."

"About what?"

"That Eddie would want to go off with some stranger rather than come have dinner with us."

"Eddie liked adventure."

"Why did he do it?"

"Maybe he liked the guy."

"No. I mean, in general."

"He was always searching for something."

"Something or someone?"

"What do you mean?"

"I feel like I abandoned him."

"You mean when you married me," said Maura with tightness in her voice.

"No. Before that. Long before that. Something happened."

"Tell me about it."

"I've never told anybody. I was so freaked out at the time that I denied it happened for years. It became one more secret in a house of secrets. Eddie and I were real close, you know, when we were growing up. We depended on each other a lot, especially after our father died, and Mom went in the hospital. At Hazel's we had to sleep in the same bed and when we got back with Mom, we continued to do that sometimes. It was nice having someone close. When I got old enough to masturbate, Eddie wanted me to show him how to do it. I was thirteen and he was only eleven so he couldn't come yet, but he was really impressed when I did. A couple of times we masturbated together, but that was the extent of our sexual experimentation.

"Then the summer before I went away to college, Eddie seemed depressed all the time. Mom had married Albert by then and he was pretty well off, so he told us we could go to college any place we could get in. I had decided to go to San Francisco State because I wasn't accepted at U.C. Berkeley. It had been a dream of mine to go to San Francisco, and I had always thought of Eddie coming, too, when he was old enough. Still, he was upset about me not being around for a couple of years.

"One night when Mom and Albert were out of town—the summer before I was supposed to leave for college—we got into the liquor cabinet. And boy, did we get plastered. Eddie passed out on the couch, so I got him up, took him to his room, and put him into bed. Then I went to my room and lay down. When I closed my eyes, the room started spinning and I thought I was going to get sick.

"Then I felt someone pull back the covers and try to crawl in bed with me. In the darkness and my drunken haze, I didn't realize it was Eddie and I hit him so hard he fell to the ground. I'll never forget the sound of his body slamming against the floor and the whole room shaking. When I grasped what I had done, I jumped up and went over to him. I told him I was sorry. But he punched me back and then went running from the room. I sat on the floor with a bloody nose, attempting to figure out what had just happened. Someone standing over my bed had brought up bad memories from my past and I reacted automatically, violently.

"I got up and went to the bathroom to stop the bleeding. Then I went to his door and knocked. 'Fuck you,' he said. 'Go away.' Things were strained between us until I left for college a few weeks later. He didn't even show up to say goodbye. We eventually made up, but we never talked about that night, and after that, things were different. He became much more independent and outgoing, and those last two years in high school, he was wild, lashing out at the world. Mom kept calling me and saying she didn't know what to do with him. He was getting into drugs, staying out all night, always in trouble. She was glad when he finished high school so they could send him out to me. They thought I could do something with him. His grades were so bad he couldn't get in to S.F. State, but they took him at City College and we got a place by the ocean. I feel like I failed him."

"You can't blame yourself."

"He shouldn't have been with that guy."

"You're not responsible for a traffic accident because of something that happened thirteen years ago."

"He needed me the night we fought. Maybe he needed more than I could give him. But I could have helped get through what was going on. If I had just handled it differently—"

"You mean maybe he wouldn't have turned out gay?"

"No," he said a little too quickly. "I don't have a problem with that. I just think he might have been more cool about it if I hadn't punched him. He thought I was rejecting him for being gay. It wasn't that exactly. There were things about the past that we had never talked about. It might have helped him, or at least helped him comprehend why I reacted the way I did. If I had been more understanding, he might have been, I don't know, less wild in his sex life, more discriminating about who he picked up. If I had told him I loved him for who he was and didn't care about him being gay, maybe he wouldn't have gone off with some crazy Arab who probably drove like a maniac, a guy who would just walk away from an accident and leave Eddie dying, trapped in the truck. God, if I ever find that asshole. . ."

"We don't know that, Dave. Don't torture yourself. It was a highway accident, a terrible thing. There's no sense in casting blame on anyone, especially not yourself. But there's one thing I don't get. What's this thing in the past, what you needed to talk to Eddie about?"

"Oh, Christ, Maura. There are things about my father, my real father, not Albert, that I've never told anybody."

"You can't tell *me*? I'm your wife, we've always shared things, at least I thought we did. I've told you all the shit about my family."

Dave thought back to the day when his life changed, when he and Eddie were left to fend for themselves. They were just kids. It was the day one nightmare ended and another began.

Fresh from the hairdresser, Joan Bates picked the boys up from school in the family Country Squire wagon with fake wood paneling.

Carwash water dripped from the bottom of the door as Dave asserted himself in the front seat while Eddie crawled in the back and returned his mother's smile through the rear-view mirror.

"Hello, my little munchkins," Joan sang out. Her voice sounded just like that Good Witch of the North in *The Wizard of Oz* they watched over the weekend.

"Jeez, mom! Munchkins? That's so corny," Dave said.

"Don't say 'Jeez,' honey." She reached over and patted Dave on the leg. "I'm just happy to see you guys."

"You look pretty, Mom," Eddie said.

"Thanks, sweetie."

Eddie was perched on the edge of the back seat with his arms on top of the front upholstery. Dave watched his brother lean close to their mom and stare at how each hair of her head was glued in place. The car smelled like hairspray and Dave hated it, but Eddie sniffed as if he liked it. Then he lightly flicked her big hoop earrings and made them swing.

"You look pretty, Mom," Dave said in high voice, mocking his brother. "You sound like a girl."

"No, I don't. Mom?"

"Dave, don't be mean. There's nothing wrong with a boy telling his mother she looks pretty."

Dave bumped Eddie's arms off the seat with his elbow. "Sit back."

Joan gave Dave a dirty look, and then smiled at Eddie in the mirror. "Your brother's right, honey. I might have to stop suddenly and I don't want you going through the windshield."

"Can we go straight home? I have to work on my science project," said Dave.

"No. We most certainly cannot. We have to go by Kroger's to pick up something for you kids' dinner. Your father and I are going to the Swenson's cocktail party and Connie is going to baby sit. After Kroger's I have a couple of errands at the shopping center, but after that we can stop for ice cream at 31 Flavors."

"Oh, boy," Eddie let out in a high-pitched scream.

"There you go again, sounding like a—"

"David! Stop. I mean it."

"Mom, I really need to work on my project. Please, can't you just drop me off?"

Joan was silent a minute. She both admired his independence and worried about him being so somber and serious for a boy of nine. "All right. I can drop you off. Don't open the door to any strangers and don't eat a lot of junk to spoil your dinner. No TV."

"I'm just gonna work on my project. I'm not a baby, mom."

"Well, you aren't all grown up either."

Dave extracted the key from under the flowerpot and opened the back door. He went right to the fridge and took out a carton of milk, folded open the spout, and put it to his mouth, letting the cold liquid run down his throat. No one was around to yell at him for drinking out of the carton.

The house was so quiet he heard the tail of the black cat clock tick back and forth on the wall. There was a tinkle of bottles as he closed the refrigerator door cutting off the white light from the refrigerator bulb. Then on the edge of the silence he heard a droning sound. Was it a lawnmower down the street? He walked over to the door to the breezeway and opened it, making the motor noise louder and closer than he thought. It seemed to be coming from the garage, and he recognized it as the idling of a car engine. His mother couldn't be home yet and his father never came home before 6 o'clock.

On cautious legs he approached the door to the garage at the other end of the breezeway, each step bringing him closer to the sound that he now realized had the angry rumble of his father's Thunderbird. He thought of escaping, but kept going until his hand touched the cool doorknob. He'd better not open it, he thought, but he tried it anyway. It was locked from the other side. Close to the door the burnt smell of car exhaust hurt his nose and he backed up. Unlocking the breezeway screen door, he pushed it open and ran around to the back window of the garage. He crouched along the wall, and then slowly lifted himself up to peek in through the glass. It was his father's red T-bird all right and he was in it, leaning back against the headrest, staring right at Dave. The boy felt a sharp pain in his gut and slumped to the ground. He didn't like being alone in the house with his father. It was useless to run though. His dad had seen him, was probably getting out of the car right now to come around to him. But wait. If he ran like hell, he could make it to the woods behind the house, scramble up his favorite climbing tree, hide in the high branches among the new spring leaves. He chanced another look and found his father in the exact same position, gazing not at him but at something behind him, way in the distance. Dave raised a heavy arm and waved. There was no reaction. A tingling sensation rushed over his skin like getting out of the bath into a cool room. He was hot and cold at the same time. It was like the time his father had brought home dry ice and he touched it: hot and cold. His body was trying to tell him something, but his head couldn't figure it out yet.

Later that night Dave and Eddie were eating their TV dinners at Mrs. Johnston's house, the next-door neighbor. They pushed the peas to the side, made craters in the mashed potatoes, and poked holes in the Salisbury steak sauce that was beginning to congeal. Bea Johnston hovered over them, asking if they wanted more milk, and then if they wanted Jell-O or Oreos for dessert.

Aunt Hazel walked in the back door and let the screen bang shut, making Bea start and nearly drop the plate of cookies she was carrying to the table. Hazel pursed her lips and stared at the half-eaten dinners, and then with a softer look focused her metal-framed eyes on the boys.

"Oh, gosh. Hazel," said Bea. "You got here quick."

While Eddie twisted an Oreo open and scraped the cream out with his teeth, Hazel took Dave into the family room and sat him down on the sofa. She was Joan's older sister, but with her graying hair pulled back in a bun, she looked more like a grandmother than an aunt. "David, I know this is hard on you, but I'm counting on you to be strong."

"Where's Mom?"

"She's not feeling too good. She's going to the hospital. You boys are going to stay with me a while."

That began the silence, and the "while" turned into almost a year. Eddie had been told that his father had gone on a business trip, later that he had taken a job in another state. Dave thought that what his father did was his fault, and he squashed his guilt down into a little ball where it sat in the pit of his stomach. In times of crisis it came to life like a rat trying to escape its cage, gnawing at the lining of his belly.

Dave felt the rat at work as he told Maura about his past. He had been reluctant to tell her much before, only saying that their father had died when they were young and Aunt Hazel had taken them in while their mother got over it.

He took a breath like drawing up water from a deep well and continued the story. "Hazel made me promise not to tell Eddie. He was too young and sensitive, they said. He was having a hard time dealing with mom being gone, sometimes crying himself to sleep at night."

Maura put a hand on his arm. "And what about you?"

Dave answered in a shaky voice. "I had to be the man. Hazel kept telling me how grown up I was, even though I was dying inside. We lived with her almost a year. When mom got out of the hospital, we sold the house, moved away, and the loss of our father was swept under the carpet, never to be mentioned again."

Maura took his hand, brought it up to her mouth and kissed it. "I'm sorry, honey. You've had to carry that all these years. And Eddie never knew how your father had died?"

"I was crazy to tell him. I figured he should know, but I always thought, 'What's the point?' After so much time had passed, it seemed better to not drag it up, which was only going to bring pain."

"It seems so unfair."

"Aunt Hazel kept saying it was for mom's sake, that bringing the past up could put her back in the hospital. And that was the last thing I wanted as a kid. When Eddie got older, we told him that dad had died in a car accident."

Dave paused and yawned so loud it sounded like a groan. He rolled over on his side, facing the other way. "I guess I'm ready to sleep now. We can talk more tomorrow." Maura wanted to hold him, but it wasn't time. She, too, rolled on her side and soon fell asleep.

Dave's eyes popped open and he stared at the face of the clock. It was a strange time to be waking up. Usually by 8:30, he had been up for four hours, worked for three. It must be Thursday, the Saudi weekend. But when the memories of the previous day began to stack up, each ugly one on top of the other, he knew it wasn't Thursday or Friday or any day that he wanted to be alive. He felt nauseous and short of breath. He sat up and gasped for air, and then found his way to the bathroom where he caught his blanched face in the mirror. He leaned his head against the glass and stared at the shiny white porcelain of the sink. Then he broke into a sweat and the room began to breath with him, the walls contracting and expanding. He reached into the shower and turned on the water.

With the warm water beating down on him he began to feel better, and a few minutes later he was dressing hurriedly in the bedroom. Maura rolled over, her face wrinkled with confusion as she peered out through the little slits of her eyes. Dave watched her face go through the same changes he had, and finally settle on an expression that reflected how much their lives had changed.

"Where are you going?" she said in a gravelly voice.

"I have to talk to somebody. There's a guy down at the Al-Shula Center who might be able to tell me something about Khalil."

"Who?"

"The Lebanese guy Eddie was with."

"Are you sure you want to do that? What if you find him, this Khalil? What are you going to do?"

"I'm just going to talk to him. Don't worry. I won't do anything crazy. I can't sit around and do nothing."

"What time is the flight tonight?"

"Midnight. I'll be back in a couple of hours to help you pack."

The recently opened Al-Shula shopping mall could have been built by the same architects as one in Cleveland or Sao Paulo. But the people wandering its passageways clearly differentiated it, giving it a crossroads-of-the-world flavor. Saudi men in their white robes and women in their black veils were interspersed with other Arabs, Westerners, Pakistanis, Indians, Thais, Turks and Filipinos. The stores carried the latest stereo and video equipment from Japan, fashions and perfume from Europe, nearly everything you wanted to buy except alcohol.

At the intersection of the two main passageways of the rectangular structure, there was an open foyer with skylights three floors above. In the middle of the foyer was a simulated outdoor cafe with a self-service bar and tables grouped around a plastic Italianate fountain. The seating area was sectioned-off from the rest of the mall by planter boxes filled with fake greenery. Dave headed straight for the cashier at the service bar, a Lebanese man Dave knew from his frequent visits there with Eddie.

Dave approached the counter with a fabricated smile. "Hello, friend. How are you today?"

The cashier didn't smile back. "You want cappuccino?"

"Sounds good." He paused a minute and watched one of the Pakistanis go to work on the espresso machine. "By the way, do you know—"

"Four riyals, please."

"Here you go. Do you by any chance know a man named Khalil?"

The cashier laughed. "I know many Khalils."

"A Lebanese."

"I know many Khalils who are Lebanese."

"He drives a green pickup truck."

"Oh, that one." The tone of his voice made Khalil sound vaguely criminal. Dave felt a chill up his spine.

"Do you know where I could find him?"

"No," he answered in a clipped manner. "Where's your friend?"

"You mean my brother?"

"That your brother?"

"He's not here today," Dave said, working hard to appear relaxed. "Look, it's very important I find Khalil."

The cashier stared at him suspiciously.

"Not for what you think," Dave added.

"What do I think?"

"Never mind. Just tell me where I can find him."

The Lebanese shrugged his shoulders and appeared bored with the matter. "At ten o'clock some friends come here. They know Khalil. You will recognize them."

"Thanks." Dave took his cappuccino and sat down at one of the tables. The place was empty except for another foreigner, who sat alone reading the *Arab News*. A little after ten, three young Arabs, confident of their attractiveness and European-style charm, strutted in wearing tight jeans and T-shirts showing off their well-muscled torsos. They sat at a table right across from Dave's and looked around to see who was watching. Dave glanced their way and they picked up on it immediately. They were used to being stared at. After talking among themselves, they all turned to look at Dave. He nodded at them and they looked away. The other Westerner had lowered his paper and took an interest in the scene. Dave gave the man a friendly nod, then got up and went over to the Lebanese table.

"As salaam alaykum," said Dave, touching his heart in the Arab manner. He felt awkward to be speaking a language he knew so little of, and using the religious greeting preferred in Saudi Arabia. He wasn't sure how more European Arabs might react. One of them looked at him, nodded, then looked at the other two who appeared to be suppressing nervous giggles. "May I sit down?" Dave indicated the empty chair and the one whose arm was resting on it removed it. "Do you speak English?"

Their black eyes darted back and forth across the table. "A little," said one of them.

"Good," said Dave. "I'm looking for a man named Khalil who drives a green truck. Can you tell me where he is?" Dave glanced at the man at the other table, who had gone back to his paper, though he didn't seem to be concentrating on what he was reading.

There was no response, not a single reaction on their faces. Dave focused on the one who said he spoke a little English. "Do you understand? Khalil. . .who drives. . .American. . .green. . .pickup truck."

"I understand you. And I'm not deaf."

Dave laughed at his own absurdity. If anyone should know that shouting at foreigners didn't help them understand, it should be an English teacher. "Sorry. This is very important."

"Why you want Khalil?"

"I can't tell you right now." Dave looked over at the cashier who watched the scene with reserved amusement.

"If you can't tell me why you are looking for him, then I can't tell you where he is."

"I just want to talk to him." The one who spoke English said something in Arabic to the other two and they all burst into laughter.

"What's so funny?" They continued to laugh and Dave felt his head about to explode. He figured he'd better leave. In getting up quickly, he knocked his chair over and the laughing stopped. The Lebanese he had been talking to grabbed his arm.

"Wait. Don't be angry with us. If you really want to see Khalil so much, he works at European Designs nearby Safeway." The man smiled and dropped his arm. Dave took his hand and shook it. "Thank you. Thank you very much."

European Designs was an expensive clothes store for women carrying the latest fashions from Paris and Milan. Many Saudi women would spend small fortunes on their wardrobes even though they would never have the pleasure of displaying them in public. Only in the women's sections of the their homes could they cast off their *abayas* and model their new purchases for their female friends.

Dave hesitated outside the boutique, not sure if he was allowed to go in a women's store by himself. He put his hand on the door handle and noticed, through the large store windows, a pickup truck parked at the side of the store. He let go and walked around to the side of the building. The dusty air and the heat made his movements seem slow and dreamlike. The truck was a 1986 Chevy and in near-perfect condition. It was covered with a thin layer of desert grit. Dave ran his finger across the top, revealing a streak of shiny forest green. His brain began to tick like a bomb. He stared at his reflection in the passenger window and saw the dark circles under his eyes and the lines on his brow. He pictured Eddie sitting in the truck, bouncing down the road, smiling and feeling high while caught in the rapture of a new adventure. An accident? This truck hadn't been in an accident. It had to be Khalil's. Then his brain took the path of hope, elated with the possibility that Eddie wasn't dead at all, that it had all been a mistake. He turned around quickly and saw a salesman watching him through the window. Something in the man's eyes took away the short moment of hope. The salesman walked away from the window and began arranging some belts on a rack.

Dave entered the store and the salesman was under his nose immediately, a short wiry man with thinning hair and a thick moustache plastered across an ordinary face. He knew this couldn't be the Khalil he was looking for. He wasn't the type Eddie would have gone off with.

"I was looking at your truck," Dave began nervously. "I used to have one just like it back in the States."

"Oh, no, sir. Is not mine."

"Maybe the owner of the truck is around. I'd like to talk to him."

"As you can see, there is only me. Could I interest you in something for the madam?"

Dave looked around and spotted a long green dress in the corner away from the windows. "Perhaps. My wife has been looking for a long dress. She likes green and her birthday is coming soon."

"Yes. Follow me, sir. I have something she might like."

When they reached the out-of-the-way corner of the store, the salesman removed a long green gown from the rack and asked Dave what he thought.

"Nice," said Dave, ignoring the dress and staring at the man. "Where's Khalil today?"

"Khalil?"

"Khalil who works here." The little man shrugged his shoulders and returned to examining the dress as if he was the customer. Dave interrupted him. "I asked you a question."

"Only I am here today," the man answered patiently. But he wouldn't look at Dave.

Dave's eyes widened and his voice became fierce. "I can see that. His truck is here. I want to talk to him."

"I don't know." The salesman was matter-of-fact. "You don't like the dress? I show you something else."

"Forget it. All I want is to talk to Khalil." Dave took a step closer to the man.

"Impossible," he spit out.

Dave grabbed the man by the shirt collar and shoved him up against the rack of dresses. The green dress fell to the floor as the man gasped, "What are you doing? You crazy."

"Shut up," said Dave in a voice that sounded strange even to him. "You little faggot. I know people you've been with. You have alcohol and marijuana in your apartment. I'm sure the police would like this information." Dave tightened his grip as he growled his accusations.

The man stared at Dave with bug eyes. "Please," he said. "You're hurting me."

"Where's Khalil?"

"He left the country." Dave loosened his hold slightly.

"Why?"

"I don't know. He came in yesterday morning. Some men were with him. They gave him money and told him he had to leave the country."

"Who were the men? People you have seen before?"

"I don't know them."

"Saudis?"

"They wore Saudi dress."

"Where did Khalil go?"

"Paris, I think. He said he would write and tell me where to send things. The truck, he wants me to sell. Let go of me, please."

Dave released him, feeling guilty about the loathsome method he had used to get information. He apologized silently to Eddie and his voice softened. "Do you know anything about an accident?"

"Accident?"

"Forget it." Dave walked out the door.

4

EDDIE'S ROOM

Maura was putting the last few things in suitcases when Dave burst into the bedroom. "I found the green truck."

"God, you scared me. You what?"

"I found Khalil's green truck." He noticed the two airline tickets sitting on the dresser. "There wasn't a scratch on it. You know what that means?" He stood in the middle of the room with his arms akimbo, challenging the whole world, while his head bobbed on his neck as if he was going into a fit.

"What are you saying?"

"There was no accident, at least not in Khalil's truck."

"Maybe it was another truck. The report was so vague."

"But Maura, listen to this. Yesterday, Khalil left the country, was forced to leave the country. He's in Paris." He picked up the tickets. "I wonder if we can get a stopover in Paris on the way back."

"The way back?" Maura whined. "Dave, I've been thinking. Wouldn't this be a good time to be rid of this place, once and for all? We've got some savings now and—"

"Maura, don't you see? There was no accident in the green truck, maybe no accident at all. Somebody's lying, but why? The last person we know that was with my brother has suddenly left the country. And something else. When Khalil came back to the shop yesterday to square things away before leaving, there were two Saudis with him, making sure he got on his way."

"What shop?"

"He worked in a clothes store over by Safeway."

She took a step back and landed on the bed. "A clothes shop near Safeway?"

"What's the matter?" said Dave.

"Nothing. This is all just a little too strange."

Dave's tone became grave. "I'm beginning to feel that Eddie's death wasn't an accident. Maybe it had something to do with the prince they were going to see."

"Prince? What prince?"

"That night, Eddie told me Khalil was taking him to meet a prince. I thought it was bullshit, that the guy was trying to impress him. Maybe he did take Eddie to meet a prince and something happened."

"Some other kind of accident?"

"Or murder?"

"Jesus, Dave, you're getting carried away."

"I'm just saying that there is something that's not right and I want to find out what it is. It could have been some kind of accident that was an embarrassment to Saudis. We've got to find Khalil."

Maura picked up the envelope of Eddie's things off the bed. "We haven't opened this. Maybe there is something here." Dave took the envelope and held it a moment, feeling an icy cold in his veins. He opened the flap with care and let the contents slide onto the bed. There was Eddie's watch, wallet, keys, handkerchief, Chapstick, and some change. Dave picked up each article and turned it over in his hands. He opened the wallet and saw a picture of him and Eddie taken some years before. They sat on a pile of driftwood at Jenner-by-the-Sea, California, and they had their arms around each other. Dave slumped down on the bed next to Maura. His body was very still. The bounce-thomp of tennis balls could be heard outside and beyond that the white rush of traffic on the Gulf Road. Tears came into Maura's eyes, but Dave just stared at the picture. "Don't you think it's weird?" he said.

"What?"

"They told me I wouldn't want to see Eddie because. . .because he looked so bad. And yet everything here is intact. The watch isn't broken. There's no blood on anything. Nothing is charred."

"I don't get it."

"When we get back to the States, I want to order an autopsy. If my suspicions are confirmed, we're definitely going to Paris to find Khalil." Dave started putting everything back in the envelope and then stopped. "I just thought of something. His pack's not here. If he was going out in the desert looking for something, doesn't it seem logical that he would take his daypack? He took it everywhere, and his small tape recorder, too." Dave picked up the keys. "It's time we go have a look at his room."

Eddie's room was on the third floor, a corner room by the outside stairs, "for quick entrances and exits" Eddie used to joke. Dave and Maura had wanted him to live with them, but it was against Saudi rules. Each single man had a studio unit with a kitchenette and a bathroom.

As they entered the room, Dave tripped over a laundry basket full of clean and pressed clothes, which the houseboy had probably stuck inside the door, unaware of Eddie's fate. He turned on the light and they looked around the small neat room. Eddie had decorated it with rugs, wall hangings and bags from the Middle East. On the dresser was a collection of Bedouin jewelry—thick handcrafted bracelets, heavy bangle necklaces and large earrings.

"I don't remember Eddie being so neat," Maura said as if to fill the horrible silence.

"It's the houseboys. They do everything—make the beds, do the laundry, empty the trash, even change the toilet paper."

"Why don't we get a houseboy?"

"Because married men have wives."

Maura let out a loud, "Ha." Then the silence was back.

"I don't like this," she said. She kept her hands close by her sides, hesitant to touch anything in the room.

"Me neither. Let's see if we can find his daypack and tape recorder."

Though the search didn't produce the pack or the tape recorder, it did lead Dave through an agonizing journey of remembrances. There were the things he recognized from the life he and Eddie had shared. And there were the unfamiliar things—several new cassette tapes still in the plastic wrapping, a book on jogging, a kite from Pakistan and a small throw rug from Eddie's trip to Qatif a few weeks before. Then Dave's attention was drawn to Eddie's desk and the project he had been working on. On one side of his electronic typewriter was a pile of poems, thoughts and impressions hurriedly scribbled on scraps of paper, notes from his recordings, feelings that hadn't been shared with anyone. On the other side were the typed pages of a journal with dated entries. Dave started reading a page from a couple of months after they arrived in the country.

November 26: It's a coffee-colored afternoon, thick, murky, unsweetened, slightly bitter, getting cool.

It's a coffee-colored afternoon, the color of Arab skin, cardamom, their eyes.

It's a coffee-colored afternoon—they all are when the rising time is 4:30 a.m., in darkness fumbling to strangle the alarm beep-beep. I see the days, weeks, months stretched out in front of me, a path paved in riyals, leading deeper into the colorless desert toward an oasis, or is it just a mirage?

I see an orderly line of men in identical blue shirts and gray pants, looking toward, reaching for trays, their outstretched hands a strange hue under the fluorescent lights, almost matching the eerie blue of the walls.

I see tables for four, Formica, blue plastic chairs arranged in neat rows by guest worker hands only recently trained to provide order.

I see clouds of DDT wafting over sand-colored boxes with curtained windows (closed, I hope), settling on an alien grass that fights the good fight with the sand, brushing like a furtive kiss the petals of flowering oleanders.

I smell a moment of sweetness from white frangipani before the death clouds come and we run for cover.

I smell another man-made cloud, this one ammoniac, sailing over from the fertilizer plant, burning nostrils when the wind is against us.

I feel the flies, undaunted by the chemicals, crawling over my drying skin by the pool, thriving.

Eddie's writing painted a frightening picture of their world in the Kingdom, far more sinister than anything he had ever expressed to Dave. Everyone complained, pointed out the absurdities, made jokes about their hosts. It was part of their survival. It troubled Dave to read the words put down in print. He knew he shouldn't read on, that he was going into territory he might later regret. But the next entry was a poem screaming to be read. Eddie had never shared any of his poems, not even with Dave.

December 9:
Stop your Ka'ba stone eyes stop
Your flirtsmiles stop
Your rumblingdeepvoice stop
Reeling me in to hear stop
Those crossroom glances stop
That followme walk stop
Timely reappearances stop
Your howdoyoudosirs stop
Your furtiveglances stop
Your strongarms stop
Relieving me of my tray stop
Rollingblackwaves of your hair stop
Your coffeehands stop
Robbing me blind stop
Without touching stop
Your leaningonabroomstick stop
Your radiationstares stop stop stop.

A screech from Maura cut into Dave's second reading of the poem. He looked over and saw her drop a box of cookies, and then frantically brush off the insects crawling up her arm.

"What's the matter?" said Dave.

"Ants." She found the trail and followed it to the door where it passed into the hallway. "What are you reading?" she said over her shoulder as she opened the heavy door to look outside in the hall.

"His journal."

"Do you think that's a good idea?"

"I'm sure it's not, but I can't stop."

Dave found an entry just a few days before Eddie's death. He scanned the work and the name Khalil popped out at him.

February 4: The green pickup hurtled along at speeds that felt like we were on a suicide mission. I sat in the death seat with the disco music pounding against my chest. No seatbelt bound me. One wrong move by this crazy Arab at the wheel could leave our bodies mangled in a wreck of twisted steel. I had come to the conclusion that Khalil had lost his mind. And then it hit me that I didn't care. The thrill of being close to the edge was like a rush of amyl nitrate in my heart. I felt alive.

I thrust my sweaty palm out the window as if it were a wing ready to take flight and felt the heat rising up from the softening asphalt of the two-lane road. A gritty wind seemed as if it could sandblast the hair off my arm. Khalil shouted over the din and pointed at the wisps of sand, which danced like ballerinas along the ridge. A devilish smile crossed his face as he stomped on the pedal, sending the truck in a flying leap over the crest of the hill. Our bodies bounced off the seat, hung a moment in the air, and then slammed back against the upholstery with the tires rejoining the pavement.

We began a free fall down the steep grade on the other side, but a sudden letting up on the gas jerked me forward. Khalil reached over, squeezed my leg, and pointed with his chin at the view opening up before us. A great fiery ball was low on the horizon, the dusty sky a constantly changing palette of blazing hues. Under the sky was an endless sea of sand dunes like a crowded beach of curvaceous naked bodies cast in shadow and soft light.

When we got near the bottom of the hill, I spotted a gas station, a blemish on the flesh-colored sands. It buzzed with the activity of Friday evening, the Moslem holy day. I could see the shabbiness of the station, the cinder block structure whose outer walls had never been finished, and two old pumps on a dusty lot, the kind you see at a last-chance Texaco on a bend in the road in west Texas. I chuckled to think that just under the pitiable filling station, deep in the earth, was a vast honeycomb of spongy limestone unique to Ash Sharqiyah, the Eastern Province of Saudi Arabia. Black crude gushed through the rock, bringing immeasurable wealth to the desert land, the same wealth that had brought me, Dave, Maura, Khalil, and a host of other foreign workers to the Kingdom. So why wasn't there enough money to spruce up this desert filling station?

"Why you laugh?" Khalil said.

"Nothing. Are we going to stop?"

He jerked the wheel of his Silverado to the right and cut in front of a Mercedes so loaded with passengers that its chassis nearly touched the ground. We roared along the narrow side road and passed a line of late-model European and oversized American cars waiting to buy gas. The truck skidded to a halt in the gravel next to the grit-splattered phone booth at the edge of the lot. As the cloud of dust settled, we broke into laughter at the commotion we caused. Michael Jackson's "Thriller" blared from our speakers and everyone on the lot turned to gawk at the intruders and our Western music

After a brief stare, the Saudis returned to their families, the men sitting in the front seats, alternately gesticulating and resting their hands and arms on the shoulders of their fellows as they talked. The women sat in back like covered statues with their black veils hiding every part of them except their hennaed hands. They spoke to each other in a high-pitched cackle while bright-eyed, happy children in the latest Oshkosh and Gap fashions crawled over their laps.

Some of the men began to shout at the slow-moving gas attendant, but the small leathery-skinned man ignored their jeers as he shuffled back and forth from one side of the pumps to the other. He wiped his hands on the front of his grease-stained thobe, a shirt-like garment that hung down to his ankles, and stared at his two companions who sat nearby. They smoked cigarettes and drank Pepsis as they watched a TV resting on a crate, the long extension cord snaking into the cinder block hut. The attendant stared at the screen and tilted his head as if he sensed something, a far-off sound just beginning.

I jumped out of the truck, and shook out my legs.

"You got any change?"

Khalil thought it was funny I was asking him for change. His head jerked back and I saw the laugh lines on his tanned face. I had a feeling we were around the same age, but he had lived a lot more.

I found the Pepsi machine inside the station. Through the dirty glass I watched Khalil sit back in the truck. He pinched his full nose and pulled on the dark, thick hair of his moustache. Then he ran his fingers through his bushy black hair, finishing the swept-back style the wind had started.

When I came out of the station, I heard, "Allahu Akbar, Allahu Akbar, God is great," the opening lines of prayer call. At first I couldn't imagine where it came from. The closest mosque was miles away. Then the unnatural brilliance of the TV caught my eye. I watched images of Saudis in their long robes move across the screen, forming into lines on a plush oriental carpet in a marble hall. "Ashhadu an la illallah. I bear witness that there is no god but Allah."

The two loafers watching TV got up, snubbed out their cigarettes in the sand, and walked over to a stainless steel water container that stood outside the rough building. The man who had been pumping gas abandoned his customers and joined them. The three kicked off their sandals and washed their feet before proceeding to a small area, sectioned off by a low wall of cinder blocks on the west side of the structure. They stood in a row on a worn rug that covered the concrete of the walled-in area, and faced west.

Several of the cars at the pumps pulled out of line and got back on the road, unwilling to wait the twenty-five minutes before they could get gas again—traveling was one of the legitimate excuses for not participating in the otherwise mandatory prayer time. The rest of the men got out and joined their fellow Moslems praying toward Mecca. The wailing voice called out from the one official Saudi channel of the TV set and the sound fanned out over the dusty little gas station and then across the desert, connecting with the other callers, forming a blanket of security over the nation.

Khalil turned down the disco tape and said, "Come on. We go." I hopped in the truck and we took off with the heavy tires kicking up little stones and sending up another cloud of dust. When we had joined the flow of traffic to the east, I took my micro-cassette recorder out of my backpack. I pushed the button and began to record. "I'm being driven down a road through great sand dunes by a Lebanese guy who looks at me now with dark questioning eyes. There is so much in his face to take me places I've never been. I wish he'd look at the road though. He's driving very fast. The world is flashing by and I feel wrinkled by the balmy gulf air and pressed by the wind. Khalil, watch the road!"

"What are you doing? What's that?"

"It's my life. I'm recording my life."

"Is your life so small it can go into that little box?" He winked at me.

"How big is a diamond, oh one-who-thinks-he-is-so-wise? Jesus, watch the road!"

The right tires went off into the gravel of the shoulder and then back onto the hard surface. Khalil laughed and pressed harder on the accelerator. He pulled into the left lane and passed one, two, three cars before an oncoming truck became visible. I looked over and saw what I thought would be my last sight on earth—a camel riding in the back of a Toyota pick-up truck, its thin legs curled under its heavy body and its nose in the air enjoying the wind. Khalil squeezed the truck back in line, avoiding by mere seconds, a head-on collision. I leaned back and tried to look unimpressed. I took a deep breath and started talking into the recorder again.

Khalil has promised me that next week we will go deep into the desert to dig for desert roses, stones made up of radially symmetric crystals, which look like the petals of a rose. You have to dig down into the sand to find them. He tells me they are formed from camel piss seeping down into the sand and petrifying, but I don't believe him. He also wants to take me to meet a prince, or so he says. What kind of land is this where camels ride around in the back of pick-up trucks and their piss turns into roses in the sand, and princes are around every corner, living in marble palaces by the sea? Well, I'm ready for anything. I want to see the real Saudi Arabia.

Khalil turned off on a road heading toward the Arabian Gulf. The Friday evening sunset was coming on quickly and it gave me a pinch of the doldrums the way Sunday evenings used to back home. Here in the land of Islam, Saturday was the beginning of the workweek.

"Do you always drive so fast?" I asked.

"We Arabs are in a hurry to catch up to the world that has left us behind." The line sounded practiced.

"Let's not try so hard to catch up we leave the world right behind."

Dave gathered up all the papers and held them together with a clamp. He had a better picture of Khalil now and knew he had to find him. "We should go," he said.

"Look at this," shouted Maura from the bathroom. "A branch of the ant trail has found something they like on the bathroom floor." The swarm of ants was so thick in one area that they it looked like a big black spot, a spot of teeming life in the otherwise lifeless room.

5

UP IN THE AIR

The Pan Am flight to New York was scheduled to leave at midnight from Dhahran. Instead of sending one of the Pakistani drivers, Bud drove them out to the airport. It was a cool night and the breeze carried the smell of the sea inland. Off in the distance, the refineries, all lit up like space stations on a desolate planet, sent out ribbons of flame and white smoke against the black sky. They had an ominous appearance, as if the noxious substance they produced could destroy the universe.

Dave noticed that Bud was antsy in the cool silence of the car, shifting in his seat, acting as if he wanted to say something, but didn't know how to begin. Then Bud cleared his throat. "Stay as long as you need to." Dave thought that it sounded like a generous offer for Tanley. "And if you decide you don't want to come back, we'll just pack up the rest of your things and send them."

"We'll be back," Dave said dryly. Maura looked out the window and sighed.

"Think it over. You can always change your mind."

"Gee, Bud, you'd think you were trying to get rid of us." Dave spoke as if he was joking, though his jaw was clenched and Bud, smiling slightly, seemed to feel the tension.

"Nonsense. Just trying to do what's best for y'all, give you options. We want our employees, and former employees to be happy." Dave thought of a hundred things he could have said, things that would let Bud know of his suspicions about Eddie's death, but he held his tongue. Maura looked over and saw Dave's mouth open but frozen, and she breathed another sigh, this time of relief.

They had an hour and a half wait in the Dhahran terminal, a drab warehouse-like structure that looked as if it had been hastily thrown up to be practical while plans were drawn up for a modern, state-of-the-art airport. There was one large waiting room and nearly all the plastic seats were taken by travelers making their midnight escapes, foreign workers going home and Saudis going to study, do business, or just play abroad. Bud insisted on sitting out the wait with them, which seemed to Maura and Dave like a punishment. Lucky for them he spent a lot of time going back and forth to the refreshment counter, bringing them coffee, donuts, fruit juice and Pepsi. The plane was ready for take-off only fifteen minutes late and they said goodbye to Bud who looked relieved to see them go.

As soon as the heavy 747 lifted off, a cheer went up from the passengers and they began to joke about how long it would take before the liquor started to flow. The desert land was holy, but the airspace above it was not. When the "No Smoking" sign went off, heads raised all over the plane, looking around expectantly, only to see the "Fasten Your Seatbelt" sign still lit. A few minutes later, it too went off and the tinkle of little bottles could be heard from the flight attendants' stations as they dislodged the carts from their moorings. A wave of anticipation spread over the compartments of the plane and thirsty eyes fixed on the curtain behind which the attendants prepared the potions. Then the curtains opened and the metal carts began rolling and bumping down the aisles while the flight attendants asked the first passengers in a pleasant singsong if they would like a drink. Several young Saudis emerged from the smoking section in back, and headed for the restrooms in their traditional white *thobes* and red and white *ghutras.* Dave put his hand on Maura's leg and she started. She must have been the only person on the plane who had already begun to doze off.

Dave pointed to the Saudis and said, "Watch this."

"What? Saudis going to the john?"

"Just wait." About five minutes later, these same men began to exit the washrooms one by one in designer jeans and dress shirts with the top few buttons unbuttoned. Gold chains glistened around their necks. They hurried back to their seats in order not to miss the drink cart.

"Strange chameleons," said Dave.

"Oh, don't be so hard on them." Now that they were off the ground, Maura was being sympathetic.

"Just amused. I hope they get plastered and puke their guts out."

"No, you don't. We've got fourteen hours on this thing. It'll be bad enough without that."

Dave and Maura's turn came, and Dave's first swig of Scotch in six months rolled over his tongue and down his throat like a velvety flame. His eyes watered slightly and his nose felt raw to the briers of the alcohol. He laid his head back and closed his eyes, savoring the sensations. He didn't want to think about anything, but his mind, given free rein, drifted to the night before they had left for Saudi Arabia, when he and Eddie had gone out for a drink. Eddie had accused him of being upwardly mobile, on the verge of being a young urban professional for his choice of Scotch. Dave, in turn, accused Eddie of slumming, having aspirations of mingling with the peasants for his choice of vodka. Eddie liked to glorify the common man, but every time he encountered a true Philistine, he ran away in horror. Dave wondered how they would have related to their real father as adults. From what he knew about their father, Stan was an only child from a working class family in Oklahoma. His parents had died and he had made a clean break from all his relatives back there. Since no one would talk about their father after he died, Eddie had nurtured a fantasy about him—a romantic gypsy who their mother, straight-laced Joan, had fallen in love with.

When Dave thought about his parents getting together, it was always his Aunt Hazel's voice he heard telling the story. She never mentioned *him* in front the boys, but once Dave overheard her talking on the phone, and the conversation stuck in his brain.

"Joan is like a daughter to me," Hazel explained about her much younger sister. "I would have done anything to keep her from that marriage. Oh, hum. She had a mind of her own. And Stanley Bates was good looking, I'll grant you that. Turn heads he would, and a real charmer. My Lord, he was a first class salesman. He coulda sold an igloo in Florida. But he didn't cotton much to the married life. If you ask me, she's better off without him. And the boys, too. Sometimes he was like the perfect dad, but there was something weird. Davy didn't look at his father the way a boy oughta."

That first night when Hazel brought them to live with her, she tucked them into the big bed she had abandoned so many years before when her husband died.

"Is Mom going away like Dad did?" asked Eddie.

"No," Aunt Hazel said. "She's just tired and needs a rest."

It was a hot night and the crickets chirped outside the open window. The curtains didn't budge. There was a soft white glow over the room from the nightlight, which Hazel had taken from the hall and put in their room in case they woke up in the middle of the night, not knowing where they were.

"Do you miss Dad?" Dave asked his little brother, dying to tell him what he saw that day in the garage.

"Of course, don't you?"

"Nope."

"Yes, you do."

"No. I don't really. We don't need a Dad."

"What do you mean?"

"I can be your Dad."

"And when I get bigger, I'll be your Dad."

"That doesn't make any sense. You'll never be bigger than me."

"How do you know?"

"Because I'm older. Anyway, when Mom gets rested, I can go back to my own bed. Then I won't have to listen to your dumb ideas."

"They're not dumb."

Dave opened his eyes and saw the stewardess smiling at him. She asked if he wanted another drink. He nodded and handed her the glass. His first Scotch, though warming, hadn't calmed his mind, which raced about as if trying to clean house before going back to the hometown and facing his mother and stepfather. He looked over at Maura and wondered that she could sleep so peacefully. She hadn't even finished her white wine. It was going to be a long flight and Dave guessed he would be awake through the brunt of it.

The voices of several of the men around them had already raised to the tell-tale level of intoxication and other passengers wandered the aisles, greeting friends, flirting with the flight attendants, trying to keep up the party atmosphere. Dave got his second Scotch and began to sip it languidly as he stared out the window, watching the large jet chase the darkness across the sky.

In the dim light of the cabin, Dave slipped his hand into his bag and pulled out Eddie's journal as if it were a secret missive. He pushed the button of his reading light and hoped that Maura wouldn't wake up.

January 13: A few thunderstorms flashed out of the desert pummeling this lowland with a long rain. For days a ceiling of gray sky pressed down on us its sinister design, alternately dropping and holding back its holy water quickly sullied by its touching of the land. A chain of dirty puddles, set down upon an unwilling ground, hurried to stagnation, beckoning mosquitoes to come perform their pagan rituals of breeding. The wet garbage strewn across the sand summoned flies and maggot producers of all types. Stepping gingerly along the beach to avoid broken bottles and rusting cans (being less vulnerable in my sneakers than the Saudis in their sandals) my eyes, squinted against the gritty air, plucked from this soiled landscape a fine-featured Urdu speaker. His entreating smile cleansed the air and calmed my rancor, transforming it to the far more dangerous trap of desire. What had I been angry about? I don't remember. No doubt a minor annoyance due to an inexplicable part of this culture. In this country, opposing cultures collide for two reasons: money and sex. Yet we, my new friend and I, play this game of wanting neither from each other. I bed down with but the sand I've brought home from the beach.

January 20: Adil, the Pakistani, screeched to a halt outside the gate to pick me up for a trip to Jubail. A couple of his Pakistani friends were going to join us, so we stopped to pick them up at a camp in the industrial area of Dammam for third country nationals working at a pipe factory. We entered a hall lined with shoes, haphazardly kicked off, but more or less matched. Taking off ours we went into a small room where four people lived. A tall man, who had been reading the Qur'an, greeted us warmly. The book lay open on his cot. Adil kissed his two friends whom he had told me were "real villagers." They were small, dark, funny and playful with each other, a spiritual brotherhood of two. They spoke almost no English and I couldn't get their names right. I called them Ash and Az. Since it was custom that guests couldn't leave a house without having something to eat, Ash rushed out and came back with some apples and under ripe bananas. We ate and then got on the road to Jubail as the others headed to the mosque to pray.

After a few minutes on the road, Ash and Az decided they must pray, so we stopped at a beautiful mosque made of large white pipes pointing to the sky and cut out at the top like organ pipes. The dome was constructed of shiny green panels and the effect was one of hi-tech simplicity, unusual in Saudi-gaudy architecture. Adil and I sat in the car by a giant murky puddle and listened to a Bette Midler tape I gave him. When Ash and Az crawled into the back seat after their holy experience, they were nearly blasted away by the Divine Miss M. at full volume. All the way to Jubail, it was high volume and high speed, zipping past the huge desalinization plant seen for miles with its flashing lightshow against the night sky.

As we got to Jubail near the Kuwait border Adil pointed out Camp 4 where he lived—a large plot of identical prefab boxes arranged without trees or vegetation on streets named Avenue A, B, C, etc. Lightening flashed across the sky, brewing up a new storm.

Adil's three-bedroom, two-bath unit was filthy and the carpet looked like Khomeini's army had marched over it. Empty soda cans were everywhere and the coffee table was thick with crud.

We left the rec center after a game of pool and walked to the car in a raging storm. On the drive back to Camp 4, we got a spectacular performance from Mother Nature—thunder, lightening and a fierce wind blowing a ready-mix of sand and rain across the road. As Bette wailed we drove through a giant puddle spraying water like a fountain, and then he turned around and drove through it again, howling with laughter.

Back at his house we were in bed. Are you sleepy? No, are you? Not really. Silence. Are you going to sleep? I think you want to sleep. No, just thinking. About what? Nothing really. You? And then I have enough and think we need to get this over with and put my arm on his. Lock the door, he said. It was on my side. The act was clumsy and over quickly, much less interesting than the buildup. He said he felt the satisfaction and wanted to sleep. That made one of us.

Money and sex. Sex and money. Within a week this seeming innocent had taken me for both. Since we were now intimate, he felt comfortable borrowing 500 dollars to buy a better car. He was poor, and I relatively rich. He promised to repay me soon, smiled and waved, and went back to Jubail, to his job in a fertilizer plant. That was the last I saw of him. Today I found out that he has quit his job and gone back to Pakistan. Usually they walk away with a piece of my heart. I guess I should consider myself lucky that this one only got 500 dollars. My intuition was right; my guilt about being a privileged Westerner was wrong. Money or sex? Sometimes both.

Dave threw the journal down and shook his head. Eddie had told him nothing of this story. It occurred to him that Eddie picked his men as their mother had, at least before Stan's death and she met Albert. Eddie had been charmed by the good looks and exotic sensuality of the Pakistani the way Joan had been swept off her feet by Stan. Neither of them were relationships that could be sustained. He was almost certain that Stan had married Joan because she was pregnant. Somehow she had managed to keep him around for nine years, though Dave remembered that he was often away "on business."

He got up to go to the restroom and passed the flight attendant station where there was a halo of light around the curtain. He smelled eggs and toast, their microwaved breakfast. He opened the first restroom door and was nearly knocked over by the odor of vomit; it was splattered over the floor of the compartment. He closed the door quickly and went to the next one. This floor was strewn with toilet paper and the bowl hadn't been flushed. The trash bin was overflowing with paper towels and water was splashed all over the mirror, counter and floor, the soap dispenser empty. It was just as Maura had predicted.

It was beginning to get light when the plane touched down at JFK Airport in New York, more than fourteen hours after they left Saudi Arabia. They had a two-hour layover before they caught the next flight to Chicago, and from there it was one more short flight to the central Illinois city of Greenbrier.

Through the large windows of the waiting area, Dave and Maura had a view of Manhattan and the paling February full moon over it. The twin towers, dwarfing their neighbors, picked up the rose color of the rising sun while the rest of the skyline stretched out in front of them in various shades of gray. Everything was coated with a chilly mist and small patches of snow could be seen between the runways. It had been an emotional, dreamlike voyage from the other side of the world, and he found it hard to grasp that in New York, life was going on as normal. Jets roared then streaked across the sky in their daily routine.

Maura picked up the *New York Times* and started reading while Dave stared blankly at the scenery in front of them. He thought of the hundreds of movies that had pictured the skyline of Manhattan, yet none quite in this manner. It was a waking giant, sleepily reaching up to rub its tired eyes as the light changed from night to day. Maura let out a groan and dropped the paper to her lap.

"What is it?" Dave said.

"They let him out. They let the asshole out."

"Who?"

"There's a story in here about Dan White. He got out of prison a couple of weeks ago and is resettling in Southern California. They don't say where, of course, but they do point out that he seems lacking in remorse."

Dave thought of the scar above Eddie's left eye from a gash he had received from a police baton during the White Night Riots in 1979. He had gone down to the city to protest with thousands of others the light sentence White received after shooting Mayor George Moscone and Supervisor Harvey Milk. Dave was terrified when Eddie arrived home with a bloody head and blood-splattered clothes. Dave bandaged his cut, and then took him, defiant and enthralled, to the clinic for stitches.

The reflection of the sun turned to golden now and the various landmarks of Manhattan emerged from the gray mist. Maura went back to reading her article and Dave continued to watch the city wake up.

It was not until the third leg of the journey, the 45-minute flight from Chicago to Greenbrier, that Dave fell into a deep sleep. Maura suffered the bounce and vibration of the small jet-prop above the barren corn and soybean fields. It was a cold day, but Maura could see no snow as she looked out over the vast acreage of large farms with an occasional creek passing through. Small clusters of trees dotted the landscape and farm buildings huddled together in groups along endless strips of unbending road. By a small river, there were large wooded areas with rooftops amongst the trees, and on the other side, uninterrupted tracts of new homes plotted on treeless grids. There were huge parking lots and low rectangular buildings connected by little moving dots which crept along at a snail's pace. At one point in the river, it looked as if a large hand had reached down from the sky and pinched it, causing it to back up into a long narrow lake with fingers sticking out into the wooded and populated area around it. And there was a downtown, a small downtown neatly quartered by two main arteries that connected it with the beltline and the several factories that were the lifeblood of the city.

The heavy airplane tires hit the runway with a thud, making Dave's eyes spring open. For a moment he was in a panic about what was happening, and then the sinking feeling hit him as it had each time he had woken up in the last two days. Maura took his hand. "We're there," she said.

"I'm worried," Dave said.

"About what?"

"Mom doesn't take catastrophes very well."

"Nobody does."

"She has a history. She hardly said anything on the phone last night. I expected her to break down or something, but she just got real quiet." It had been the hardest phone call Dave had ever made. He had hoped that Albert would answer, but it was his mother. She had detected something in his voice immediately. When Dave told her about Eddie's death, she fell silent and then quickly handed the phone to Albert who took the details of their flight back to Greenbrier.

"She's got Albert," said Maura. "She'll be all right."

6

HOME TO GREENBRIER

A brisk northerly wind chilled Dave and Maura as they walked the hundred yards across the tarmac to the Greenbrier terminal, a low, neat, brick building with a coffee shop at one end. Dave looked up and saw his parents glued to one of the large windows. He had imagined them to be dressed in black from head to toe, stark mourning figures from an Edvard Munch painting, but his mother wore her heavy camel's hair coat with a flowery scarf on her head. She held a lace-trimmed handkerchief under her nose and even through the thick window glass he could see that her eyes were red and puffy. Albert had a good grip on her left arm and looked like a giant in his brown corduroy parka with the fake fur trim. He was a tall, thin man, slightly hunched over, and with very little hair left on his head. His sensitivity showed in the dark bags under his eyes. The tufts of hair above his ears were grayer than Dave remembered.

His mother looked much the same as she always had. The chestnut hair color, which covered her own mousy brown and gray, had been a part of her for so long that it seemed natural and it went well with her gray-green eyes. Her face was only a slightly weathered version of the pretty co-ed who had played Emily in a college production of Thornton Wilder's *Our Town.*

As Dave and Maura walked through a double set of automatic doors into the waiting room, Joan broke away from Albert's grip and fell into her son's arms. She seemed heavy, not quite able to support her own weight. Dave wavered a second before he could plant his feet solidly on the ground.

"I'm sorry. I don't want your old mother to embarrass you," she blubbered. "I've cried almost constantly since you called. I keep thinking I have it under control, and then something sets me off again. I'm so glad you're here now." Dave felt her wet face against his neck. He stroked the back of her head and said, "I know. I know." He looked over her shoulder at Albert, trying to get an indication of how she was doing, but Albert just stared at them sadly. His eyes, too, were watery. Maura stood awkwardly to one side clutching her shoulder bag.

Albert walked over to Maura and gave her a big fatherly hug, which took her by surprise. Enveloped by the spindly arms of the man, she smelled his Old Spice. They separated and Dave stuck out his right hand to Albert as he continued to hold his mother in his left arm. Then Maura leaned over to kiss Joan's wet salty cheek.

With the luggage collected, they headed out the main door toward the parking lot. Dave was the first to step outside the building and he stopped cold. Everyone else followed suit. Parked in front of the terminal was a J.T. Durbin and Sons hearse with the back door swung open. Dave and Maura had managed to forget that Eddie had been traveling on the plane with them. On seeing the scroll on the door of the hearse, Dave thought of the fans they used to find as kids in the pews at church during the summer. They were green cardboard with "Courtesy of J.T. Durbin and Sons" printed in Gothic script across them, and stapled to something which looked like a scalloped tongue depressor. Eddie had written a little poem about the fans for an English assignment at St. Ambrose. The teacher, an aging humorless nun, had found it unacceptable and made him do the assignment over. It was about meeting a girl at a school social and being afraid to ask her to dance. It began:

Get a Durbin fan and fan me
I think I'm getting hot
You'll find one in the last pew
I sit back there a lot.

Several men came from around the side of the building and loaded the coffin into the back of the hearse. Like four statues the Bates stood, bags in hand, turned to stone by the loneliest of all possible scenes.

"I think I should ride with Eddie," said Dave, breaking the spell.

Albert reached over and put his hand on Dave's shoulder and said softly, "I think your mother needs you. Eddie'll be all right." Dave nodded consent and Albert walked over to talk to the driver. Dave put his hand at the small of his mother's back and led her, stunned, to the car.

After a lunch of ham and cheese sandwiches Joan had put together that morning, Dave took Maura aside and told her he was going to the funeral home to try and see Eddie. Maura agreed to stay with Albert and Joan, and then went in to help clean up the kitchen. Albert sat in the breakfast nook working a crossword puzzle.

"Albert, could I borrow your car?" Dave felt the proverbial teenager. Albert didn't answer immediately, but turned toward Dave as if he had been awakened from a deep sleep.

"Why don't you take mine, honey?" called his mother from the kitchen. He always had to ask Albert even though it was his mother's car he usually ended up taking.

"Where are you going?"

"Just for a drive."

"Maybe Maura would like to go too. I can finish up here."

"No, I'd rather stay," said Maura.

Dave parked the car in front of the J.T. Durbin Funeral Home on Oak Street and walked into the building. The gloomy Gothic decor took Dave back to his grade school days when walking into church instilled him with fear. The silence of the reception room and the muted colors of the stained glass windows created an otherworldly atmosphere, a way station between here and the beyond. Under a veil of overly sweet floral essence (was it fresh-cut flowers or air freshener?), he tiptoed across the brown tile floor and peeked into side rooms expecting to see Eddie's coffin. Rounding a corner, he almost ran right into Mr. Durbin.

"May I help you?" Durbin said in a reverent but suspicious manner.

"Hello, Mr. Durbin. You probably don't remember me. I'm David Bates."

"Oh, Dave. Yes, I do now." There was a long dramatic pause. "Dave, I want to express the deepest regrets from me and my family to you and yours."

"Thank you. And how is your family? I haven't talked to Danny in a long time."

"Everyone's fine. Danny's in the business now. You ought to give him a call. He'd love to hear about your experiences in . . .where was it?"

"Saudi Arabia."

"Yes, Saudi Arabia. He had a friend in college from over there, you know, Iran."

"Oh, really? Well, that's quite a different place. But sure, I'll give him a call." It was odd that Durbin acted like he didn't know where Eddie had died. He stared into the emotionless eyes of the short, barrel-chested man for an awkward moment. "Mr. Durbin, I have a request to make."

"What is it, Dave?" His voice was soothing, hypnotic, seeming to be computer generated.

"I'd like to see Eddie."

Durbin's perfectly calm demeanor cracked ever so slightly. "I'm afraid that's not possible. Eddie's remains have been laid out in the coffin which your stepfather chose this morning and it's been sealed up as requested."

"Requested by whom? No one in the family has identified Eddie and we haven't requested a closed casket."

"But that's the information I received in the communiqué from the consulate that accompanied the body. Eddie had been identified and a closed casket had been requested due to the poor condition of the remains. I've done the best I could, but. . ."

"And what was the condition of the rem. . .Eddie, Mr. Durbin?"

"Well, like one finds after. . .after a bad auto accident."

Dave squinted, twisted his lips and continued staring Durbin down. "What if the family requested an autopsy?"

"That's a legal matter, Dave. But the funeral is scheduled for tomorrow morning. Don't make things uncomfortable for your parents." Beads of sweat formed on the man's wide forehead.

"I'm just not convinced that Eddie was killed in a car accident and that his body is in that coffin. I want to be sure. The Saudi police report was a little suspicious."

"Legal matters are not my concern. I have two funerals scheduled for tomorrow and lots of work to do. You'll excuse me, please. Don't forget to give Danny a call."

A plan was already forming in Dave's head. "I don't want to keep you from your work. Thanks for your time. Goodbye." Durbin's shoulders relaxed and he began to breathe easier.

When Dave got to the door, he turned around and saw that Durbin had already disappeared into his office. He opened the outer door and closed it, making the little bell ring, but he didn't go out. He stood in the vestibule out of sight for a moment, and then walked softly over to the office door, which had been left slightly ajar. There was a shuffle of papers and then a phone call.

"Hello. . .Yes, this is Mr. Durbin of J.T. Durbin and Sons Funeral Home in Greenbrier, Illinois. I was told to call you if there were any problems concerning the Edward Bates affair. . .Yes, I'm afraid so. There's some talk of an autopsy. . .his brother. . .Yes, tomorrow. . .I will. . .You're welcome."

Dave hurried to the door and tried to hold the little bell as he went out. When he let it go, it tinkled slightly. Durbin came out of his office saying, "Hello. May I help you?" But there was no one there.

Danny Durbin had been a good friend of Dave's in high school. When he was sober, he was one of the nicest guys around. Alcohol brought out a wild streak in him. In the old days he loved to party and his drinking frequently led to fights. In his junior year he was expelled twice for being drunk at school. Danny had said he would never join the family business; the last thing he wanted to do was mess around with dead people. Dave decided to give him a call and see what had changed his mind.

"Hi, Danny. This is Dave Bates."

"Dave! This is a surprise. Gee, I'm real sorry about Eddie. Must be a real. . .mindblower. How ya doing?"

Mindblower? Dave thought. Interesting choice of words. He almost hung up. "It's been really tough, Danny. Can't even begin to describe it. Say, think you could get away for a beer?"

"You mean now?"

"Sure. Why not?"

"Let me ask Mary if she has anything planned." Even with Danny's hand on the mouthpiece, Dave could tell that Danny and Mary had words. Danny came back on the line. "Sure, Dave. Why don't we get together at the University Pub? I could meet you in half to three-quarters of an hour."

"Great. See you there."

As soon as they met, Dave could tell that the old Danny had been tamed. His face was tired and puffy, and he had a substantial beer belly—signs of the successful family business, a wife that Dave had heard was a shotgun marriage, and two kids. The strain of maintaining it all was evident in his face.

"Something must agree with you over there, Dave. You look great."

"Looks like you're not doing too bad yourself. Wasn't that a BMW I saw you pull up in?"

"Ain't that a honey? People die and get buried and I end up with a BMW. Life's strange, huh?" That was about as philosophical a statement as Dave could imagine from Danny.

They talked a little about old times, but it fizzled quickly as Danny went through the old gang, most of whom hadn't left Greenbrier. Dave bought time by telling all his strange stories of Saudi Arabia—how Maura had gotten whacked on the legs, how the students burrowed into their P-coats on cool winter mornings, and how he had no idea what Saudi women looked like. He figured if he got a few beers in

Danny, he'd be more amenable to the plan Dave had in mind. After they finished their third round, Dave couldn't wait any longer.

"Danny, I've got a favor to ask of you. It's a big one. I want to see Eddie." Danny got a serious look on his face and started to speak, but Dave held up his hand. "Before you tell me it isn't possible, just hear me out. There are some unusual circumstances concerning Eddie's death. They wouldn't let me identify the body over there and the police report was sketchy, as if it had been falsified. I went to see your father this afternoon and he got nervous and defensive when I asked to see Eddie, said it wasn't possible. The more I think about it, the closer I come to believing it wasn't an accident at all. Certain people seem to want to keep the whole affair under the rug."

"Wait. Are you accusing my father of being involved in some kind of—"

"I'm not accusing anybody of anything. I just want to know what happened. You're the only one that can help me, Danny."

Danny stared into his beer and said softly, "I can't, Dave." Then he looked out the window at his car. "I can't go against my father." Dave wanted grab him and shake him. What happened to the rebel? There was a time when he went against his father at every turn.

"Danny, listen to me. If your brother Pat died, wouldn't you at least want to know how it happened?"

"I thought it was an accident."

"That's what I'm telling you. I have reason to believe that it wasn't, and every time I try to find out what really happened I run into a brick wall. I just want to go in there, open up the casket and look at Eddie. Whatever we find, we can close it up and proceed with the funeral tomorrow."

"Don't ask me to do that. You and Eddie were always good friends. I'd like to help you, but if my father found out. . ."

Dave had one last card to play. "Danny, remember that time we saved your ass, the time the police came looking for you for being involved in a fight at the Steak 'n Shake and breaking several windows? We swore in front of your father that you had been with us all evening. You owe me, man." Danny hung his head like a scolded dog. They drank in silence.

"All right, Dave." He looked up with an impish smile from out of the past. "When it's done, it's done. We seal it up and say nothing. The funeral goes on tomorrow, okay?"

"Thanks, Danny."

"I'll need some coffee."

As they entered the back door of the funeral home, Dave was hit again with the sickly-sweet flowery smell. He was fighting nausea at what they were about to do and the floral smell nearly put him over the edge. Danny hastened to turn off the alarm system and then they followed the beam of his flashlight into one of the windowless parlors where he turned on some low lights. A coffin rested on a platform surrounded by flower arrangements. As Danny got the tools he needed and started working on the coffin, Dave paced the room, feeling the sweat rolling down from his armpits though the room had the coolness of death.

Dave was reading one of the cards from the family of his high school sweetheart when he heard Danny say in a low voice, "Dave, I've got it open. Okay. Here we go." The lid creaked.

Dave jumped. "What was that?"

"It was the lid. Come take a look."

He held back, but strained his eyes in the low light to peer around Danny's large frame into the shadowy opening. Danny turned and took Dave by the arm, pulling him closer.

The first thing Dave noticed was the way they had combed Eddie's hair. It was too neat and swooped down over his forehead in a style that he had never worn. The face also looked peculiar, as if it had been forced into a position of repose when shock had been his last living emotion. But it was Eddie's face and Dave felt the blood draining from his extremities until he looked more deathlike than the made-up corpse. Danny took hold of his arm to keep him upright.

"He looks in pretty good shape, Dave. I read the report from the consulate and they said the body was badly damaged, something about a fire in the accident. It's strange. My father took care of everything himself. He's good at what he does, but he can't work miracles. He doesn't usually do this stuff anymore." Danny began to examine Eddie more closely. Dave stood, his mouth agape, unable to speak or move, though inside he realized that what he had suspected was proving true.

"Look, Dave," Danny said excitedly. He pointed to a line across Eddie's throat. Dave bent down closer. Danny turned to Dave, their noses almost touching. "His throat's been cut," said Danny in a mysterious whisper. Dave reached out and shakily touched the scar on his brother's throat. It was heavily coated with make-up and cold to the touch. The room was like a freezer and he began to shiver.

"Okay, Danny. You can close it." His voice was barely audible.

"Are you all right, Dave?"

"Yeah. I just need to get out of here."

"Why don't you go on home? I'll finish up here."

Dave arrived home about midnight. Maura and his mother were waiting up for him. His mother had obviously been crying.

As he came in the door she confronted him as she had so many times in the past. "David Bates! Where have you been? You should be ashamed, leaving your family for hours on end like this. We were worried half to death."

"Sorry, Mom. I needed to be alone for a while."

"Well, you might think of someone besides yourself for a change. Have you been drinking?"

"I had a few beers, but you're surely not going to get on my case for that. I'm sorry you worried."

"I just think it was terribly inconsiderate." She was on the verge of tears again "Are you hungry?"

"I can fix something. You should go to bed, Mom. Tomorrow will be a tough day."

"Don't you kids stay up too late, either." Her anger had faded away. "I've put you two in your old room, Dave. Sorry about the single beds."

"We'll manage."

"Goodnight, honey. Goodnight, Maura." She kissed them both and went up the stairs to where Albert could be heard snoring.

As soon as she was out of range, Maura asked, "Are you all right? You look horrible."

Dave slumped down into a stuffed chair in the living room. The cat came from out of nowhere and started rubbing up against Dave's legs. "I saw him."

"Eddie?" Maura fell to her knees on the floor next to him.

"His throat was cut. He wasn't in an accident." The words came out slowly and without emotion.

Maura gulped and put her hand to her neck. "You're sure?" Dave explained the afternoon's events—the phone call Durbin made, the conversation with Danny and finally the shock of seeing Eddie, the strange look on his face and the cold touch of his skin.

"We have to go to Paris to find Khalil and then back to Saudi."

Maura shuddered. She was sure Dave wouldn't be satisfied until he knew the whole story. How could she save him from himself, from a search that would be the most dangerous thing he had ever done? "I'm worried, Dave. I think we should go to the police."

"The police can't do anything in Saudi Arabia."

"I mean the government, the CIA. . .somebody?"

"Don't you see? There's a cover-up going on here. That call Durbin made had to be to someone in the State Department, or maybe the CIA. They probably threatened to revoke his license if he didn't go along with them. If the funeral proceeds as normal, they'll think everything is okay, the evidence is in the ground."

"This is getting too involved."

"We just have to play dumb and act smart. That's the ticket." He thought hard a minute. "Maura, you don't have to go with me if you don't want to. You don't have to go back."

"Right. You think I'm going to sit around here in the States while you're off chasing murderers around the world. I'm going with you. Just promise me one thing. If it gets too dangerous, you'll stop this, get some help, not do anything foolish."

"The last thing I want to do is get myself killed. We just have to use our heads." Dave put his arm around her, trying to quiet the anxiety on her face. "You look tired. Should we go to bed?"

"I don't really feel tired. Do you?"

"It must be like nine in the morning for us."

"We should try and get some sleep, though."

"Or at least get into bed. It's getting kind of chilly down here."

"Single beds, remember?" she joked.

The following day was one of the rare Midwestern February mornings that teases, making one believe for a moment that spring is on the way. The sun shone brightly in a clear blue sky and it was unseasonably warm. Maura got up to open the window, anxious to hear the song sparrows and finches chattering and chirping. She was met by the smells of thawing earth, brown grass being hit by the sun and evergreen giving up its fragrance. Even with the bare trees, naked shrubs and the broken brown stalks of the garden, it seemed a beautiful and vibrant land compared to the desert where they had been living. She dreaded going back there, and she turned to look at her husband. Though asleep, his face was not relaxed, would not be until he had solved the mystery of his brother's death. And then what? Would they be able to go ahead with their lives or would the full weight of Eddie's absence come down on them once the search was ended. Dave's preoccupation with Eddie's death allowed him to stave off the depression of loss, but the investigation Dave talked about could very well put them in serious danger.

The crisp clean air of winter filled the room. Dave stretched, and then opened his eyes. "That's nice," he said. Maura looked beautiful in her nightgown, fresh and defiant like an Irish princess as the breeze gently rustled her hair and the sunlight picked up her freckles. For a moment, Dave thought of sex, a fleeting notion that stirred then quickly dissipated.

She smiled at him as if to say, "Me, too, but I understand." Just as Maura started to get up from her crouching position by the window, there was a light rap on the door.

"Dave? Maura? Are you awake?" called Joan softly.

"Yes, Mother."

"Can I come in?"

"Yes, Mother." As she opened the door, Maura sat back on her heels by the window.

"Maura! You'll catch your death of cold with the window open like that."

"It's really quite warm today," said Maura as she closed the window.

"Not at all like it's supposed to be," said Joan.

"Meaning?" asked Dave.

"Oh, you know, rainy and gray for a funeral day; sunny and bright on the other side." She tried to be in control, but turned away to hide the tears that were coming. "I almost forgot what I came for. Oh, I have some breakfast cooking." They could smell the bacon and cinnamon rolls wafting up the back stairway from the kitchen, reminding Dave of Sunday mornings from his childhood.

"Not the cinnamon rolls, Mom. You didn't!"

"I did. Eddie used to love them so."

"We used to get out the food coloring and make the icing all kinds of inedible colors—purple swirls, pea green and canary yellow stripes, and one we called black licorice."

Joan put a hand over her mouth and hurried from the room.

The air at the funeral mass was pungent with incense, an odor that Dave used to find mysterious, and as he got into his teenage years, sexually exciting. Now it seemed oppressive, sucking out the air that he needed so much these days. At the same time it set off a spell of reminiscing about their school days and especially the many times he and Eddie had served at Mass together, all the times they had to suppress giggling fits when the priest, who was prone to farting, would let one go. Dave thought of the time that Eddie had dropped the water cruet and it broke in the middle of Mass. Dave rushed into the sacristy to get a replacement and the Mass continued with Eddie in a state of shock, a look of horror on his face. After the Mass was over and he apologized to the priest, Dave teased him about it as they took off their cassocks and surplices. He told Eddie that he had committed a terrible sin and that he was sure to go to hell. When Eddie started to cry, Dave continued to taunt him for his "sin," and then for being a crybaby. Eddie would get a kick out of recalling the incident now, though he still wished he had the opportunity to apologize for his meanness, that time, and a hundred others when he had taken advantage of being the older brother.

Barely aware of what went on in the Mass, Dave instead concentrated on memories of Eddie, falling into a dreamlike state from the incense, the heaviness of the day, and the overheated church. At the gravesite, in the open air, Dave perked up, took in the surroundings, the day still sunny and warm, the bare trees, crunching gravel as each new car arrived. He also didn't miss the stranger. Turning to Maura, he said, "Don't look now, but there is a man standing at the back of the crowd in a navy suit. He's wearing sunglasses. What's your impression?"

A couple of minutes later, Maura whispered, "Official."

"CIA, if you ask me."

"Let's not be paranoid."

"I haven't been wrong yet."

"Should I try to talk to him? He might be a distant relative."

"Let's just watch him."

Joan looked over and gave them an admonishing glance.

When Eddie had been lowered into the ground, they had thrown their roses on the casket—Dave threw Gerbera daisies—and the air had cleared of incense, Dave and Maura looked around for the man in the sunglasses. He was gone.

"Just stayed around long enough to make sure Eddie was in the ground," Dave guessed.

"Let's say you're right," Maura proposed as they walked toward the waiting limousines. "What interest could the CIA have in Eddie's death?"

"That's what I want to find out."

"And if they are interested in Eddie's death, don't you think that it would make things a little beyond us?"

"If we don't do something, nobody will. Eddie's death will be covered over and forgotten. We'll never know why he died. I don't care what kind of games the Saudis and Americans want to play with each other, but why should Eddie have to die because of them?"

"You think Eddie's death was political?"

"Well, put the things we know together. Eddie was on his way to a prince's palace. His tape recorder is missing. He was killed. And some people pretty high up have an interest in keeping the whole thing quiet. There's one person who can fill in the missing details."

"Khalil."

"We've got to get to Paris and find him. He's the key."

"That's not going to be easy. When should we go?"

"If Mom doesn't throw a fit, we'll leave in a couple of days. I'll tell her I have to get back to work."

"If we're going to Paris, I have to do something about Beth. I can't go to Paris and not see her."

"We'd better not involve her in this. The less people who know about it the better."

"I haven't spoken to her since the wedding flap, but she's still my sister. After what happened to Eddie, it makes me want to repair things with her. Just like that," she snapped her fingers, "a person can be taken from your life forever."

7

ABOVE AND BELOW PARIS

The three days after the funeral were agony for Dave, who was wound up like a racehorse, his mission keeping his muscles taut. He took long walks and jogged in the early morning cold until finally one day at breakfast he bit down on his guilt about leaving and told his mother they had a flight booked for the following day. By that time winter had returned to the Midwest. Layers of ashen clouds hung low over the city, and the brown grass was laced with frost each dawn. With the gray backdrop, the Greenbrier airport looked more dismal than ever, filled with people who wore the expressions of refugees anxious to escape. In the waiting room Joan stood, gripping the handkerchief that had become a nearly permanent fixture in her hand. "I hate to see you go," she said, "but I know you have obligations. You won't stay over there any longer than you have to, will you?"

"Don't worry about that. Maura wouldn't let me. My contract's up in June and we'll come back for a nice long visit then." A flight announcement drowned out Joan's response. Her lips trembled slightly as she formed the parting words that they didn't hear.

"That's our plane," said Maura. They hugged Joan and Albert hurriedly, and proceeded to Gate 3, the third break in the chain-link fence.

On the one-hour flight to Chicago and then the eight hours to Paris, Maura was the one who stayed awake this time. She trudged through the waste of her family history, recalling each hurt and missed opportunity. Her relationship with her sister, Beth, had been strained for as long as she could remember and she concluded that she had to do something about it. Whereas Dave and Eddie had been almost inseparable, Maura and Beth spent little time together, even when they were growing up. Beth was four years older and wanted nothing to do with Maura and their little brother, Max. They rarely saw her after she went to college, though she remained close to their father and defended him on the few occasions that she and Maura spoke.

In Maura's eyes their father's drinking was the disease that never allowed them to be a real family, a condition that became even worse in the years after Beth left. He was often out of control, and he treated their mother horribly. The abuse was more psychological, but a couple of times it became physical with their mother ending up with bruises and a black eye that she tried to hide. After twenty-five years of marriage, Maura finally convinced her mother to file for divorce. Beth was furious at Maura and the tension exploded when she flew over from Paris to attend Maura's wedding. She called Maura a heartless bitch, blaming her for destroying their parents' marriage, and then berating her for not inviting her own father to her wedding.

They had managed to get through the simple ceremony and most of the reception, without any mention of their dad. As Dave and Maura got ready to leave for Cancun, their mother invited Beth back to the house. Beth didn't answer, but instead asked her mother if she had talked to their dad.

Maura overheard and blew up. "He has nothing to do with this," she said.

"Except that he happens to be your father and should have walked you down the aisle instead of Uncle Mike who could barely stand up."

"What makes you think Dad would have been any better?"

Maura clutched the colored beads around her neck that went with her honeymoon outfit, and let fly a bitter synopsis of those years after Beth left for France leading up to their parent's divorce. Beth stormed out, and without saying goodbye to anyone, packed her bags and returned to Paris. They hadn't spoken since.

Dave and Maura landed at Orly airport outside Paris with their internal clocks so confused that the time of day hardly seemed more relevant than the day of the week. It had only been one week since Dave had been notified of Eddie's death, though it seemed like eons had passed.

In a bargain hotel in the Latin Quarter they dropped their bags and looked around the shoddy room with its stained carpet and smell of old tobacco. Dave sat down in a creaky desk chair and Maura sunk into the bed. They looked at each other as if the low ceiling had fallen down about their shoulders. "How the hell are we going to do this?" said Maura.

"I have no fucking idea."

"Trying to patch up five-year rift with a sister, who could probably care less, seems like a breeze compared to finding Khalil, no last name, in a city of eight million people."

"There must be a Lebanese community, an area where they live. We can start there."

"Beth has lived here a long time. If she doesn't hang up on me, maybe she could help us. She always had an adventurous streak."

"That's a big if."

"Wish me luck," she said, picking up the phone like it was an unfamiliar contraption.

"Beth, it's me, Maura. I'm here in Paris. Please don't hang up." She heard a heavy sigh on the other end. "Are you there?"

"I'm here."

"You probably don't know what to say, so just listen. Dave's brother, Eddie, died in Saudi Arabia. We went to Greenbrier for the funeral. Now we are on our way back over there."

"My God! What happened?"

"An accident, they say."

"They say?"

"It's a long story. Beth, I've been doing a lot of thinking lately. I don't want to continue like this. I mean between us."

"You think I do? I feel terrible. You were right."

"About what?"

"Dad. He's in a 12-step program."

"I heard that."

"The last time I saw him he told me everything. That's part of the process, you know. He admitted how horrible he was to Mom, and you and Max. I had no idea. I guess I didn't want to believe it. He and I were always close."

"I know."

"I'm glad you're here. It's time we put this behind us. Are you going to be in town for a while?"

"A few days. We have some business to take care of."

"So it wasn't just to see me." Her voice lost its wind temporarily. "But that's okay. You called. That's the important thing. I want to see you as soon as possible."

The reunion of the two sisters was civil, unemotional. As they were never close, there were no tears, long hugs, or laments about lost time. They simply talked. Maura agreed that she would ask their mother to talk to their father. Both Maura and her mother had refused to see him when he attempted to make amends and ask their forgiveness. Now it was time to leave it all behind. While Maura and Beth discussed family matters, Dave wandered around Beth's large apartment off Haussmann in the ninth arrondissement. Except for the living room, which she kept relatively uncluttered so she would have a place to receive guests and clients, the rest of the apartment was filled with old furniture and paintings of all sizes and in various stages of restoration.

Dave paused in front of a painting propped up against an easel, a good-sized eighteenth century portrait of a Rubenesque madam in her garden. It looked perfect.

Beth came up behind him. "I've been working on it every day for two weeks, but of course, it's not finished," she explained. "They're supposed to pick it up tomorrow." She showed him a photograph of what it looked like when she first got it. It had two large gouges and several worn patches that had nothing left of the original color.

"I can't believe it is the same painting. This place is like a museum."

"Very few of the pieces are actually mine, and even the ones that are, I'd sell for the right price. Sometimes I want to have a huge bargain sale and get rid of everything, take off like a gypsy and travel around Italy."

"You have a great talent," said Maura.

"Thanks." She picked up a music box off a Louis XVI ebony side cabinet and examined it as if it was the first time she had seen it. "You know, I still don't get what you two are doing in Paris."

Maura looked at Dave and he nodded. They had discussed it on the way over to Beth's place. If things went well, they would tell her the truth and ask for her help. "We have reason to believe that Eddie's death was not an accident," said Maura. "What we have learned so far makes us think he was murdered, and that there's been an official cover-up. Possibly the last person to see Eddie alive was a Lebanese man named Khalil. Dave went to his place of work and found out that he was given money and sent to Paris."

Beth hugged the music box to her stomach and let her eyes open large. "So you want to track down this guy and see if he'll talk?"

"That's the gist of it," said Maura. "Pretty far-fetched, huh?"

"Damn! I'm the one that is supposed to have the exciting, adventurous life and you are making my life look dull as dishwater. You guys have me completely intrigued. Tell me everything from the beginning."

"We don't expect you to get involved," said Dave. "Just point us in the right direction. We also might need your translating abilities from time to time."

"Nonsense. You're going to need someone who speaks French on this full time. I'm prepared to do everything I can. I love a good mystery."

"But this could get dangerous," said Dave.

Maura rolled her eyes. "That's what I've been trying to tell him all along."

Beth cast off the threat of danger with a careless wave. "We'll find him. There are lots of Lebanese restaurants and cafes in Paris, a few right here in my neighborhood. We can start with them. I don't know, though, a Lebanese man named Khalil who recently came from Saudi Arabia. That's not much to go on. How long can you stay?"

"The company told us to take as much time as we needed, so that's what we're doing," Maura said.

"The truth is, they don't care if we come back at all," Dave added. "They'd just as soon forget the Bates brothers ever existed."

Beth put her hand on Dave's arm. "I'm really sorry, Dave. I only met Eddie briefly at the wedding. He was so beautiful and full of life."

Dave, Maura and Beth walked along the Boulevard des Italiens in the cool, damp air of Parisian winter. After the isolation of Saudi Arabia and the drabness of Greenbrier, Dave and Maura felt besieged by the sights, smells and sounds of the city. The streets were alive with movement, the cafes bustled, and giant movie marquees flashed brilliantly in the electric air. The high-pitched nasal sound of French car horns burst constantly from the traffic, geese honking their way home. With natural grace, waiters moved about the many restaurants lighting lamps and candles as they prepared the tables for the evening dinner crowd, and the rapid Parisian tongue rolled off moist lips, surrounding them in a sensuous web of foreign sounds. The loose-fitting clothing, with particular attention to hats, gloves and scarves swirled about them like a fashion show gone haywire. Everyone seemed in a rush, and the three of them were swept along the few blocks to the restaurant where Beth was friendly with the Lebanese owner. The plan was to discreetly pick his brain as to where they might find Khalil.

"What do I tell him?" asked Beth.

"That Khalil left his truck behind in Saudi Arabia and we want to buy it. He neglected to leave the necessary papers to make the transfer," said Dave.

Maura scrunched up her nose. "Is that believable?"

"We can't tell the truth."

"I guess not."

When they stopped in front of a window with a huge display of fresh fruit, people pushed by them on the narrow street with bags of fresh produce, wine and naked loaves of bread stuck under their arms. Beth explained that the restaurant was North African and featured couscous. They saw a number of couscous restaurants on the street.

"Where we're going," said Beth, "is on the rue du Faubourg Montmartre, a restaurant called Chez Beirut."

"Doesn't sound very appetizing," said Dave.

"Not these days," agreed Maura.

"Is anybody hungry?" asked Beth. "We're likely to get more information if we sit down and eat something."

"I'm starved. We haven't eaten anything since the pitiful lunch they served on the plane. . .or was it breakfast? Maura?"

"I could eat something, sure."

They opened the carved mahogany door of Chez Beirut and saw that the restaurant was completely empty. Beth looked at her watch. "We're early for dinner, at least by Paris standards. Would you believe that in the summer you see people eating as late as midnight?"

A man wearing a street coat over his white shirt and black bow tie hurried out from the kitchen, and recognizing Beth, greeted her with a series of cheek kisses. Andre directed them to a table by the window and held Beth's chair. She asked him if he was cold. He looked down at his jacket and apologized, and then dashed off to the kitchen. Maura commented that Andre looked like Marlon Brando in *Streetcar Named Desire.* He even had a Brando voice, speaking French with a peculiar, breathy tone.

"You're right. It never occurred to me," said Beth. "I've got an idea."

When he returned coatless, Beth asked him if he had ever seen *Last Tango in Paris,* a film he more likely had seen than *Streetcar*. He answered no with an expression of suspicion on his face. She told him they thought he looked like the star of the film, though when the star was much younger. He smiled shyly and seemed pleased that they thought he looked like a movie star. Beth continued with a story about Dave and Maura being movie producers, who had just come from working on a film in Saudi Arabia. A young Lebanese man had worked with them on the set, but had suddenly left for Paris before the shoot was finished, something about visa problems. They had become friendly with the man and they would like to find him, possibly offer him more work in their next film.

Maura leaned forward and gave Dave a confused look. She understood enough French to know that Beth had shifted stories. Dave didn't have a clue. When the waiter had gone, Beth repeated in English what they had discussed, admitting that she glamorized the story slightly.

"Slightly?" said Maura, remembering from their childhood how much Beth liked to invent stories.

"In any case, he said it was unlikely that such a young man would come to this quarter. Andre has been in Paris for twenty years and knows what he is talking about. Most of the new immigrants in this part of town are North African. The young Lebanese go to the Latin Quarter, looking for work in the clothes stores and restaurants there. He told me to check his uncle's restaurant on boulevard St. Michel and his cousin's on boulevard St. Germain. We can head over there tomorrow."

They dined on humous, tabouleh and shish kebab, and were well taken care of by the man who reminded them of Marlon Brando. No one else came in the restaurant while they ate, drank wine and talked of their lives. Several times Maura had to put her hand on Dave's leg to stop its nervous vibration. Then she would squeeze his thigh as if to say, "Try to relax a little. We'll find him."

The three of them spent the better part of Sunday talking to Lebanese restaurant owners in the Latin Quarter who referred them to relatives, friends, and friends of friends, but no one had seen or heard of this Khalil from Saudi Arabia. They had had their fill of Lebanese food, for at each place, even when they didn't order anything, the Lebanese they befriended kept offering them tastes of their house specialties. As friends or relatives had sent them, it would have been unthinkable to let them leave without having eaten something.

Beth played beautifully the role of information-getter. She delighted them with her compliments, her smiles, and her "charming" accent. Whereas true Parisians were at best tolerant of an American speaking French, these immigrants hung on every word. Exhausted,

Beth left them at a cafe on the boulevard St. Michel in late afternoon. They planned to meet for dinner later that evening.

In the cafe, Dave had fallen into the other end of his personality spectrum, quiet and morose, and even two espressos hadn't snapped him out of it. From his shadowy mood, he scrutinized each passer-by. After a half-hour of his silence, Maura spoke, "What are you looking for, Dave? You don't even know what he looks like."

"I can guess," he mumbled.

Maura wrapped her hand around her coffee cup and held on for support. "I can do more than guess," she announced. She had thought a lot about what she was about to reveal. Since the day Dave had mentioned that Khalil worked in a clothes store near Safeway she had imagined ways to ease the fact that she had met him into the conversation. But she always came up with a frozen tongue. Her brief encounters with him had been innocent, but her attraction and the bathtub fantasies still left her with a knot of guilt in her stomach.

Dave took his eyes off the street and turned to her. "Would you care to elaborate on that?"

"I think I've met this man, Khalil. I never knew his name."

"What are you talking about?"

"Remember the night of the *mutawain?* While you were busy giving your information, a very nice-looking Arab man was standing near me and urged me to stay quiet, just when I was about to explode. Later when I turned around he was gone. A few weeks later I saw him in Safeway. I tried to say hello, but he ignored me as was proper. I wanted to thank him for what he did that night, so I followed him into a nearby clothes shop. Once inside the store, I realized that he worked there. I felt awkward and didn't know what to say, so I left. It must be the same Khalil."

"You chased a stranger around the shopping center, the very man we have been knocking ourselves out to find, and you didn't think it was important enough to tell me?"

"I didn't chase him. . .I just—"

"I don't get it. There's something you're not telling me. Are you hot for this guy?"

"Don't be ridiculous. I didn't even talk to him, and we aren't absolutely sure it is the same person. You are starting to sound like a Saudi with the attitude that women can't be trusted, that first chance we get we'll attack any man. You have no idea what it is like being a woman in a country where you can hardly take a shit without asking your husband's permission."

"Too bad for Eddie that this guy was more interested in my brother than my wife! Either way I lose." He stood up and peered down at her. "There are times I wonder where your brain is!" With a dramatic pirouette, he stormed out of the cafe.

Maura sat fuming in the hard metal chair, aware of the other patrons' eyes upon her, holding an empty but still warm cup in her hands. She wasn't anxious to go outside as she saw the people on the street huddled up in their heavy winter coats with steamy breath coming out of their mouths. Staring out at the late afternoon crowd, she saw a man who looked like Khalil and she stood up quickly. He disappeared into a group of students and she sat down. A minute later she saw another man who resembled Khalil, and then another. The street was filled with Khalils going this way and that. In her confusion she began to doubt if she could even recognize the real one anymore. She called the waiter to pay the bill.

She left the café and walked down the boulevard St. Germain. She'd had enough of the boulevard St. Michel that day and without paying much attention to where she was going, she walked along, thinking about what she would say to Dave when they met back at the hotel. She should have mentioned from the beginning her brief encounters with the man that could be Khalil. But why was Dave being an asshole about it? Their relationship had been on rocky ground even before Eddie's death. The tension of living in Saudi Arabia—she had to admit a lot of it was her fault—had crept into their day-to-day life and lovemaking had become an infrequent and somewhat delicate task. She wasn't cut out to be a *hausfrau,* baking cakes and waiting for her hubby to come home so she could please him between the sheets. One of the reasons she had married Dave was because he wasn't the kind of man who would expect a doting wife. Something about Saudi Arabia had changed him, both of them.

A couple of times she looked up to see that the stores were getting more elegant, the window displays more elaborate. In front of one, she saw a tall dark man wearing a jacket too thin for the cold weather. He was hunched over and seemed to be shivering as he examined the women's clothes in the window. Maura stopped to look at the display too, and chanced a glance in his direction. She quickly looked away because he also looked like Khalil. Having been too long without a good night's sleep, she felt the need to stretch out and relax for a while, and it seemed like good a time to go back to the hotel and face Dave.

Both she and the man pulled away from the window at the same time, going in opposite directions. They collided, and for a split second, Maura found herself looking into a familiar face. She gasped, but he looked right through her and continued in his direction with a hurried, "*Pardon*." Her next move was pure instinct as she was much too shaken to think clearly. She followed him, staying as close as she could behind him while they made their way through the crowded streets. When he stopped to peer in a window, she stopped and stood at the one next door. She could feel her heart pounding and she no longer felt the cold.

At boulevard St. Michel, Khalil turned left toward the Seine. Maura followed him up the boulevard, then across the Pont St. Michel to the Ile de la Cite where he turned right and walked along the river toward Notre Dame. It was getting dark now and there were fewer people on the streets than there had been in the Latin Quarter. Maura dropped back. Once, while walking on the north side of Notre Dame, Khalil stopped to look up at the menacing gargoyles of the old Gothic church. Maura followed his gaze up to the grotesque creatures and a chill went up her spine. Before the man walked on, he looked back and saw Maura standing ridiculously in the middle of the street, head tilted toward the sky. She turned and went in a nearby cafe. When she exited the café a minute later, he was gone. Her panic paralyzed her for a moment, and then she ran in the direction he had been walking. At the corner, she saw that he had crossed the small bridge to the Ile St. Louis and she hurried after him.

The main Street of the Ile St. Louis was empty except for an unmistakably American family coming her way, the kind of American tourists that Parisians love to hate. The father, mother, son and daughter were all overweight and eating ice cream cones in the middle of February. Their twangy voices seemed to carry for blocks as they echoed off the 17th century facades of the narrow street. "This is the best thing in Paris," said the little girl, brandishing her ice cream cone against anyone who would disagree. Maura tried to slip by them unnoticed, keeping an eye on Khalil about fifty yards ahead. But just as she passed, the woman reached out with her down-home voice.

"Honey, do you speak English?"

"*No. Je ne parle pas Anglais,*" came out of Maura's mouth before she had even realized what happened.

"I guess not, Mother," the man said.

As Maura walked on she heard the woman say, "Gee whiz, they told us lots of people over here spoke English, but I'll be darned if I can find a one. I just wanna know where the Eiffel Tower is. We at least gotta see that."

After a short distance, Khalil disappeared into one of the buildings. When she got up to it, she saw that it was a small hotel and through the glass door she watched him collect his key from the desk clerk. She retraced her steps until she found a cafe about half a block up the street. In her excitement, she could hardly hold the phone and she prayed that Dave would be at the hotel. It rang three times.

"Come on. Don't be an asshole. Answer the goddamn phone."

"Hello." His voice was sullen.

"Dave, don't be angry. And whatever you do, don't hang up." She pushed each word out over her excited breathing. "I've found him."

Silence.

"Dave? I found Khalil."

"What are you saying?"

"Khalil. I've found him; at least I'm pretty sure it's him. I saw him on the boulevard St. Germain and I followed him back to his hotel."

Dave started to say something, then stopped. "You really think it's him? Where are you?"

"The little island near Notre Dame. He's in a hotel here. I'm up the street at a cafe. You better call Beth and have her bring you over. Write this down. The hotel is number 75 rue St. Louis. I'm at number 66."

"Okay. Wait there."

"What if he leaves again?"

"Just stay there. And Maura?"

"What?"

"I'm sorry."

"Forget it. Just hurry."

Maura took a table by the window in the deserted cafe and ordered a *croque-monsieur* and a coffee. Due to the several different Lebanese dishes floating around in her digestive system, she wasn't hungry when the sandwich came, but she didn't feel comfortable sitting there just drinking coffee. About twenty minutes later, Khalil hurried by on his way back toward the Ile de la Cite, and Maura abandoned the project of trying to eat the sandwich with a knife and fork. "What'll I do now?" she said out loud. A minute later, Dave and Beth arrived.

"God, you just missed him," Maura said, jumping up. "He went that way." She looked out the window and pointed to a lone figure in the distance.

"What's he look like?" said Dave heading back out the door.

"He's wearing a tan jacket, blue jeans, and he's tall, dark. . ."

". . .and handsome, right?" Dave winked at her and took off after the man. "I'll call you at the hotel," he shouted back. Beth collapsed into the chair next to Maura. "This is too much," she said, still panting. "We ran the whole way from the Metro station, figured the Metro would be quicker than trying to drive at this hour. How in the world did you find him?"

"That's another story. The first thing we need to do is to find out if that's really him."

"You're not sure?" said Beth in shock.

"I only saw him twice in Saudi Arabia, and very briefly both times."

"Why didn't you mention that before?"

"I wasn't sure he was the same guy we were looking for. I never knew his name. And both times that I saw him were embarrassing situations."

"This is sounding more interesting all the time."

"Not really that interesting, but it would be hard to forget a face like his. Of course, now that I've sent Dave running after him, I'm a little bit doubtful. Let's go over to the hotel and see what we can find out. We'll make up a story. Come on, you're good at that."

"You make me sound like a con artist or something."

"You know, con artists, used car dealers and antique dealers," Maura teased.

"How would you like to wear that *croque-monsieur*?"

"Two *croque-madames* might be more appropriate," Maura joked as they stepped out into the street. Despite the strange circumstances, or perhaps due to them, they were beginning to find their footing with each other.

Beth told the elderly man at the hotel desk that she was an English teacher and she had seen a notice inquiring about English lessons on a bulletin board at the American Center. He only left the name Khalil and this address, so she stopped by to see if he was still interested. The clerk said that there was a Khalil Shariff in room 206, but he had just stepped out. Perhaps she would like to leave a message. Beth took the paper and pen and wrote down a false name and number. While Beth talked to the short, bright-eyed man, Maura noticed the key for 206 on the counter; the man hadn't put it away yet. Maura slipped it into her pocket. Beth said goodbye and as they walked out, Maura drew up close to her and whispered, "I got the key to 206."

"No," said Beth, incredulous.

"Yes."

"I better think of something fast." She turned around to the man who smiled after them. "By the way, I've always been curious about this little hotel. Would it be possible to see some of the rooms? My parents might like to stay here next time they come to Paris." The man was quick to offer a tour of a couple of rooms.

Outside a room on the first floor, Maura asked to use the bathroom and the desk clerk pointed to a door at the end of the hall. While Beth engaged the man in conversation in one of the rooms, Maura hurried up to the second floor and slipped into 206. The first thing she noticed when she opened the door was a sharp odor of man.

Most likely he had not opened the window in the time that he had been there, unable to tolerate the fresh chilly air of the Paris winter. The curtains were drawn, making the room dark, and she tripped over a pair of shoes while looking for the light switch. In the harsh light of the overhead lamp, the room seemed even more distasteful—strewn with clothes, the bed unmade, and empty coke bottles sitting on the dresser.

Her eyes fell on the night table where there was a small worn blue backpack. It looked like Eddie's. She walked over and picked up the pack and noted that it was unusually heavy. It seemed to hold a hard, solid object. She unzipped the bag, and with goose bumps rising on her arms, reached in and pulled out a peculiar-shaped stone. Holding it up to the bedside lamp, she sat on the bed to examine it more closely. It had a grainy, sand-like texture and was in the shape of a rose, with petals of petrified sand. "A desert rose," Maura said to herself, dropping it on the bed as if it was a cursed object. What did it mean? Was it related to Eddie's death? Was this clump of hardened sand valuable? Why had Khalil carried it all the way from Saudi Arabia? None of it made any sense. One thing was certain—she had found the man they were looking for. Hearing voices outside the door, Maura dropped the stone back in the pack and switched off the lights. She recognized Beth's voice and heard them head up the stairs to the floor above. Maura left the room as she had found it and hurried up to the third floor where the man was showing Beth a room with a magnificent view of Paris.

Beth noticed Maura's white face as she came in and at the first opportunity told the clerk that they had to be going, thanking him heartily for being so kind. Maura eased down the stairs ahead of them and placed the key back on the counter.

Beth took her sister's arm as they left the hotel. "Are you okay? You look like you've seen a ghost." A car started up somewhere down the street.

"In a way I have. I thought that Dave was being paranoid at first, thinking that Eddie had been killed. But it was all right because it kept him going, involved in trying to figure out what had happened. Now all his worst suspicions are proving to be true and I'm getting a little scared."

"What did you see in Khalil's room?"

"Nothing really. I mean, nothing that tells us anything definite. Eddie's missing backpack was there with a piece of stone, petrified sand or something. It was shaped like a rose and it startled me because the last thing that Eddie said to Dave on the phone was something about a desert rose. He had been out in the desert that day looking for these stones. But why would Khalil carry it all the way to Paris? And in Eddie's pack? That could be evidence against him." The knock of a diesel engine could be heard progressing slowly behind them.

"How are we going to get him to talk? Do you think he's dangerous?" said Beth.

Maura seemed preoccupied and didn't answer. At the corner, she steered her sister to the right, and once they were around the corner, stopped.

"Now face me like we're having an animated conversation. Use your hands," said Maura.

"What? What's going on?"

"Just do it. I'll tell you later." A Peugeot came around the corner, hesitated, then continued past them and pulled over to the curb up the street. "Tell me, Beth. Is it common for Parisians to wear sunglasses after dark?"

"Not unless they sell drugs or guns."

"Is there a Metro station nearby?"

"Across the bridge," she pointed in the direction that the Peugeot was parked.

"Is there another way?"

"We could go over to the Ile de la Cite and catch one there. What's going on?"

"Let's go that way," she pointed toward the Ile de la Cite and took Beth's arm.

"Would you please tell me what's going on?" They heard a car door open and close.

"I think we're being followed."

"Maybe we should find out who it is?" Beth had a tendency to tackle things head-on, without fully considering the consequences.

"I don't want him to know we know. Besides, I think I know who he is."

"You've seen him before?"

"He was at the funeral. No sooner had Dave and I figured out that he looked official and out of place than he disappeared. Let's go back to your place."

"But I thought Dave was going to call the hotel."

"If this guy has done his homework, he already knows I have a sister in Paris and where you live. Chances are he doesn't know about the hotel unless he's been following us since we got here and I don't think he has. Anyway, if Dave doesn't reach us at the hotel, he'll call your place."

Dave stood on the rue Louis-le-Grand near the Boulevard des Italiens, looking at the glass door that Khalil had entered. The discreet gold letters on the door said, "Continental Opera" and the hours were given just below. Dave guessed that the "Opera" part of the name came from the district rather than anything to do with its function. It looked to be a private club of some sort, and in the short time that Dave watched the door, several men went in and out. The clientele seemed to have little in common, though many of them appeared to be foreigners.

Just inside the door was something like a movie theater ticket window behind which sat a heavily made-up bleached blond who looked to be in her mid-forties. She didn't acknowledge his presence as he stood at the window trying to figure out what to say. Finally, she looked up, but not really at him and said with an ennui that only the French can properly muster, "*Soixante-cinq francs.*" Dave pushed the money into the tray that went under the glass and in return was given a nylon wristband with a small metal tag attached. A number was stamped on the tag and a little key dangled from a hoop on the buckle. Dave stepped away from the window and stared at the band that lay across the palm of his hand as if it were an exotic artifact.

He started down the wide staircase and was overtaken by warm, moist air and the slightly stale odor of a much-used locker room. He was thrown back to high school when he would escape the cold winter afternoons and descend the steps of the gym for swim team practice. But instead of the old metal lockers at the bottom of the stairs, he found neat fiberboard ones covered in beige and brown Formica, which closed with a dull thud rather than a raucous metal clang. Instead of bawdy jokes and back slaps echoing from the walls, he could only hear low voices, mostly drowned out by the beat of disco music.

His feet sank into the brown carpet as he shuffled down the row of lockers, looking for the number on his wristband. His nose detected a potpourri of French colognes that mingled with but didn't quite mask the damp musty odor. To his right was a cherub in a stone fountain and next to it an imitation palm. Dave stood dumbfounded, an alien dropped down onto another planet. Several men with towels wrapped around their waists walked by, glanced at him, and went on. One of them looked back and smiled. From around the corner came a large beefy Frenchman in a tank top and very brief gym trunks plastered to his thick thighs. His view was obstructed by the pile of clean white towels he carried, so he didn't see Dave until he was almost on top of him.

The man stopped short and said, *"Je peux vous aider?"* Dave shrugged and started to speak, but the Frenchman repeated quickly in English, "I can help you?" Still unable to speak, Dave held out his wristband. The man smiled and said, "This your locker number. Over there. Come." And he led Dave to his locker.

"Merci," Dave said.

"It is nothing," the Frenchman mumbled and hurried off with his bundle of towels.

With the key on his wristband, he opened the locker and inside found a clean-smelling towel that was still warm. Dave took off his clothes slowly, looking around to see if anybody was watching, then quickly wrapped the towel around his waist. As he was about to close the locker, he noticed some pay phones nearby and reached into his pants pocket for some change. When there was no answer at the hotel, he called Beth's.

Maura answered. The sound of her voice immediately boosted his confidence.

"It's me. You'll never guess where I am." His voice was full of mischief, like a kid who's sneaked off to the circus to see the freak show.

"Don't make me guess. I'm too nervous."

"A gay bathhouse," he whispered.

"Oh, great," Maura responded unimpressed. "Are you having fun yet?"

"I followed Khalil here."

"Guess who else is in town?"

"King Fahd."

"Don't joke. This is serious. Mr. Sunglasses."

"Oh, shit."

"He was following Beth and me. That's why we came to Beth's. I'm hoping he doesn't know about our hotel room."

"Good thinking."

"He's outside the building right now, sitting at a cafe. Dave, I'm scared."

"Just stay calm, Maura. We're very close to something. I'm going to try and get Khalil to come back to the hotel. You think there's any way you can loose Mr. Sunglasses and meet me there?"

"We'll figure out of something. Beth and I are getting pretty good at sneaking around. While she occupied the desk clerk at Khalil's hotel, I visited his room. He's definitely the man we're looking for. Eddie's pack was there. There was a stone in it, shaped like a rose." The news punched him in the stomach and drained his enthusiasm for playing the naive detective in a gay bathhouse. He remembered that he was after his brother's killer. "Dave?"

"I heard you." His voice sounded very serious now. "Try to get to the hotel. I'll be there as soon as I can with Khalil." He hung up and headed in the opposite direction from where he came in, passing a hair salon where a pale, gaunt stylist lounged in one of the chairs, smoking a cigarette and waiting for customers. Just past that, in an alcove with more lockers, was a row of low stools in front of a long mirror. At each place was a hair dryer. Dave sat at one of the places and looked at his curly brown hair. It looked like it hadn't been touched in days and he ran his fingers through it, wondering if he should get a haircut, though he doubted he could sit still long enough. He leaned in closer to the mirror and saw dark bags under his gray eyes. He practiced a smile. It looked fake. At least his body was still in good shape, not paunchy like some of guys he had seen so far. That's what they went for in these places anyway, wasn't it? The body?

He got up and walked through a doorway into a dim hallway where the disco music was uncomfortably loud. Off the hallway were a number of trysting rooms and lounge areas with couches where men talked or watched or stared off into oblivion. He shuddered at the sound of moaning coming from one of the rooms and from another room he heard slapping, an open hand on ample flesh. In one of the lounge areas, a thin young man had fallen asleep in a sitting position with his head fallen back and his mouth agape. From his marble throat, on which a wall lamp focused, a gravelly breathing emanated. Despite the way his hands lay protectively between his legs, the pale young man looked vulnerable and Dave imagined, for a moment, a knife sliding across the exposed throat. The image sickened him and he hurried on, past saunas, showers, a steam room and dark niches from which came more moans of pleasure.

At the end of the long hall was a brightly lit area where he came upon a kidney-shaped swimming pool presided over by a Greek statue, a disk thrower of perfect form. On one side of the pool were tables and chairs where men dined on gourmet French dishes, clad only in their white towels or terrycloth robes. On the other side was a row of chaise lounges and on one of them a couple was entwined. One man broke away from a passionate kiss, jumped up, cast off his towel and dove into the pool. The sleek figure glided under water to the end where Dave stood, and hoisted himself out of the pool with a single effort. He smiled at Dave, then walked back and threw himself dripping wet onto his partner. There was a curdling squeal, then laughter.

Dave stood hunched over, looking as if he might fall into the blue rippling waters of the pool. Then he lifted his eyes, and in the mirror on the opposite wall, got his first good look at the man he was after. Next to the waiter's station was a small bar and sitting on one of the bar stools was Khalil. Dave imagined going over and sitting next to him, smiling, saying a few clever lines, and then inviting him back to the hotel. The scene played so easily in his head. He took a deep breath and walked over to the bar, but ended up taking a stool a few seats away from Khalil.

Dave ordered a Scotch. "You want ice?" the bartender asked in English.

"Please."

"British?" he asked.

"No. American." Khalil glanced in his direction.

"Cool." The bartender smiled. "Your number?"

Dave panicked. "Well, I'm staying at a hotel. . .and. . ."

The man started laughing and took hold of Dave's wrist. "No. This number," he said, pointing to the wristband. "I write down your number and at the end, you pay. If you want to eat, drink, get a haircut, any service, you tell your number." He walked away chuckling and wrote Dave's number on a pad. Dave blushed and took a big swallow of Scotch. He could feel Khalil's dark stare falling on him, increasing the tingling heat rising to his face.

As the first drops of Scotch began to work their magic, Dave reminded himself that this was the encounter he had planned for over a week; this was his chance. He turned to Khalil and tried his best to smile, then quickly returned to his drink. The first sight of Khalil's eyes sent a shudder up his spine. The man's thick eyebrows rose slightly, forming arches over what looked like two dark tunnels. Dave wanted to crawl away and forget the whole thing, but instead he got up and moved to one of the small tables in the corner, still within eyeshot of Khalil.

From a distance Khalil seemed not quite as threatening, and Dave smiled. This time, Khalil's square face cracked into a brief smile like the first sign of deterioration in an outer wall. Dave couldn't help feeling a sense of pride that people found him attractive, but it quickly changed to alarm as Khalil slid off his stool and came over to him.

Dave looked up at the man's broad hairy chest, and then to his lips that said something. Because of the music, it was hard to hear and the man's voice was much softer than expected.

"May I sit down?" Khalil said a second time. He locked in on Dave's eyes, and Dave felt drawn in as the liquor took hold. He nodded.

"You speak English well," said Dave. "Are you French?"

"No. Lebanese. You are American?" His voice had a dark mellow tone, like an aged red wine.

"I'm here on vacation. I don't speak any French, so it's a little difficult to. . ."

"No matter. Here, language is not so important. Only the language of the body." He looked at Dave intensely. Dave felt naked and took a big gulp of his drink. Khalil continued to search his eyes. After a minute of silence, the Arab broke his stare, finished his drink and set it down on the table. "Anyway, I must go," he said.

"Go?" Dave's voice rose and cracked slightly.

"I just take a walk around. Maybe see you later." He got up and left.

Khalil disappeared into the dark hallway and Dave was overtaken by a sense of rejection. Had he said something wrong or not said enough? Did he need to throw himself at him? He had thought that all he had to do was make himself available and Khalil would take the bait. Was there some element to the game he didn't know about? But overriding all his questions was the notion that he'd better do something quickly. He downed his drink and took off in the direction that Khalil had gone.

He began a frantic search through the hallways and saunas, looking in each open room, and as best he could in the dark places. It now seemed that the men he passed paid him little attention. What was left of his confidence drained away. In the steam room, he came upon a group of men huddled like in a pagan ritual around a god-like figure, one of them on his knees in front of the man in the middle. He fled from there in a panic, going back to the bar for another drink.

Fortified with the second Scotch, he continued his search and found a wing of the underground maze he had not yet discovered. It included another sauna—he had counted three in all—showers and more small rooms. He sat down on a couch and arranged his towel like a woman arranging her skirt. From there he watched the parade of men, many of them gazing at him and making him feel that his desirability had returned. An older, overweight gentleman sat down next to him. He gradually inched his hand over and touched Dave's leg.

Dave jumped up and continued his search. As he hurried around one corner, he ran right into Khalil's solid frame. Khalil grabbed Dave to steady himself and they stood face to face.

"Oh, hi," said Dave with a parched throat. Khalil neither smiled nor said anything, only continued to stare at Dave with his deep brown eyes that appeared surprisingly sad up close. Dave was hit by a peculiar dizziness mixed with a doubt that Khalil was Eddie's killer. There was something about his manner, his sad eyes, his gentle masculinity that made it hard for Dave to imagine him running a knife across Eddie's throat. Khalil took Dave's hand and led him to one of the rooms, but Dave pulled his hand away and stopped at the threshold. "I can't do this," he mumbled to himself.

Khalil went on in and sat on one of the two wood framed cots fitted with plastic-covered mattresses. He reached out his hand, palm down the way Arabs do, and rapped his fingertips against his palm like a small child waving. "Come," he said. "Sit."

Dave entered the small cubicle and sat down on the edge of the cot. Khalil then got up, closed the door, and moved the other cot in front of it, forming a barricade.

"What are you doing?" Dave said, short of breath.

"If we don't do that, people will come in. Relax. I won't hurt you." He sat back down and took Dave's hand. Dave pulled it away and wiped it on his towel. His palms were damp. His leg started to jitter.

"It's awful warm in here," said Dave. Sweat dripped down his sides. He could smell the odor of his anxiety. "Maybe I should go shower."

"You don't have to for me. But if you want to go, you can, of course. You are not prisoner."

"It's not that. It's just. . .strange, you know."

"This is your first time?"

"No. Of course not," Dave said, but not very convincingly.

"You're married, yes?" Khalil took his hand again and touched the ring.

Dave nodded. He didn't pull his hand away this time though it took all of his control not to.

"For an Arab, it is not so unusual to be married and be here. For an American, I think is different."

"It's different all right." Dave broke into a tight smile. "Are you married?"

"Not anymore. My wife was killed in Beirut. She was very young. While she was sleeping a shell came and hit our house."

"I'm sorry."

"I was sleeping with a friend that night. . . an American teacher from the university." He sighed heavily. "I'm sorry, too. We are married only short time. We had no sons." Khalil tilted his head and looked hard at Dave. "You make me think of someone."

"No," said Dave, a little too quickly. "I mean, probably another American you met. I suppose we all kind of look alike."

Khalil laughed. "But no place has such variety. Some look like my brother and some look like your brother. Some are white as snow, these I like very much, and some are as black as a goat. Some are big like the cedar trees and some are small like rabbits. Every one is different."

Again Dave had the impression that this soft-spoken man couldn't be Eddie's killer. And if he was, how could he be holding hands with him in a little sweatbox, almost naked and discussing America's melting pot? Dave looked at himself in the mirror on the opposite wall and wondered who he was. He felt no connection with the image of a man with brown curly hair and gray eyes, this imposter who would do anything to find the truth. At the same time he was a sentient being having friendly, but unsettling feelings for a man he was supposed to hate. He enjoyed the attention he received from Khalil, and hated himself for enjoying it. He wanted to break out of the close little room, thick with their masculine smells, and yet it was warm and protected from the harsh reality of the cold world outside.

"What are you thinking?" asked Khalil. "You look so serious."

"Many things."

"Are you thinking about your wife?"

"No."

"Do you want to go someplace else?"

"Yes. I'm not comfortable here."

"Evidement."

"What?"

"That's not English? Oh, I confuse."

"I think you mean 'evidently.'"

"Right. Always I confuse French and English."

"Let's go to my hotel." Dave blurted out

"Or mine?"

"Mine's closer."

"How do you know?"

"I mean, it's just a couple of blocks, on the Boulevard des Italiens."

"Let's go then." When they stood up, Dave's towel, which had worked itself loose, fell to the floor. He reached down hastily, picked it up and held it in front of him. Khalil was amused by the display of modesty and took advantage of it to put his arms around Dave and plant a kiss on his lips. Dave pulled back at the strangeness of the man's moustache and beard touching his face.

"You don't like this?" Khalil asked.

"It's just different, that's all. Your beard feels funny."

"Yes, to American men who only shake hands, I guess it is strange. In my culture we always kiss our brothers and fathers." There was sadness in his voice, a sadness for the great distance between himself and the American men that he liked, a distance that could never really be bridged except by a brief moment of intimacy. He dropped his arms and removed the barrier from the door. "After you, my friend," he said.

The two sisters had an escape plan for Maura. Beth had decided to dress in Maura's clothes and act as a decoy. She tucked her lighter hair into a hat and pulled up the collar on the coat.

"How do I look?" she said.

"You might get rid of some of that makeup," Maura suggested. "I never wear much myself."

"Oh, it's dark and he won't get that close to notice." Beth hesitated and looked at her sister with her hands on her waist. "Are you trying to tell me I wear too much makeup?"

Maura laughed. The sister who always seemed so confident and didn't care what anybody thought was being defensive. "It's none of my business."

"Hmm," said Beth. "Shall we go?"

Beth walked out the front door of her building, making sure the man in the sunglasses saw her before she turned and walked toward the opposite corner from the cafe where he sat. Maura waited inside the door until she saw the man go by. When they were around the corner, she stepped out and walked toward the cafe. Beth went quickly, staying as far ahead of her pursuer as she could. She walked over to the rue du Faubourg Montmartre where she bought a newspaper, then circled back via the rue Montmartre to her apartment.

Maura arrived safely at her hotel, and once inside the room, she began to pace. Though she rarely smoked, she found a cigarette in Beth's coat pocket and lit it up. It wasn't long before she heard voices outside the door and she ran into the bathroom.

When Dave opened the door, he was surprised to smell cigarette smoke, but he didn't let on that anything was unusual. He waved Khalil in ahead of him, then closed and locked the door, even putting on the safety chain. He took Khalil's jacket and offered him a chair. His manner was very cool. "Would you like something to drink? I don't know if we have anything. Maura," he shouted, "is there anything to drink?" Khalil looked surprised, and then shocked as Maura came out of the bathroom with her hands behind her back. "We have a visitor," Dave said triumphantly. Khalil looked at Maura and a flicker of recognition crossed his face, but he still hadn't put things together yet.

"This is my wife, Maura. But I guess you've already met."

"I don't remember," he said, getting up. "I must go now."

"Let me refresh your memory," said Maura in a sharp tone of voice. "It was several weeks ago at the clothes store in Saudi Arabia, and then of course this afternoon on the street."

"You must make mistake. I really need go." He started for the door.

Maura pulled a gun from behind her back and said hoarsely, "Sit down, Khalil. We want to talk to you."

Dave stared at the gun in disbelief. "Where did you get that?"

"From Beth. How did you think we were going to keep him here? With cheese and crackers?"

Khalil had stopped. He and Maura looked at each in the mirror near the door. "You don't shoot me, I think." And he started again for the door.

Maura aimed the gun above his head and fired. The terrific boom made Dave jump, more startled than any of them. "Jesus Christ, Maura!" he shouted.

Khalil turned around and looked her in the eyes. She had the gun pointed with both hands right at his forehead.

"I'd hate to ruin your beautiful face," she said. Khalil walked back to the chair and sat down. He slouched down and folded his arms across his chest. "Okay. Tell me."

Dave swallowed hard and finished the introductions. "My name is Dave. I'm Eddie's brother."

"Eddie?" He was confused for a minute, and then smiled. "Is Eddie here?" His seeming innocence shook Dave. He looked at Maura, but her face was cold, unchanged, not buying his act. He was troubled to see her play the bad cop so effectively.

"You're a good actor, Khalil," said Dave, trying to keep up with her. "Why don't you tell us what happened?"

Khalil lost his patience. "And who is actor to get me here? What is all this about? Why you point a gun at me?"

Dave softened his tone. "We just want to talk. We want to know why. . ." he took a deep breath, ". . .why Eddie was killed."

"Eddie? Killed? I don't believe this."

"Come on, Khalil. We just want the truth."

"I didn't know. I swear. Eddie is my friend. You think I—"

"Why are you in Paris?" asked Maura.

"They give me money, a ticket. They tell me go or they put me in prison. I didn't know why. I thought they were angry me because I bring American to the palace."

"Who is 'they'?" asked Dave.

"The Prince Muhammad's men."

"Is that who you took Eddie to see?"

"No. I took him to meet Majed, Muhammad's brother. What happened to Eddie?"

"That's what we're trying to find out. The police told us he died in an accident, in a green pickup truck."

"My truck. But is not true."

"We know. We also know that his throat was cut. We were hoping you could tell us what happened. You were there, weren't you?"

"The last time I saw Eddie he was alive, talking to Majed."

"Why don't you tell us what happened that night? Maura, I think you can put the gun down."

"They were only blanks," she said, dropping the gun on the bed and feeling proud of herself. "Beth just keeps it around because she's afraid of burglars. You know, with all that expensive stuff in her apartment." They all breathed a sigh of relief.

"Okay, Khalil. Go ahead."

"It seems so long ago. It was one of the days when the sand is everywhere—the land, the air, the sky—because the wind is blowing. I am driving down the road in the desert and is difficult to see. But I see a man and I think this is beautiful man. His blond hair is blowing as he stands by the road trying to get a ride like Americans do with thumb—not like Arab way. I slow my truck and I see his blue eyes. How can I see his blue eyes when the sand is everywhere? I can feel them, asking me to stop and I stop. He gets in my truck and smiles big like a little one, a child. He is liking me, I think. He tells me he is looking for a desert rose and he knows the place. He has map. I don't have time to go that day. We plan for the next week. I pick him up and we go there, many times taking the wrong road and finally find the place. There are no people there, but many holes in the ground. We dig and dig and talk and laugh. I think Allah is very good to me this day. Finally, we find a rose and the smile on the face of Eddie is like the moon when it is new.

"I am not so interested in this looking for roses and am happy we can go now. But Eddie wants find another one. I say the sun is going down and we should drive to beach and watch this. Then I get idea. I have friend who is Saudi prince and lives in palace on beach. He is crazy guy and has drink. He likes to meet Americans, especially with the blond hair and the blue eyes."

"Oh, so you do pimping for him?" Dave said angrily.

"What's this 'pimping'?"

Dave sat clench-fisted, saying nothing.

"Pimping," Maura explained, "is when you arrange meetings for sex and the pimp gets a share of the payment."

"What's this? I don't take *baksheesh*. What do you think? Why you say this? I don't want this kind of money." Khalil showed the lines of insult in his face and his temper increased the intensity of his eyes.

"Dave didn't mean anything by it, Khalil. Go ahead with your story," Maura said calmly. "We want to hear your story."

"Yes, but don't say these things to me. I want to help you. Eddie was my friend." Dave nodded his head and Khalil continued with the story.

"I only take Eddie to meet the prince because I think maybe he hasn't met a prince before and is interesting for him. He likes the idea. On way to prince we stop at beach. The wind dies like often it does near sunset, but there is still much dust in the air and we look at sun like through a veil. We sit close in my truck and he tells me about America. He talks much about his brother." Khalil paused and glanced at Dave as the words sank in. Dave sat on the floor now with his back against the bed, his eyes closed. Maura picked at the peach-colored carpet.

"I continue," said Khalil softly. "When the light is gone, we drive to Majed's palace. The guards know me, but they are suspicious to see Eddie. They don't like Americans to see the compound. I talk to Majed on gate phone and of course he want to meet Eddie. The guards let us through, but they are not happy of this.

"We meet Majed in the *majlis,* like meeting room, and drink tea. Eddie has big open eyes and watches everything. Majed talks about the days when he was a student in California. He is happy I have brought him an American visitor. We talk and then he must go for prayer time, even Majed, yes he never misses prayer time. He is Al-Saud. After prayer, he invites us for eating. I think Eddie doesn't like very much the lamb and rice, always the food of Saudis. He keeps staring at the lamb's head in the middle of the big plate and Majed laughs when he sees this. He cuts off piece of kidney and gives to his guest on a knife—

it's like honor—and Eddie says, '*Shukran,*' but I don't think he is really thankful. Majed laughs and says, 'You speak Arabic now.' We have nice time. Everybody happy. Everybody smile.

"After dinner, Majed ask us if we want drink, American drink. Eddie looks at me thinking, 'What he means? Pepsi?' Then Majed says, 'Come.' And we follow him through a door and down some marble stairs. At the bottom of steps, Majed reaches into wall and touches some buttons. Two big wooden doors open and we are in disco. There is dance floor and big ball hanging with the little mirrors all covering it. There are colored lights and speakers and of course bar with drink—Johnnie Walker, Jack Daniels, what you want. I take Johnnie Walker Black and Eddie takes vodka. Majed opens freezer and pulls out frozen bottle Stolichnaya. He says, 'No problem with Russian?' and Eddie says it's okay. Majed takes gin and tonic. We go with our drinks and sit on a carpet platform with many cushions. After short time, other Saudis come in and sit near us. They don't drink anything. Majed doesn't talk to them and he doesn't introduce us."

"Who were these other Saudis?" asked Dave.

"One is his brother Muhammad who is younger and does not like this. The others are Muhammad's friends and maybe some cousins. They talk to each other and watch us, but Majed ignores them. He is older and they must respect him no matter what they think. Then the doors open again and four or five Filipino boy-girls come in. They are all small and pretty. They are boys, but they dress and act like girls. Majed hired them for different jobs around the palace. One of them sees our empty glasses and gets us new drinks. His name is Rico and he fixes an extra pillow behind Eddie when he brings the drinks. He is one of Majed's favorites and is always there when Majed drinks which is every night. Rico used to work in a house in Al-Khobar, but the police came to stop this house was like prostitution. Majed got him out of jail and brought him to the palace. You can see that right away Rico likes Eddie, but he is shy because his English is not too good.

"Majed then pushes some buttons in the floor and disco music begins. It is the same tape as always from American DJ in New York who make the tape for Majed. The DJ was friend at university, I think. The first song is 'Beat It' of Michael Jackson—you probably know this song maybe—and the boy-girls are excited. They jump up and dance. Majed is laughing and turns the music louder, but the other Saudis don't like I can see. They say nothing and drink tea.

"The music is too loud to talk now so we just watch the boy-girls dance. Rico comes over to us and takes Eddie's hand. He tries to pull him out to the dance floor, but Eddie doesn't want. He is red, like embarrass. When Majed motions him to go, he lets Rico take him. Maybe he wants to please his host, which is a good idea when you visit a prince. He dances good, you know, like a man, not like the others.

"I am feeling very happy and I think is good I bring Eddie. Maybe it is drink. I don't know. Then just when I am feeling most happy, Majed's brother Muhammad looks me and there is cold in his eyes like death. Eddie comes back and sits down beside me. I reach for his hand and it is cold as ice and this thing like the night wind runs through me. Eddie sees my face and says, 'What's matter?' and I say, 'Nothing. Why your hand so cold?' 'The glass,' he says and smiles. His smile warms me again. Rico, who followed Eddie back there from the dance, turns around and walks away like an angry girl. She is jealous. I look at Majed and he is laughing. But this laugh is far away and I know I am getting drunk. I am. . .how you say. . .cheap drunk, not like Majed who drink all night. I look at Eddie and. . ."

Khalil's words were cut off by a loud knock at the door. It startled the three of them and they all looked at their surroundings as if suddenly remembering where they were. Dave looked quickly at the window and the fire escape beyond it, then at Maura.

"See who it is," Dave whispered.

Maura got up and went to the door. "Who is it?" she asked.

"*S'il vous plait, madame, ouvrez la porte.*" It was an official-sounding voice.

"*Qui est-ce?*" said Maura.

"*Les gendarmes. Ouvrez la porte.*"

"*Un moment, messieurs. Je dois. . .je dois mettre. . .les vetements. Un moment.*" Maura turned her panic-stricken face toward Dave. He nodded as if to say, "Good work." He had their shoulder bag by the strap.

"Get your purse," he whispered.

Khalil stood up, but seemed frozen in place. Dave was already at the window. Maura grabbed her purse and then Khalil by the arm. In a few seconds they had scrambled out on the fire escape, and then they climbed the steps to the roof. They ran across the roof of the hotel and jumped over a low wall to the next building. Maura started for the door leading to the stairwell, but Dave shouted, "No. That's too obvious. The next one."

They ran to the next roof that was several feet lower, but they all made the jump without hesitation. Dave got to the rooftop door first and grabbed the handle. He yanked it, but it wouldn't budge.

"Christ, what do we do now?" said Maura.

Dave ran to the edge of the building and looked two stories down to the next one. He hurried back to Maura and Khalil, dragging them out of sight behind the stairwell.

"Don't panic," he said. "The next building is too far down. There's a way out of this though. I know it." They both looked at him with doubt.

"Wait a minute," Maura said. "What are we running from? We haven't done anything wrong."

"Maybe not in your mind. Try looking at it from a cop's point of view. You're carrying a gun which, blanks or not, is rather frowned on in this country, especially when you open fire in a hotel room. We've also got this mysterious character wearing sunglasses following us around who may or may not be among our pursuers. But worst of all, we just ran away from the French police. That just doesn't look too good."

"Shhh," said Maura. "I hear something." They all three put their ears to the structure they leaned against. Someone was coming up the steps. Dave hung his head and Maura melted down into a sitting position on the cracked tar of the old rooftop. "They've got us now," she said.

"Wait," said Khalil. "I think the police don't move so slowly." The steps were a monotonous, heavy shuffle coming toward the roof. They reached the top and then stopped. There was a long pause before the metal latch clanged and the door screeched open. A middle-aged woman emerged behind a huge laundry basket with which to collect the sheets hanging in the cold dark night.

"Bonsoir, madame," said Maura as they slid by her and through the door to her amazed look. Once she had a moment to think, she put her basket down and began to yell after them. But they were already down the stairs. Just as she returned to her basket and leaned over to pick it up, several policemen came running across the roof. They asked her if she had seen any strangers on the roof. She looked puzzled, then pointed in the direction of the long drop-off. No one could have gone into her building, she said. She had just this second unlocked the door.

When Dave, Maura and Khalil reached the street level of the apartment building, they left one by one and agreed to meet at a café on Haussmann.

From the café Maura called Beth. "Oh, God, this is so exciting," Beth said when Maura explained what they had just been through.

"Great! I'm glad you're enjoying this, but what the hell are we going to do?"

"Don't worry. I've got it all worked out. I can't leave here, right? They're probably still watching my place. I'll call my girlfriend Camille and ask her to drive you to my house in the country. No one knows about it since it's not really in my name. You should be safe there. As soon as I can get away, I'll meet you there."

"Khalil's with us, you know."

"Take him with you. I'm dying to meet him. Good luck!" Beth gave them Camille's address, a couple of Metro stops away. Again they left separately and agreed to meet at Camille's.

8

HIDEAWAY IN TONNERRE

Camille drove her old Peugeot with a death grip on the steering wheel and her sky-blue eyes glued to the rode. Her sleek hair hung like a helmet around her determined china-doll face and was cut straight across at the shoulders and in a perfect line across her wrinkled forehead. Maura sat next to her in the front and kept glancing over, wondering if the petite blond knew about the danger they were in, or if Beth had invented a story why they needed to go to her country place. In the back seat Dave and Khalil fidgeted, and as the Peugeot crawled onto the *Periferique* that circled the city, Maura heard a dull drumming of fingers on a padded armrest coming from Dave's side of the back seat.

Camille spoke English in a halting manner, painfully constructing the words into grammatically correct sentences. Maura attempted to converse with her in French, though was soon lost and allowed them to drift back into English. Still, she couldn't determine how much Camille knew of their situation. Camille did offer, in a slightly cheerier tone of voice, that it was no problem for her to drive them to Tonnerre, the small town where Beth's house was. Her parents lived there and she would take advantage of the trip to see them. But Maura stopped asking questions when she realized that Camille was having a hard time talking and driving at the same time. Each time Maura asked her something, Camille would slow down to about half speed, and then accelerate when the question was answered.

It was almost midnight when they pulled into Tonnerre and the streets were deserted. Only the main road through town had streetlights and a single cafe showed signs of life. Maura was hungry, and pointing at the café, asked if it was possible to stop. Camille became extremely apologetic, acting as if she had committed a crime by not providing for their nourishment. She would drop them off at Beth's, then immediately go pick up some provisions from her parent's place. The café was not very good, she assured them.

Maura heard the men in the back seat come to life and sit up straight when the car coughed and nearly died. Camille had neglected to downshift as she slowed the car to make a sharp turn up a dark street. Halfway up the block, she stomped on the brakes and brought the car to an abrupt stop in front of a row of small shops. She pointed out Beth's 17th century country house, squeezed between two others from the same period. On the ground floor was an antique store Camille's parents ran. Next door was an eerie storefront marked by a hand-painted sign with a horse head on it, indicating a horsemeat butcher. Beth had pointed out a similar sign to them in Paris, and Maura stared at the sign with disgust as they got out of the car. The men stretched and rubbed their hands together from the cold.

Their shoes echoed on the flagstone walkway up to the door of the shop and Maura jumped at a sudden angry bark of dog at the neighbor's upstairs window. Dave put his arm around her. Camille mumbled something about the dog, and then dug in her purse. She rummaged around before pulling out a very old but intricate iron key, which she used to unlock the door to the downstairs shop. Switching on lights, she led them through giant armoires, little round tables with marble tops, and uncomfortable-looking chairs. The furniture gave off a burnt musty smell from a long history of winter nights by smoky fires. She then threw back a burgundy velvet drape and unlocked another door that led to a small, rank-smelling courtyard. She pointed out the outhouse. Maura screwed up her nose and translated for Dave.

"That's it as far as facilities," she said. Khalil laughed at the uneasy reactions of the Americans.

They mounted the old winding staircase off the courtyard, expecting rats and bats to cross their path at any moment. Camille pushed open the door at the top of the stairs and it creaked loudly. They slid into another world, a rustic hideaway that might house the ghosts of the French Revolution plotting against the king. The furnishings of the large room were of the period, though at the front were two small alcoves—one filled with a nineteenth century brass bed and the other contained a thoroughly modern kitchenette equipped with sink, stove, refrigerator and dishwasher.

"A dishwasher, but no bathroom!" Maura said.

Camille shrugged her shoulders, and said, "*C'est bizarre, no?*"

They continued the tour up another stairway to a small dark room on the top floor. It was set up with a couple of rustic antique chairs and a daybed by a small window looking out over the street. Because of the peaked roof, the room seemed much smaller than the one below it and you could only stand up in the middle. On the other side of the stairs, Camille opened a door and turned on a light to show them the back section of the house. It had fallen into disrepair with most of the plaster gone from the walls and some of the main support beams leaning at precarious angles.

"I leave you now and come back later with food," said Camille in English, surprising them with a line that seemed as if she had been putting it together in her head for some time.

When Camille left, they returned to the first floor and Dave stretched out on the double bed in the alcove.

"I feel like Anne Frank," said Maura.

"I doubt Anne Frank had a dishwasher," said Dave. "The place does have its charm."

"And what about the outhouse? You think that's charming too?"

"Didn't you ever go to camp?"

"Yeah, and I didn't shit for a week." Dave and Maura both broke into laughter while Khalil stood in the middle of the room looking confused.

"I think we lost Khalil," said Maura. "Don't worry, Khalil. It's a bad joke." She too fell on the bed. "Let's just relax a little bit until she brings the food and then you can continue your story.

"If you can stay awake to listen," said Khalil, raising his thick eyebrows.

"Don't worry. We'll stay awake," Dave assured him with his eyes closed.

A short time later, Camille returned with a basket of cold chicken, mayonnaise in a squeeze tube, cheese, bread, and wine, apologizing for the meager provisions while she emptied the basket. Then she left to spend the night at her parent's house.

When they finished eating, Khalil patted his stomach, took a deep breath and started talking.

"Yes, we were at Majed's and I was feeling drunk, a little bit like now," he smiled. "But that night I was very tired. Majed sees that and tells me to take one of the Filipinos and go to a room. But I don't want a boy-girl this night and I think Majed is not happy with me when I say this. He likes to make his guests happy. Eddie looks at me with questions in his eyes. 'I must work early in the morning,' he shouts over the music. Majed hears and says, 'Don't worry, I will have someone take you back any time you want to go.' Eddie says, 'Okay,' and we shake hands very long time. Eddie says, 'Call me next weekend,' and I say, '*Insh'allah.*'" Khalil paused and sighed deeply. Maura felt the sadness in his voice. Dave, too, sensed it and took Maura's hand as they sat on the floor staring at the empty wine bottle, its green glass catching the light of the candles they used instead of the electric lights.

"Then I was sleeping and dreaming something very nice. I was rolling over and over the sand hills. The sky was blue and clear. I am warm, but not hot. And there is water and palm trees and I take off my clothes and swim in a lake which becomes bigger and bigger and then is the ocean and I am near the beach in my country. There is no war and my sister is alive, my wife too, but she is far away standing on the shore. I start to swim toward her, but am getting nowhere. Then something happen. I am picked up roughly and my dream is broken. I open my eyes and see bright light and Muhammad's men are shouting at me and telling me I must leave right now. I ask questions, but they don't tell me anything. They give me envelope with many riyals and tell me there is ticket to Paris waiting at the airport. I must leave country today and not come back. It will be very dangerous for me if I don't follow their orders. I ask to speak to Majed and they almost break my arm so I don't ask again. They take me to my truck and I see Eddie's bag on the front seat. But I must give this bag to Eddie, I tell them, and they say he is gone. They follow me in another car to the store where I work and I tell my friend I must leave and ask him to take care of my truck. Then these men take me to the airport, I have not even time to pack my clothes. I come to Paris and know nothing until I meet you. That is my story and it is true."

After a long silence, Maura said softly, "We believe you. Sorry about the gun." The candlelight flickered, making the room seem unstable, unfixed in time or space. The dog barked again, and then was silent.

"Why would they kill him?" Dave said in a distant voice.

"You know, the Saudis must control everything. They must show good face to the world. But the Al-Saud is a very big family and there are many who have different ideas from the brothers who now have power. Some like Majed want to open up the country to the West. He thinks is stupid pretend there is no Western influence. But he is embarrassment to family because he drink too much and he like the boys. Then on the other side there are those like Majed's brother Muhammad who would like get out all foreigners and make Saudi Arabia like before, before there was the oil and money. These people will do anything because they believe Allah is with them. They are very angry that Majed shows his weaknesses to foreigners. But Majed don't care. He enjoy the life."

"Would they kill Eddie just because he saw that? It's no big secret that certain princes and privileged people have alcohol and disco music and even boys."

"You are right. I think something happen while I am sleeping. I don't know."

"I must talk to Majed," Dave concluded. Khalil was silent.

Maura stirred from her dream. "What? Who?" she said.

"No," said Khalil. "It is too dangerous."

"What's too dangerous?" Maura asked.

"Why would it be dangerous just to talk to him? I'm not planning to come right out and ask him why my brother was killed. But if I had a chance to talk to him, I could find out what happened. I have to find out what happened."

"You will need help, but what can I do? I can't go back to Saudi. They will kill me, especially now I know why they get me out of the country."

"What will you do, Khalil? You can't stay in France," said Maura.

"I don't know. I am a man without a country, without family. I think there is only one place for me. I want to go to States."

Maura frowned at his conclusion. "Is that where people go because they have nowhere else to go?" she said. "It's not that easy. You'll need help."

"I know. I have money."

"You'll need more than money. Do you have relatives or friends there?"

"No," he said, his face falling into a pout. He reminded Dave of his students and their aptitude at provoking emotions with their facial expressions. Maura was easy prey and was on the verge of offering their assistance. They were in no position to take Khalil under wing when they hardly knew what they were doing themselves. And though they had already been through a lot with Khalil, they had only known him for a few hours.

Dave nodded at Maura and said, "It seems that you need some help from us and we need help from you. Of course, we couldn't do much in the way of helping you until we get back from Saudi Arabia. Maybe you could hide out here for a while."

"But what do you need from me?"

"I want you to tell me everything you know about Majed—his friends, his habits, everything."

As Dave and Khalil talked about a man Maura would likely never meet, she drifted off and fell into a deep sleep. It was sometime later that she felt her husband crawl under the covers."

"Where's Khalil?" she mumbled as she opened her eyes and noticed how low the candles were burning.

"He went upstairs to bed. Did you think he was going to snuggle up with us?"

"I don't know. I wouldn't want to sleep up there alone, plus it's like an icebox."

"I don't imagine it's much warmer down here. Should I have invited him to join us?"

"I didn't say anything about a *menage a trois*. I just thought it might be cold and creepy sleeping up there alone."

"I've noticed the way you look at him."

"You have to admit he is kind of enchanting."

"Enchanting is it now? I bet you never referred to me as enchanting."

He had a point, thought Maura. But how many women marry men they think are enchanting and get away with it? "Your qualities trump enchanting anytime," she said after a brief search for the right words. "You're not jealous, are you?"

"Haven't I got the right to be jealous? It's the 80's now. Men can be jealous again."

"I just think it's a little misplaced. He'd rather have you than me."

"What do you mean?" he said defensively.

"I'm the one that should be jealous. Just how did you get him to come back to the hotel room from the bathhouse? Promise him something?" she teased.

"I'll tell you about it tomorrow. I'm too tired now."

"Uh huh. . .too tired."

"I have nothing to hide."

"You're off the hook for now. Let's get some sleep."

"What hook? I'm not on any hook."

"Goodnight, Dave."

When they blew out the candles, a darkness settled over the room that they hadn't experienced in a long time, a darkness you find away from the cities, in small unlit towns and out on country roads when you turn off the headlights. It was a blackness that made the eyes useless, and imagination took control. Maura fell asleep quickly, but

Dave lay awake long enough for his eyes to start finding things in the darkness, his ears to pick out sounds from far away. He heard the sounds of sandals slapping against marble floors, coming closer and closer, and saw the door being thrown open, the shadows of Arabs in their head cloths and loose-fitting garments moving toward him...and Eddie. He tried to warn Eddie, but no sound would come out of his throat. Then there was the shiny steel catching a glint from the hall light, slicing across Eddie's neck. His body jerked and his eyes opened in a horrifying last look at life—the calm of revenge on his murderer's face—before they wrapped him up in the blood-soaked sheets and carried him down the hall.

Then Dave felt the infinite darkness of the coffin as it traveled thousands of miles in the cold of the airplane luggage compartment only to be put into the chilly dark earth. In the darkness he saw the false smile of contentment they had painted on Eddie's face, the one he had seen in the funeral parlor that night. The vision was erased when the dog barked nearby, and then fell silent.

The door creaked and Maura stirred. Dave lay completely still. If they didn't make a sound, no one could find them in the darkness. They were hidden under its cover. Footsteps moved to the center of the room and stopped. Maura bolted upright in bed.

"Who's there?" she said.

"It is Khalil," a voice said softly.

"Can't sleep?" Dave asked, now sitting up as well.

"I was thinking of something."

"Yes, what is it?"

"The little tape recorder. Eddie was talking into his recorder when we were driving to the beach. He put it in his bag, I think, but it wasn't there the next morning."

"We thought of the recorder, too. It's missing. It wasn't returned to us with the other things of Eddie's."

"Khalil," Maura asked, "why did you bring Eddie's pack with you to Paris, and the stone."

"How you know that?"

"I went in your room at the hotel," Maura admitted.

"You people are like private eyes. How you learn these things? From TV?" Maura laughed. "Anyway, when I leave to Paris that morning, I had a few clothes in the back of the store, but no bag. So I take Eddie's bag, and the desert rose, well, I keep for souvenir. I didn't know how to return to Eddie. But when I get to customs at airport, I remember it is illegal to take these stones out of the country. Those men are still with me and they push me through customs with no check. That is all I have when I come to Paris, and 50,000 riyals."

"Wow! How much is that in dollars?" Maura wondered.

"That's twelve or thirteen thousand dollars, not a bad little payoff," said Dave. "Do you remember anything else about that morning, something you noticed, but didn't think was important?" Khalil came over and sat on the foot of the bed. He and Dave went over in detail the events of the day he was forced to leave the country. Maura lay back and sank into the down pillow.

Beth arrived early the next morning with fresh croissants and jam. Khalil was curled up on the rug at the foot of the bed with a blanket and several coats thrown on top of him. Maura opened her eyes and watched Beth drag a portable space heater out of the closet and turn it on. "What happened? Did you kick him out of bed?" Beth asked with a mischievous smile.

"Don't let your imagination run wild," said Maura in her gravelly morning voice.

"Hey, you're all outlaws now. You can do what you want. How about some fresh croissants?"

"Hardly the food for outlaws," Dave growled. "I trust you weren't followed."

"My dear, you haven't ever seen me drive an MG—my other car."

"What is this? Second house, second car. Maybe we should move to France," said Dave. "Are you sure you weren't followed?"

"I drove the Renault from my house to the parking garage where I keep the MG. Of course I was followed. I parked the Renault and switched to the MG. Then I drove out the other entrance. Simple as that."

"That's my sister," said Maura.

When Beth had gone in the kitchen to make coffee, Khalil got up and started pulling on his pants. Just then, Beth popped her head back in and said, "This must be the famous Khalil. Good morning, Loverboy."

"What's this? Why she say this?"

"She's just joking," said Maura.

"In my country, women don't joke like this."

"You're not in your country, remember?" Maura said. "And besides, you're practically an American now. You'd better get used to it."

Beth laughed. "I'm sorry I missed the swearing in, or was it an initiation."

"Khalil, meet my sister Beth. Beth, Khalil."

"Pleased to meet you," he mumbled.

"Don't mind me if I seem a little brash. I've just been up for hours and all the excitement has made me sort of jumpy. I'm happy to meet you too, Khalil." She stuck out her hand and Khalil hesitated before shaking it quickly.

"I thought I heard something about coffee. Then we have to talk," said Dave.

"The coffee's coming. Talk about what?"

"Khalil. He has no place to go."

"He can stay here," said Beth without even thinking about it. "The question is, can he stand it? It gets pretty boring and I doubt the neighbors are going to rush to invite an Arab into their homes for a nice dinner and a game of cards."

"He doesn't seem to have much choice. It wouldn't be wise for him to go back to Paris right now. I'm sure our friend Mr. Sunglasses has the authorities looking for him as well as us. What do you think, Khalil?"

"If Beth doesn't mind, I could stay here for a few days. If they find me, maybe they send me back to Lebanon which is not good thing for me."

"I'll tell Camille's parents that you'll be staying here. They're very nice people and they'll help you get settled in. What about you guys?" she said, turning to Dave and Maura.

"Still back to Saudi Arabia like we planned. There are several holes in the story of Eddie's death. Khalil has given us a lot of help, but it looks like I'll have to meet with the Prince himself."

"And you, Maura?" Beth said, turning to her sister. "Are you sure you want to go back?"

"We settled this in the States," she said quickly. "We're both going."

"Well, now that we've determined that, how are you going? They'll probably be watching the airports."

"They'll be watching for a couple going to Saudi Arabia. But you're going to get us tickets to Bahrain. From there, we'll take a dhow back to Saudi."

"A what?"

"Dhow. D-H-O-W. They're old Arabian sailing vessels, which have been converted to motor-powered boats for short trips from the island to the mainland. It's a more discreet way to enter the country, but you have to be part of the group tours they have every weekend for foreigners who need a break from Saudi. People go over there to get drunk and flirt with the idea of finding whores. Bahrain is a regular bastion of liberalism. Women can drive cars, they serve alcohol in the hotels, and I think there are even a couple of movie theaters."

"Sounds like Sin City. When do you want to go?" said Beth, coming out of the kitchen with a tray of golden brown croissants, strawberry jam and a pot of steaming coffee.

"I guess the sooner the better," Dave answered. Beth caught Maura's eye and saw the worry lines in her face. Her little sister had aged considerably, and she wondered when it had happened. Beth surmised that marriage had been hard on her. She was glad that she was a free woman.

9

MIST RISING OVER MANAMA

Dave and Maura stretched out on a quiet, half-empty Air France flight to Manama, Bahrain. The flight attendant mechanically set down trays of food in front of them and Maura stared at hers stupidly. "All right," said Dave, "what's the matter? You've hardly said a word since we got on the plane and now you look like you've just been served a plate of dog food."

"I'm sick to death of airline food and I'm sick of flying. I just want to be somewhere."

"But you are. This is Air France. Isn't that Burgundy Beef shining so deliciously in your reading light? And look, little wedges of La Vache Qui Rit with French crackle bread. Mmmm. And real French wine. Bordeaux. We're in heaven."

"And we're headed straight for hell."

Dave stopped struggling with his plastic-wrapped silverware and put the package down on the tray. "Do you want to go through it all again?" he said in an exasperated tone. "I'm going back to Saudi Arabia to find out why Eddie was killed. You can stay in Bahrain if you want. Or go back to Paris and wait for me there. Whatever you want. I won't hold it against you. But please don't make me feel like I'm dragging you to a death chamber."

"I just want to know one thing," said Maura, her lips quivering as if hesitant to form the words. "Are you doing this out of love for Eddie or because of some strange guilt you feel about abandoning him? I just want to know if I'm going to have to compete with a ghost for the rest of my life."

Dave stared at the dish of food for a long time, watching the Burgundy Beef sauce congeal, before he answered calmly. "I'm doing it because I have to. I'm doing it because I wouldn't be able to live with myself if I didn't. And I'm doing it because I have a right to know if my brother was murdered. And if the U.S. Government and Tanley participated in a cover-up, I have a right to know that too. We are human beings, not cogs in a great international oil-pumping machine. At least they should have the decency to admit the truth and not try to cover up a murder with some bullshit accident report. I'm not out for blood. What recourse do we have anyway when we're dealing with some of the most powerful people on the planet? I just want to know the truth."

Maura chewed her lip and ran her finger along the edge of the tray-table. She didn't want to fight. Besides, what could she say in the face of such righteousness? But a voice called out inside her. "What about me? Shouldn't a wife have something to say about her husband poking his nose into places where there was something rotten?" Ever since their marriage, Maura had tried to hold her tongue in matters where Eddie was concerned, often feeling like a tag-along to the Bates brothers. Now with Eddie gone and Dave obsessed with finding out what happened, she was perhaps more distant than ever. The worst part was that with his headstrong mission, she ran the risk of losing Dave altogether. He so casually admitted that he was going to take on some of the most powerful people in the world. Could he come out of that alive? How could he expect her to sit back and calmly watch?

Out loud she said, "A long time ago, I said I wanted to be with you and that still stands, in Saudi Arabia or Timbuktu. But goddamit, I'm not bringing you home in a fucking box. I couldn't bear it, Dave."

The last part had come out with a little more force than she had expected, causing a hush to fall on all the passengers around them. They stopped eating and perked up their ears. An elderly British couple across the aisle didn't deign to look over and, in fact, pretended not to have heard a thing, though the slight flutter of their facial muscles indicated that they had. As quickly as possible the couple resumed eating, cutting into the silence with their metal utensils against the chinaware.

Maura's face was a fiery red and Dave took her hand. "You won't have to," he said softly. "I promise. Are you sure you don't want to eat something? It might make you feel better."

Neither of them ended up eating very much and when the dinner trays were cleared away, Maura wiggled around until she found a comfortable position. It wasn't long before her mouth gaped open and the telltale breathing of sleep came from it. Dave alternately flipped through the pages of the airline magazine and stared out at the somber night. He thought of Eddie's journal and pulled it out of his bag. He had intended to read more of it, but hadn't found an opportunity in the craziness of the last few days. And though reading made him feel closer to Eddie, it also upset him, forcing him to see things about his brother that he wasn't sure he wanted to know. Most of the passengers drifted off to sleep, so he took advantage of the quiet bubble around him to dive into Eddie's words once again.

December 15: Market day in Qatif, which sits in the middle of a large east coast oasis, means all the local farmers are going to town with their wares and daughters in the back of trucks and young girls wave to me from under their veils as I stand at the front of the bus waiting to get off. So I step off, rid of the long ride that brought me to this Shiite stronghold of poor people, second-class citizens to the dominant Sunni sect. I'm apprehensive. In 1979 Khomeini-spurred riots caught some Westerners unaware, some were injured, but the National Guard was ready and squashed the rebellion quickly and soundly and you never know what kind of bitterness lingers after that, bitterness against the government and the usual animosity toward Americans that Shiites everywhere seem to harbor. Where will all this hatred against foreigners finally lead?

Instead of animosity, some mildly curious regular guys sitting on a bench give me the eye and watch me walk toward the produce stalls, the first area in my line of sight. And I'm mad because now I know there is plenty of fresh food that we don't get in the mess hall (I hate military terminology but it fits) and it's not just the British cook cooking everything to death that's keeping us from a healthy and varied diet—it's all here, available, they just don't want to deal with going to the market to get it. Easier to open a can or a package. About everything I could think of in the way of produce surrounds me in big piles, especially melons which I haven't seen in months though I see a big one right now coming my way in the hand of a menacing-looking Arab holding a Bowie knife in the other. A flick of the wrist and the blade goes into the tender flesh, ejecting a chunk he then stabs and sticks under my nose. I take it, as if I had a choice, and taste it, the juice running down my chin. Cheap too, but I explain with my hands that they are too heavy to carry around and he wipes his knife on his thobe and lets it drop into a piece of wood, picking up two cantaloupes and holding them up to his chest like breasts indicating that I could put them under my shirt. He laughs. Hmmm, I think, and then think I'd better laugh too. He smiles showing me he is missing several teeth and walks away. I go on.

Nearby fish shimmer in pails and there are prawns as thick as your big toe and lots of other things from the sea like snapping crabs, none of which we ever see on our table, or I should say in our self-serve cafeteria line.

This isn't the main market people come to Qatif for, just the warm-up. Across the street from the food market are, as I was later to find out, some of the only handmade crafts to be had in Saudi Arabia—throw rugs and baskets made by the Qatif locals. The simplicity of the rugs interested me, their striped designs in brown, white, beige and gray and some with threads of bright color running through them. The women selling them are all in black, with hennaed hands and bare feet. Unlike their city sisters, their eyes are exposed, dark beady things on whites the color of stained teeth.

As soon as I start looking at a rug I like—all in natural hues—a middle-aged women holds up her bangled arm and shows me four fingers, meaning 400 riyals or over 100 dollars. I scoff and start to walk away and in a split second she is down to three and chattering to the wind through her veil. I hold up two fingers and she looks outraged, her babble winding up to a feverish pitch. Two I insist with my fingers like a peace sign, so she shows me a smaller, ugly rug that looked like it had been made by a five-year-old daughter and I start to walk away again. She grabs my arm. I stop cold. A Saudi woman is touching me, putting me in a social, psychological and physical trap all at the same time. She lets go and holds up three fingers again, but with a finger from the other hand cutting one of them in half. Now we are getting somewhere I think though we were still at about seventy bucks for a rug that in any other country in the Middle East would go for fifteen tops. They are desert women, but still know how to milk the inflated economy.

I take out 225 and hold it in her face, then in a flash it is gone, into her hand without me even seeing the transition and she is walking away. I roll up the rug and stick it under my arm feeling satisfied, actually thrilled with my purchase.

Next, I wander into the butcher's alley where huge carcasses hang on hooks in the heat dripping blood onto the dusty soil where here and there big cow eyes stare up at me from severed heads. There are lifeless tails too that do nothing to alleviate the fly problem, swarms forming big black spots on the sides of beef. But what they didn't cut off were the testicles so that the buyers would know these were bulls—perhaps in this male chauvinist society they put an even higher price on the male, but I remember hearing it had a religious significance. And though the bloody-aproned butchers wave me toward them with their knives to inspect the meat, I get out of there.

Then I find the main market a few blocks away, just following the crowds. It is a huge outdoor area with stalls selling the same thing that most flea markets all over the world now sell—junk and not even good junk, or old junk, but junk you can buy at any dollar store—things like cheap clothes, kitchen wares, beauty products, candy, etc. In one stall they have music boxes with Santa Claus figurines on top standing next to plastic Christmas trees which I don't know how they get away with since the administration has already informed us that Christmas decorations are forbidden on the compound.

In the liveliest corner of the market is the place where they sell birds and live poultry, where you find the boys aged six to sixty, fluttering about the cages, and the boxes with air holes cut in them. They love to hold the birds and chickens and rabbits and carry them around in some manner, which looks very uncomfortable for the animals, grimacing and biding their time until they see a chance to get away. Every so often I see a bird taking to awkward wing-clipped flight and then chased by a rabble of young boys with sticks shouting at everyone to catch the bird.

One young man in a clinging thobe and with a bare head of black curls grabs my hand and makes me hold a pigeon which is warm and I think I can feel its heartbeat, but at the same time I am sure it is going to shit its fear in my hand. I am also afraid the smiley young man is going to try and give me the damn thing—a cherished gift here which you can't refuse—but he takes it back and puts it in a tiny box where he has another one. Next to the box in the dirt sits a crippled old man with pretzel-thin arms and twisted legs and a small boy hurries by dropping a one-riyal note in the skirt of his thobe which the old man feels but can't see. Reaching down he snatches it up and hides it in the folds of his robes.

Then I reach the sheep, goat and camel market in a big parking lot. There are only two camels and they are sitting side by side in the back of a pick-up truck with legs bound to keep them from disappearing—camels are very expensive, more than cars now. To get a closer look I have to wade through a sea of brown sheep and multi-colored goats, which smell to high heaven. While I am wondering if it is worth it just to see the camels up close and touch the fur, I see a man trying to drag a goat he has just purchased toward his truck and the goat is putting up such a protest it might start a major revolt among the other animals, but the sheep all stand roped together and looking dumb without making a peep.

As I am weaving my way back through the sea of animals, one of the guys from Tanley calls out to me and though I'm not overjoyed to run into somebody from work, at least he is of similar inclinations and thus tolerable. He says he is driving out to Tarut, an island just off the coast and asks me if I want to go which I find hard to turn down knowing it might be my only chance as it is difficult to get to without a car. On the way across the causeway—it was probably less than a mile—he showed me car to car flirting which I can't tell if the Saudi guys see it as flirting or just being friendly though my guide thinks he is showing me the time of my life.

Most of the houses on the island are crumbling—dried mud on wood frames or brick or cinderblock—but they all have TV antennas and are parked next to shiny new cars. On the outer shore is an old Majedsh fort, which has mostly been reduced to rubble and what is left is all covered with graffiti in Arabic I would have given my last dime to read.

Down by the water, teenage boys are stripping down to their baggy white undershorts that become see-through when they go in the water. They are crab hunting. They walk out into the low tide muck and pick up pretty blue and orange shelled crabs which they bring over to show us and I keep having to remind my friend to look at the crabs and not other things that were also pretty all shiny wet. The sky is royal blue and the buildings of the island are all light-colored, making me think of a Greek island I've seen in pictures. And suddenly, I throw my arms up and shout, "El hamdulillah," something I learned in a Sufi dancing class years ago.

Dave put the journal down and stared out into the infinite blackness below the plane. There was no sign of life, not a faint twinkling light as far as he could see in any direction. Maura woke up and shuddered. "I'm cold," she mumbled.

"That's because we're flying over Saudi Arabia," teased Dave.

"How do you know?"

"Should be about now. We'll be in Manama in a little over an hour."

Dave shuffled the pages and came to an early entry that he had missed before. It was not long after they had arrived in the country.

October 19: It began, the low wail fanning out over the dusty desert town on the air thick with heat, sending a shiver up my infidel spine. The doleful sound grew, crackling and sputtering from the worn-out speakers mounted high on the minarets. It was the last prayer call of the day and, I had been told, prime cruising time. I had done my research. Arab men have traditionally turned to other men for their sexual pleasures. From the gay guide: A foreigner found having sex with another man can be punished with two months in jail, possible whipping, and then deportation. From my compatriots: Sex with an Arab? Sure, I've had sex with an Arab. You asked for it, you got it. Bend over. It's over in ten minutes. And from our company handbook: You might be asked certain "favors" for a ride to or from town. A polite but firm refusal is the best policy.

So here I was, standing at the bus stop in front of the shopping center, one eye on the groups of foreign workers and the non-Saudi Moslems, who were shirking their responsibility avoiding prayer time. They strolled up and down the sidewalk looking into the shops, restaurants, and teahouses, all closed due to the prayer hour.

Then there was a bustle of activity as some of the stores reopened for a final hour of business after the last prayer time. I walked over in front of Safeway, thinking of taking some supplies back to my room. Snacks mostly. A nice-looking dark man, forties, and wearing Western clothes, was entering the store. Our eyes locked and I was the first to break away. Instead of going in the store, I kept walking. But a few seconds later I heard the automatic door open as he had turned around and come out. He began following me, quickening his pace to catch up. I stopped at the curb.

"Hello," he said. "You want see my car. It's here." He pointed to the parking lot. He led the way and I followed, swept along by that powerful trio of loneliness, libido, and curiosity. We hadn't been sitting in his car for 30 seconds before he started massaging his crotch saying, "You like this?"

In an instant the adventure snapped. It was gone for me. I didn't like the look on his face, a combination of nastiness and conquest as he started the car.

"No, wait. I have to meet someone here."

"No problem. Just five minutes. We go near."

"Five minutes? No thanks," I pulled back the door handle, piercing the soft semi-darkness of the car with a beam of brutal light. The

horrified look on his face, accentuated by the overhead lamp was unforgettable.

Close the door!" he shouted. When I didn't obey, he reached over me and pulled it closed with a loud bang. "We go," he said more calmly. "Just 5 minutes."

The car started rolling backward and I was thrown into a state of panic. "Sorry," I said, "I have to go." I pushed the door open and jumped out. I then realized he was halfway out of the parking space and our little scene had held up a line of traffic. Cars honked and flashed their lights. I bowed slightly, but didn't want to stay around for my applause. At a quick pace I headed for the street. Just as I was about to cross it, I saw the bus go sailing by, the last one of the night.

Then I was in a quite different predicament. Unless I planned to walk the five miles back to the compound, I needed a ride. I cursed my luck as I stood at the bus stop in hopes that it hadn't actually been the last one. It was not the roar of a diesel engine that I heard coming my way, but the slightly less deafening approach of a Saudi wearing sandals. The slapping of leather on pavement by feet used to a slow deliberate pace of life was unmistakable. We had dubbed it "the Arab shuffle." But in this case the sandals were attached to the feet of a young man in designer jeans and a tight-fitting T-shirt, which hung well on his tall stocky frame. He was a dark-skinned Arab with wiry hair and a moustache accenting a handsome face. I watched him walk in my direction, then take a seat on the low wall that separated the sidewalk from the parking lot.

"You wait bus?" he asked.

"Yes," I answered, walking toward him. "Do you know what time the last one comes?"

"I think is finished. Where you live?"

"The navy base." He looked puzzled. "Near King Faisal University," I added.

"Oh, yes. That's too far. You have room?"

"Yes."

"Alone?"

I shook my head, not knowing how to answer.

"Oh, you have madam," he said sheepishly. Somehow the word "madam" had slipped into the Arab-English vocabulary as an alternative to "wife". "Wife" implies a sexual liaison and it would be very impolite for a stranger to use a word with such connotations.

"No, but I have a roommate." I had begun to warm to his smile and dark bottomless eyes, but I knew I had to be wary.

"Come. I give you ride."

"Thank you, but I can't invite you to my room." He just smiled and led the way to his car. Once on the road in the closed car, I could tell that he had been drinking. To be on the road in such condition was an act of extreme recklessness in Saudi Arabia. He was a rebel, I thought, and I liked that, despite the dangers involved for me as a passenger. But he drove carefully and we arrived safely at the compound gate. On the ride he told me that he worked at the airport, was single and lived with his family. Other questions like if he were Saudi or not, he pretended not to understand. At the compound gate he asked, "When I see you again?" so sweetly I was nearly charmed. But was it worth being publicly flogged or thrown in jail? I agreed to meet him the following Friday at the same place.

The new day broke just as the plane descended toward the Bahrain airport, a little north of the island's only city, Manama. It looked as if they were going to set down on a blanket of gray mist and then the tires bumped the runway and they were thrown back in their seats.

Dave and Maura stepped out of the small terminal and felt the cool, moist winter air of the Gulf though it was warmer than the other places they had recently been. They spotted the Sheraton limousine and flagged it down in anticipation of a leisurely ride to the hotel, but a wave of Sheraton goers came up behind them and they had to fight to get a place on the small bus. The Indian driver, attempting to impress the English speakers aboard, ran a non-stop commentary from the airport to the town. They had difficulty understanding him, but they didn't feel like they were missing much as they looked out the windows and saw nothing but the dry flat scenery, unbroken except for an occasional stand of palm trees.

The barrenness of this part of the island turned, in a few short minutes, to housing developments in various stages of construction, many of them having been occupied before the construction was finished. Railings were unpainted and wires stuck out from poles where streetlights were supposed to be. Piles of brown dirt waited for landscaping while sidewalks started and fell off at random. The tracts of identical apartment buildings then gave way to the city, modern and busy, with several large hotels rising up out of the mist on the northern end of town.

The Bahrain Sheraton was a beige monolith, indistinguishable from other Sheratons except for the hotel name in Arabic lettering on the front. Dave and Maura dodged the bellmen trying to steer them toward the check-in desk, and moving quickly across the polished marble floor of the lobby, they entered the dining room. As it was still too early to go knocking on doors, they intended to stuff themselves at the breakfast buffet. They had come to the hotel to contact one of Dave's co-workers who arranged the dhow trips, and they needed to kill time. Most people on the weekend getaways partied well into the night, and Dave knew they wouldn't appreciate an early wake-up call.

In the dining room, laid out before them was a buffet decorated with a variety of exotic fruit, birds of paradise, anthuriums and tiger orchids. The buffet itself included everything from fava beans in a large copper pot to six kinds of freshly squeezed juices. Dave and Maura circled the tables and gaped at the sweet rolls, toast, potatoes, caviar, hot and cold cereals, eggs cooked to order, and even bacon and ham, which were outlawed in Saudi Arabia. Hovering around the buffet tables, a number of Filipino waitpersons and food servers, stood ready to make everything perfect for a crowd that was still in bed, trying to sleep off the hangovers from the night before. And then they noticed Joe Fester, a loud-mouthed boor who specialized in bad jokes, sitting in a corner by himself. Maura cringed, but he had already spotted them.

"Bates and the lovely wife," he shouted in a voice that killed the early morning serenity of the room. "I didn't know you were on this trip. I thought you were back in the States." Then Joe seemed to remember why they were supposed to be back in the States and respectfully lowered his voice a notch. "Say, who's car was it anyway? Anybody I know?"

"I'd rather not talk about it, Joe," said Dave.

"Oh, yeah. Sure. Really a shame. What a place to die in!" Then he leaned over and tried to draw them in by speaking sotto voce, "Hey, you know how you can tell when a Jewish American Princess is having an orgasm?" He didn't wait for a response. "She drops her. . .her. . .oh shit. . .her whatchamacallit. . .the nail thing. . .emery board. . .that's it." Then he broke into a wretched laughter. "You two aren't Jewish, are you?" And that sent him into an even more grotesque laughter at the thought that Jews might have gotten through the screening process and were working in Saudi Arabia.

Maura looked at him hard and said, "Joe, shut up."

"Jeez," he said, looking at Dave for male camaraderie. "What's eating her? We're all here for a good time, aren't we?"

"We aren't," said Dave. "We're just trying to get back to Saudi. We're not in the mood for jokes, especially not your jokes."

"Aw shit," said Joe, stabbing a big piece of ham and shoving it in his mouth. Then Dave and Maura noticed the sweating, half-empty cocktail glass on his table and realized that he was already drunk at 8:30 in the morning. After a few minutes, he got up and weaved toward the door.

"You can unclench your fists now," said Dave.

"Do they behead you for murder here like they do in Saudi Arabia?" Maura asked bitterly.

"I can't even imagine they'd punish you for it. They'd probably give you a reward."

"I can't wait to see the rest of the crew. You might have to knock me out for the boat trip across."

"That's if Billy Boy will even let us join his select little group. He'll probably make us go through some kind of Club Med type initiation."

They waited until 10:30 to knock on Bill Preston's door. The second knock brought a response and Bill was still zipping up his baggy jeans when he opened the door. "Jesus Christ!" he said. "I was expecting room service." He wasn't wearing a shirt and his torso looked like a hairy ski jump with his flat chest scooping down over a beer belly. The plugs of his hair transplant shot off in every direction, and his eyes too, looked like he had made an early morning raid on the mini-bar. In the background a whiney voice said, "Is that our eggs, Billy?" Her question was quickly followed by a yelp as if she had been pinched. A third occupant of the room let out a low chuckle and then there was the smack of a hand on bare flesh.

"Cathy isn't up yet," Bill explained as he stepped out in the hall and pulled the door behind him, reddening slightly. "What a surprise! What brings you here? Everything go okay back in the States?"

"As well as can be expected. We're on our way back and couldn't get on a flight direct to Saudi. We wondered if we could take the dhow with you all," Dave proposed.

"Gee, I've just contracted for a certain number of people. Why aren't you flying over?"

"We thought it might be fun to take the dhow trip. We've never done it. We'd pay of course, even extra for the inconvenience."

"Well, as a matter of fact, a couple of people weren't too crazy about the trip over," he said rubbing his stomach and making an achy face. "They have decided to fly back. I guess we could fit you in. You'd better be ready for the time of your life, Maura. It gets pretty wild on the trip back." He winked at her as if they shared some secret sexual knowledge.

"I think I can handle it," she said, holding her mouth in an artificial smile.

"Meet us in the lobby just after noon," Bill said as he slipped back into the room.

"And if you see room service on the way down, tell them to get their asses up here."

"Sure," said Dave. "And thanks."

"God, what a creep!" said Maura after he closed the door.

The Gulf was calm as the old sailing vessel, looking like something out of a bible history class picture book, set out from the small bay at Manama. Some of the romance was lost, however, when Dave and

Maura realized that the rigging and lateen sails had been removed and replaced by the motor that rumbled deep in the bowels of the boat. Still, the clouds had cleared and given them a perfect day—blue sky, warm air and a gentle breeze—a world away from the bare trees and gray skies of the Midwest. They found an open place on the deck and looked forward to the upcoming adventure across fifteen miles of open water.

There was no seating on board save for the folding chairs that a few of the seasoned travelers had thought to bring with them. Everyone else was sprawled out on deck like seals basking in the sun. A low rail on the sides of the ship came up about two feet above the planks to keep them from rolling into the sea as the boat swayed from side to side.

Dave and Maura had joined the majority of the passengers who were clustered in the bow. They began, like weary travelers, to look for land on the horizon. Those with folding chairs set them up more toward the stern and a few sat atop a roughly framed structure in back, which a tarp could be thrown over in rainy weather. At the highest point of the boat, atop the crude shelter, the simple red and white flag of Bahrain flapped in the gentle breeze.

Of the thirty people aboard, there were only four women besides Maura—two Tanley wives and two young British nurses, who attracted considerably more attention than their average looks would warrant under normal conditions. The crew was made up of two well-weathered Arab seamen who fussed about the boat like aunties serving tea, showing particular care for some aspects of entertaining and appearing absent-minded about others. As one sat at the helm, the other popped in and out of the hold where the engine puttered away, bringing out the welcome offerings of a sugary fruit drink and cookies. The server had to spend a good deal of time just rolling up and down the skirts of his thobe to facilitate his movements. Arab attire was much more suited to the desert than the sea.

As the dhow moved from the relative calm of the large bay to open waters, the wind picked up and they could see a blanket of whitecaps stretched out between them and the Saudi coast though the far shore was still too distant to be seen. The festive air on the boat kept the passengers from giving much thought to the condition of the sea and as soon as Bill gave the signal, a champagne cork popped. It was followed by a chorus of pop tops while a bouquet of plastic glasses rose up to catch the overflow of champagne and a cheer went up from the crowd. The captain and his first mate hardly took notice; their attention was focused on some indiscernible point way off in the distance, perhaps a storm brewing, but more likely it was Allah, as the fingers of their free hands danced over strings of prayer beads.

One of Bill's naval training buddies jumped to his feet, spread his legs on the deck for balance and put a beer to his lips, pouring the cold bubbly liquid down his throat. As his Adam's apple bobbed, a few enthusiasts began to chant, "Go. Go. Go." In the middle of the chant, the boat bucked against a wave and the guzzler lost his footing, nearly falling on top of several innocent bystanders who might have been crushed by his big frame and huge belly. But he regained his balance without losing a drop, finished off the can to the applause of the group, smashed it against his forehead, and then threw it overboard.

Dave and Maura seemed to be the only ones who had neglected to bring any alcohol onboard, everyone else being well supplied for the two and a half hour trip. But since all the alcohol had to be drunk or thrown overboard before they arrived at the dock in Al-Khobar, the other travelers were willing to share from their exaggerated stockpile of drink. When a wine bottle came to Maura, her first reaction was to decline; she hadn't drunk from a passed-around wine bottle since college. But when Dave suggested that it certainly couldn't make things any less tolerable, Maura agreed and took a swig. Then just as she handed the bottle to Dave, the dhow hit a wave, sending a spray of salty water over the revelers in the foremost part of the boat. There was a momentary astonishment, then laughter. Within seconds, the boat crashed against a much larger wave and a considerably bigger splash leapt over the side, dousing the people on the starboard side of the bow. Some of the drenched victims scattered quickly amidst squeals of laughter, while others sat steadfast, licking the salt from their lips and pushing back the hair plastered to their foreheads. Then a regular series of jolts sent spray as far back as where Dave and Maura were sitting. There was a charade of panic as everyone began moving back to the center of the dhow, many of them crawling so as not to have to stand up in the rocky boat.

The captain jumped up, secured the steering wheel with a piece of rope and started rolling up his skirts. Motioning for Bill to help him, he grabbed a tarp, which they rigged up on the starboard side of the bow. The canvas wall saved the passengers from being totally drenched, though the salty spray still reached most of them. Before long they had salt-lacquered hair and a layer of seawater drying on the skin already raw from a weekend in the sun.

Someone from the visual arts department documented the passengers' antics with a small video camera. The footage was significantly incriminating that it would never be shown outside private parties. But the most delicate taping was yet to come as the call of nature began to circulate around the boat.

"I have to piss," whined Dave as he finished his second beer. They both looked toward a line of merry, but antsy waiters outside a crude little compartment at the back of the boat. Considering the alternative of leaning over the edge to pee and possibly being dumped overboard when the dhow hit a big wave, Dave took his place behind the five men already waiting. As he joked with the co-worker in front of him about their predicament, the flimsy door of the compartment, which hadn't been properly latched, swung open revealing the torture-like conditions of the tiny box. One of the nurses was squatting over a hole in the floor with her back to the rest of the boat and didn't realize that she was mooning everyone until a few of the men started hooting. Then the dhow shifted and the door swung closed. Seconds later, it swung open again and this time a large white ass was deliberately thrust toward the entryway. She wiggled it back and forth as she pulled up her shorts to the tune of whistles and catcalls. When she emerged, she was red-faced, but smiling.

Dave wondered how he was going to relieve himself in a shed too small for anyone over four feet tall to stand up in. The next person came out, a tall blond Nordic-type who unwrapped himself from his crouched position and lifted his arms over his head in a Rocky salute. To challenge his victory, someone pointed to the wet stains down the front of his pants and the crowd started yelling and laughing. He quickly brought his hands down to cover the spots and waddled away cursing the boat and everyone on it.

Dave's turn came and he was careful to latch the door and make sure his pants were out of the way as he crouched down and watched the water rushing under the dhow through the hole in the floor. The water had a mesmerizing effect and the box seemed detached from the boat, as if it were ready to topple off the back into the sea. Then there was a pounding on the door.

"Christ! Hold your horses," he said.

"It's me," said Maura. "I've got to go bad."

"I don't think there's quite room for a duo," he said, wondering what Maura's reaction was going to be when she saw the inside of the box. He finished and opened the door.

"Oh, my God!" Maura had a horrified expression on her face. "I've changed my mind."

"No, you don't," said Dave, turning her around and pushing her into the compartment. "All these people were nice enough to let you go ahead of them, so you can't back out now."

"Isn't it funny," Maura remarked later. "The two company wives haven't moved from their lawn chairs the whole trip?"

"And have you noticed that neither of them has drunk a drop?" replied Dave.

"I thought they were just being stuffy. They've obviously been on these trips before. Look at them. They look like two queens, sitting back and musing over the foolishness of their subjects."

The merriment continued throughout the trip, but there was a brief moment of solemnity as everyone stopped to watch the first mate climb up the pole to change the flags about halfway across. Down came the red and white Bahraini flag with its jagged edge between the colors, and up went the bright green with crossed swords under which was scrolled Arabic writing from the Qur'an. Not long after that, they spotted the small town of Al-Khobar on the horizon. Though no one was too pleased, it was especially unsettling to Dave and Maura who stood and stared with a foreboding of what the land would offer on their return.

About half a mile out from the shore, Bill spread the word to "drink it or dump it." By the time they reached the dock there wasn't a sign of alcohol anywhere save in the eyes of the passengers. As they reached the shore, they were a rag-tag group of crusty sailors, salty, sunburned, red-eyed, and unstable on their feet. When they stepped into the makeshift customs house, the nostrils of the officials, some in thobes and some in uniforms, flared with anticipation, as they were sure they were going to find contraband. They set about meticulously searching everyone's luggage. Not finding a trace of liquor, they began to pick on other things objectionable, if not really illegal, in the Kingdom. The man in front of Dave and Maura was accused of bringing disco tapes into the country. His "disco" collection included Dolly Parton, Tammy Wynette, and George Jones.

"No disco in Saudi Arabia," the official said, confiscating the tapes.

"Disco?" the man laughed. "That's Country and Western and I bought 'em here. There are hundreds of these damn things in the cassette souks all over town. I paid good money for those tapes and I want 'em back."

"No disco in Saudi Arabia," the official repeated and waved him on with tapes in hand. The man ambled away cursing under his breath and the official tossed the tapes in a box on the floor.

The customs agent eyed Dave and Maura suspiciously. They had only Maura's purse and the shoulder bag, containing little more than their passports, toiletries, and a change of clothes they had bought in Tonnerre. The rest of their clothes, as far as they knew, were still in a hotel room in Paris. The man with a green uniform and a suspicious eye looked perplexed at their few belongings and spent a disproportional amount of time checking through them. He ended up taking out a tube of toothpaste, squeezed a dab on his finger, smelled it, and then threw the tube back in the bag with a disgusted sigh. And leaving a blouse half-draped over the edge of the bag, he looked toward the next person.

At the exit, a Saudi in traditional dress sat on a battered old chair and made one final check. He allowed Maura to pass, but stopped Dave, patted him down and asked him to remove his shoes. Dave looked down. He wore a pair of sandals he had borrowed from one of the guys on the boat. He slipped them off and started to show the bottoms of his feet before he caught himself. He remembered that it was an insult to show the sole of one's feet to an Arab and though he had a strong urge to do it anyway, he figured this was no time to be attracting attention.

Maura was waiting for him as he came out of the building, standing uncomfortably again on Saudi soil. "What was that all about?" she said.

"Oh, he wanted to see if I had little bottles of Bacardi rum taped to the bottoms of my feet."

"Well, did he find anything?"

"I think he just liked my sandals and wanted to have a better look."

"It's a wonder they didn't confiscate them too. They took all of George's videotape, you know."

"That's a shame. I was looking forward to seeing a rerun of the expression on your face when you came out of the john."

Two company vans were waiting for them in the parking lot, and Dave and Maura got in the one that Rajab was driving. Rajab, a young Sri Lankan, was everybody's favorite compound employee. He lit up when he saw Dave and Maura, flashing his famous smile of perfect white teeth. "I'm so happy to see you. I miss you," he said. He had a flirtatious innocence, ebony eyes, and skin like the finest milk chocolate. He took Dave's hand and said, "You know, I never get to tell you I am sorry about Eddie. I like him very much."

"Thank you, Rajab," said Dave. Then Rajab turned his eyes on Maura and smiled shyly. She felt a true affection for him, one of the few people in Saudi Arabia she was happy to see again.

As they took a seat, Dave said in a low voice," I wonder if he knew that Eddie would have hopped in bed with him in a minute."

"Who wouldn't?" said Maura teasingly.

"Who wouldn't what?" asked Billy as the group plodded onto the bus and took seats all around them. Dave turned his face to the window.

10

BACK IN THE ARMS OF ALLAH

Darkness fell as the van pulled up to the compound gate, the sun having gone down like a big orange balloon behind the fertilizer plant with its constant ribbon of smoke trailing off toward the town of Dammam. Rajab honked and the Pakistani security guard came out of the gatehouse in a starched white shirt and blue pants. He unwrapped the chain, which encircled though was not locked around the two poles of the double gate. Terrorist acts against Americans in other parts of the Middle East would temporarily stir up talk of increased security, but concern quickly subsided in the safe atmosphere of Saudi Arabia where the people were held in a tight rein.

They passed through the gate and stopped in front of the dining hall where the single men piled out in hopes of getting their evening meal. Since Dave and Maura lived right near the maintenance building where the vans were parked, Rajab told them to stay on and he'd drop them off in front of their house. They drove through the grid pattern of concrete, boxy houses that looked like they had been dropped neatly from the sky rather than constructed. It was a shock to be back in this artificial world, the compound, which had a fraction of the character of its supposed model, suburbia, and all the functional aspects of its closest kin, military housing. Personnel could be moved in or out at a moment's notice.

They stepped off the bus and looked at their house with suspicions. Something was not right. The first thing they saw when they walked in and turned on the lights was the bare walls. Then they passed through the hallway into the living room where two large shipping boxes occupied the center of the floor. It reminded them of the sterility they faced that first day they walked into their new quarters months before.

"It's a good thing we didn't get here a minute later or they would have had us shipped out," said Dave. He turned around and walked directly back out the door.

"Where are you going?" Maura yelled after him, though she had a pretty good idea already.

He went straight over to Bud's house and pounded on the door. The outside light flipped on, the bolt turned and then he was face to face with an astonished Bud in bathrobe, holding a *Reader's Digest* with his index finger stuck in it to hold the place.

"Dave!" he said, trying to appear his cool, good-natured self. "Well, I'll be. How did you—"

Dave cut him off. "What is going on here? Obviously, you weren't expecting us."

"What do you mean, Dave?"

"I mean the two big boxes sitting in an empty living room."

"We didn't hear from you and we just figured. . ."

"You figured wrong. I told you we were coming back, and we're back. So, unless I'm fired, and if I am, I'll fight you all the way on it, I want someone at my house immediately to unpack those boxes."

Dave turned around and stormed away, leaving Bud uncharacteristically at a loss for words. He looked down at the magazine in his hand and said, "Shit."

Dave knew his threats were weightless. When Tanley decided to fire someone, there was no fighting it. You were out on a plane the next day if not the same. Back at the house, he found Maura already beginning to unpack the boxes. "Don't touch a thing," he roared.

"What?" Maura screwed up her face in confusion.

"They packed it up and they can just unpack it. Bud's going to send someone over right away." He sounded confident, but he was unsure what effect his anger had had on Bud. A minute later, there was a knock on the door. Dave yanked it open.

"Rajab, what are you doing here?" said Dave.

"Mr. Bud tell me to come."

"But I didn't mean for him to send you." Dave's anger was quickly turning to embarrassment. "I thought you were going home." Rajab lived in Dammam in a crowded house with other Sri Lankan and Filipino workers. He had already worked a long day.

"Yes, I go, but Mr. Bud tell me to come and help you."

"That's okay. You don't have to. You can go home."

"No. No. I want to help." He smiled and looked over Dave's shoulder. Dave turned around and saw Maura standing behind him looking unconsciously seductive.

"All right. I get it," he said.

"Dave!" Maura said, punching him in the back. "God, you twist everything."

"No, I don't. I really think we should make a party out of it." Dave felt his anger fading away. He put his arm around Rajab and pulled him into the house. "I wonder what they did with that rotgut wine that we made."

"Is still there, sir," Rajab said matter-of-factly.

"Rajab, please don't call me sir. My name is Dave and this is Maura. How did you know about the wine?"

"They tell me, the Filipinos who pack this. They leave it under the sink."

"Should be well-aged," said Maura, going to the cabinet. "What is that now? Three months?"

"Our finest red," said Dave, taking the bottle. "Would you like a glass, Rajab? It's okay if you don't. You're Moslem, aren't you?"

"Yes, but I can drink a toast."

"Are most people Moslem in Sri Lanka?" asked Maura.

"No. Most Buddhist. Then, Hindu. Only a few Moslem."

"When will you go back to your country?" Maura continued.

"This summer, I hope. I am here long time. Five years."

"Five years!" Maura repeated, nearly choking on her sip of wine. "How did you stand it? And you're here every day, aren't you? Do you actually work seven days a week?"

"Yes."

"Seven days a week for five years. Incredible."

"We work seven days because there is nothing else to do. Better to keep busy. And we have two weeks vacation every year."

"I just hope you were able to save some money," said Dave.

"A little," Rajab answered sadly. "But most I send to my mother. She is sick."

"I'm sorry to hear that," said Maura.

"Probably she will die soon." He spoke without emotion.

"We should get going on this unpacking. We can still talk while we're doing it," said Maura. "I want you to tell me all about your country."

By the time they finished the bottle of wine, they had learned a lot about Rajab and had emptied the boxes. With their possessions strewn all over the living room floor, they decided to call it a night and sent Rajab home.

At 5:30 in the morning, Dave reported for work with everyone else, and from the moment he signed in, he felt caught in a routine that had lost all meaning for him. Without Eddie, the plan to make money in Saudi Arabia seemed lifeless. He ached as a twin might for his other half.

Most of his fellow workers looked at him uncomfortably, and not knowing exactly what to say, just acted as if he had never left. A few of the ones he was friendlier with expressed their sympathies in hushed voices and Dave nodded and thanked them. But when all the other teachers went off to their classes, Dave found himself sitting alone in the teacher's room waiting for someone to tell him what to do.

Since another teacher had been assigned to his class permanently, they put him to work proofreading the latest update of the teaching materials. Hour after hour he sat in a small room by himself crouched over the manuscripts though very little of the time was he actually concentrating on the tedious material. He plotted his next moves in the quest to discover Eddie's killer. So lost was he in his scheme that when Jerry came in at mid-morning and stood behind him, he didn't realize it until Jerry coughed.

"Can I bother you for a minute?" said Jerry in a soft voice.

"You're the boss," quipped Dave, recovering from the surprise. Jerry chuckled nervously.

"I just want to apologize about the mix-up over your things."

"Mix-up?"

"We really didn't expect you to come back."

"I said I would, didn't I?"

"I'm sure it was a blow to you and sometimes it's better to. . ." Jerry paused, searching for the right words.

"Run away?"

"You wouldn't be running away from anything. It was an tragic accident."

"Accident?"

Jerry took a deep breath. He seemed unsettled by Dave's aggressive behavior. "You know, Dave, the circumstances of Eddie's death are a closed case here in Saudi Arabia."

"Nothing is a closed case until the truth is out."

"Surely you know by now that the only truth they recognize is in the Qur'an. Everything else is, well, sort of relative, malleable."

"Waxing philosophical are we now?"

"I'm just trying to save you some trouble and everyone a lot of headaches."

"Maybe a few headaches would shake people out of their complacency. People come over here and get swallowed up by this controlled, isolated environment. They don't have to think anymore. They let the powers that be determine what's right or wrong. Most of the guys here will tell you how much they love their country, land of the free and home of the brave. So what the hell are they doing here? But even more mind-boggling, why do they keep coming back? Just for the money? I don't think so. They are like prisoners that can't live on the outside. They like being told what to do and when to do it. No decisions. You become part of a machine, give up your free will. Employees here should be outraged that something happened to one of their co-workers and no one in administration cares enough to investigate. Americans have a slight edge over the majority of people in the rest of the world—the freedom to question, the ability to right a wrong. If we give that up, what do we have left?"

"That's all well and good. But we're not in America now. We're not dealing with Americans. We are maintaining a very delicate balance with people who have suddenly been thrust into the world's limelight, and with little preparation. I think they're doing a damn good job considering. Look at the rest of the countries in this part of the world. So I just want to warn you that if you have anything in mind that will upset that balance, we won't hesitate to ship you out on the next flight to New York."

It was the strongest statement Dave had ever heard from Jerry and he was momentarily dazed by it. He had revealed more of his attitude than he should have and it was time to backpedal or else they would stop him before he had a chance to put his plan in motion. "I just want to finish my contract and then we'll be out of your hair."

"I know you're a reasonable man, Dave. I've known that all along." He stared for a moment at the materials on Dave's desk. "The truth is I really came here to ask you a favor. We need someone to cover the last hour of Company 8, Section 6. Can you do it?"

"That's my old class. I don't know." Dave wasn't anxious to go back in the arena.

"It's only an hour, and you can take them to the lab the last half."

When Dave walked in the room, all the cadets were quietly sitting at their desks. They appeared a sea of clam and respect as they had all donned white dress uniforms for an early afternoon military review.

"Good morning," said Dave.

"Good morning, teacher," they said in unison, a chorus of bright voices with smiles breaking out on several of their faces. Saleh jumped up and pulled the teacher's chair out from under the desk and bowed slightly, indicating for Dave to sit.

Dave eased into the chair, suspicious of their best behavior. He surveyed their faces and nodded, realizing that a few of them were missing. Most likely they had fallen behind or had been kicked out for mischief. The students all seemed to be holding their breaths until he cracked a smile, and then everyone let out a sigh of relief.

"We miss you, teacher," said Fahd. Other students around the room made affirmations and nods of agreement.

Dave thought of all the frustration and annoyance the class had caused him, the times he had wanted to run from the room screaming, the rude, infantile acting out that had seemed designed to make his life miserable. But now all he could see was the warm glow in their faces, the pure joy of seeing him. "I've missed you, too," he said, and meant it.

"We very sorry about brother," said Saleh.

Their communal sympathy and genuine concern spread like a powerful wave over him, far surpassing what he had gotten from the other staff, and certainly more true than any consideration he received from the Tanley administration. He looked down at his crossed hands on top of the green manual, the place marker sticking out the top with his name hurriedly scrawled across it. His eyes welled up and his throat tensed. He tried to sniff back the tears. Saleh and Fahd leapt out of their seats and started to move forward, their eyes focused in preparation of offering comfort. Raising one hand, Dave motioned for them to sit down.

"Thank you," he said. He stood up and took a deep breath. "It means a lot to me."

There was a rustle of uniform, an unbending of bodies, and the stomp of boots on the cement floor as thirty young men in white rose to attention by their desks, and then, as if given a command, saluted him. It was an absurd gesture that at any other time in his life he might have found comical. But at that moment he was stunned by the force of their respect and compassion. It put him over the edge. Tears rolled down his cheeks as he raised his hand to forehead and saluted them back.

"Thank you. *Shukran.* Thank you," he whispered, lowering his hand to touch his heart. "I will never forget this. Please, sit down."

The first workweek back in Saudi Arabia passed slowly with Dave sitting cooped up all day in a small room proofreading and Maura at home writing letters, trying to put into words what had been happening in her life. She hadn't written to many of her old friends since they had come to Saudi Arabia and now seemed a good time to catch up with them. But she struggled with a letter to her mother, who had remarried and moved to Southern California. Maura had promised Beth that she would encourage her mother to see their father and start the process of forgiving. The words wouldn't come.

Maura found it ironic that she and her mother had both moved to California though looking for very different things. Her mother hadn't approved of her marriage to Dave and was appalled when Maura told her they were going to Saudi Arabia. Maura had called from the Bates' saying she was in the States. She had a hard time explaining that they wouldn't be able to come and visit. And Eddie's death only confirmed her mother's notion that bad things happened to people in places where they shouldn't be. With memories of her most recent conversation with her mother still in her head, Maura managed to scratch out a brief and somewhat cool letter saying that it was time to let bygones be bygones. She was ready to heal the rift with her father and hoped her mother was, too. Putting a US stamp on it, she dropped it on the pile that would go in a diplomatic pouch on the next flight out.

Dave and Maura spent the evenings quietly at home, watching movies they checked out from the company video library. Most of them had luckily been spared the censor's shears unlike the ones shown on TV. On Wednesday evening, Moslem Friday, Dave was particularly restless. He kept jumping up and doing things while they watched *Cabaret* for the third time since they'd been in Saudi Arabia.

"Should I shut it off?" asked Maura. "I guess we have seen it a lot. But I love the chance to escape."

"No. You don't have to shut it off. I like it too. I just can't sit still."

"I wish you'd talk to me about it. I can see things going on behind your eyes. I can hear you thinking at night. I know you're up to something. I just wish you'd tell me what's going on."

"I don't want to worry you."

"Look, I'm going to be worried. I can either be worried-ignorant or worried-informed. I'd prefer worried-informed." Dave got up and went into the hall bathroom. He came back with a small bag from the pharmacy.

"I probably should have consulted you on this, but I went ahead and got it. I hope it works." He pulled a box of Lady Clairol out of the bag. "Today a brunette; tomorrow a blond."

"Who? Who's going to be a blond?" She was dumbfounded.

"Me."

"You, a blond?" She cackled with distaste for the idea.

"The Prince likes blonds. And watch this." He put the bag down and stood up. He positioned himself in the middle of the room, threw his hands to the floor, and kicked his legs up into a handstand. But he had too much kick and his legs flipped over, catching a lamp on the way down and sending it and himself crashing to the floor. Her shock quickly turned to laughter.

"Are you okay?" she managed to say through her amusement.

Dave lay flat on his back in the middle of the living room floor with a disgusted look on his face. "Well, it isn't perfect yet. Sorry about the lamp."

"The lamp? I don't care about the lamp. It's a Tanley special. What is this all about?"

"The prince."

"The Prince is also into kinky positions?"

"Very funny. I happen to know that he's attracted to blond American athletes. Tomorrow is beach day. He usually goes to Aziziyah on Thursdays. So I've got to make him notice me if I want to meet him. Look," he said, whipping off his shirt. "I've been going to the gym every day this week. What do you think?"

"Well, a week at the gym doesn't a Sylvester Stallone make, but you look fine. You look great. You have a naturally sexy body. I've never had any complaint there."

"Thanks," he said and started to get up. Quickly Maura rolled off the couch on top of him, forcing him back to the ground. He struggled to get away before she found the spot, but it was too late. She was an expert tickler and soon had him writhing in hysteria, completely defenseless.

"Stop," Dave yelled. "Please."

"I can't."

"Please, I'll do anything."

"Anything? Give me a massage every night for a month?"

"Yes." Maura let up for a second, long enough for Dave to grab her arms, turn her over on her back and sit astraddle her waist. Then he held her arms above her head.

"That's not fair," Maura whined.

"All's fair in love, war, and tickling," said Dave.

"Ouch! You're hurting me."

"Ah, now the real fun starts. It's time for the neck."

"No! Not the neck," she screamed.

"Yes. Now we'll see who massages who."

"Whom, Teach." Dave buried his lips in the tender white flesh where her neck met her shoulder. He nibbled and sucked on her there until she begged for mercy. Then he moved to her ear and his tongue slipped in toward her eardrum, seeming as if it would go right into her brain. The sparks shot up and down her body and her skin was gooseflesh, bristling at each new sensation.

He let loose of her arms and took her head in his large warm hands. She wrapped her arms around his back and pulled his bare chest down to mesh with her breasts. Then his mouth was on hers, planting kisses in rapid succession on her lips. She lost count at twenty-three, distracted by something coming to life and pushing against her inner thigh. Her gooseflesh changed to a warm flush that swept over her body, taking, like a brush fire does, her oxygen. He pressed his mouth harder against hers and she could feel the beating of her heart in her throat. One sensation melted into another as his hands were somehow already under her T-shirt, his thumbs lightly brushing across her nipples. Then he lifted her up and pulled the shirt over her head, and even her own shoulder-length hair excited her as it fell down and swept against the pale freckled skin of her bare shoulders.

"Would you please get out of those tight shorts before you injure yourself?" she pleaded. Within seconds they were both naked and she could feel the full extent of his body on top of her, from the hair of his legs to the smooth flatness of his stomach to his eyes locked to hers in a smile. She was round and voluptuous, a light sandy color; he was long, lean and muscular, olive skinned. She ran her fingers over the hairy backs of his thighs, his firm round ass, and his smooth back. She was ready for him, even anxious, but she was already afraid of it ending. "Not too fast," she thought to herself.

And his eyes, still glued to hers, seemed to ask, "Is everything okay?"

She smiled and kissed him.

"Let's rouse the neighbors tonight," Dave whispered. She resented the notion that sex should be an act of rebellion, something that might touch someone outside of their immediate tangle of love, but her complaint quickly dissipated.

"It's your move," she said.

It was the first time they had made love since before Eddie's death, and if the wait was what provoked the intensity, it was worth it. But Dave was unusually quiet afterwards as he lay on the floor staring at the ceiling. Maura was curled up next to him.

She wanted very much for him to hold her right then, but he seemed miles away.

"Dave?"

"Yes."

"This is not flattery, okay?"

"Okay"

"You are an incredible lover. And more than that, I love you very much." Her voice started to get jerky. She could feel the tears coming, couldn't stop them even if she had wanted to. "Do you know what an unhappy woman I'd be if anything happened to you?"

"Don't worry, Maura," he said in a soft, distant voice.

"Oh, God," Maura wailed as the sobs rolled off her chest like the tide moving out from a deserted beach.

Dave quickly wrapped himself around her, holding her tightly. "I love you too, Maura," he whispered. And amidst the quieting sobs crept a guilt that she had used trickery to get what she wanted, at least for the moment. But as he held her tighter still, that too was quelled, and she relaxed into a blissful stupor.

In the morning, Maura awoke clutching a pillow instead of her husband. She reached out and felt the space where he had slept. It was already cool. Then she rolled over and saw that the bathroom door was closed. Why would he close the door? He never did that.

"Dave?"

"What?" came the muffled voice.

"What are you doing in there?"

"Just a minute."

Several minutes passed before the door opened slowly. In the interim, the previous evening had all come back to her—the pharmacy bag, the Lady Clairol. . .that's all the further she got as she found herself looking at someone who was familiar to her, but whom she didn't know. He was like the characters that faded in and out of her dreams, combinations of people from the past and present, people she knew well and people she'd only seen once or twice.

"Well, say something for Pete's sake," Dave pleaded.

"Dave? Is that you in there? I recognize your voice but. . ."

"Oh, come on. I can't look that different."

"You do. It's amazing. The blond brings out the Eddie in your face. Your eyes look bluer, like his. It's eerie."

Dave shrugged his shoulders and went back in to the bathroom mirror. "It's just temporary," he called back in a strange voice.

"I hope so. What are you going to do about work?"

"On Friday night, I'll dye it back."

"But you'll never get your right color."

"It'll be close enough. Do you think the guys around here are going to notice a slight change in another man's hair color?"

It was nearly noon before Dave reached the cruising beach at Aziziyah that Khalil had described to him. The directions had been difficult to follow, but after a series of wrong turns, Dave found the narrow bumpy road that curved around the wall of a compound and passed through a dumping area before it arrived at the wide flat beach. It was a hazy but warm day, and his head began to sweat under the hat he had been wearing since he left the house. He took it off and threw it in the back seat, shaking out his blond curls.

He drove by a group of families and was shocked to see a woman, fully clothed and covered with an *abaya,* emerge from the water, looking like a giant black stingray on legs, the water streaming from the dark cloth onto the sand. He continued down the thin strip of hard-packed sand that was the road. Beyond a certain unobvious dividing line, it was men only. Interspersed among the darker Arabs were a number of Westerners with pale skin and light hair. Competition, he thought.

Some of the Arabs had set up tents, less inclined to expose their bodies to the sun, while the light-skinned Westerners exposed as much skin as they thought they could get away with. Since the only places men were permitted to show their legs was at the beach, on playing fields or in gymnasiums, most of the Westerners were in brief trunks. Many of the Saudis sat fully clothed in their cars or pick-up trucks with the doors open. Khalil had explained that the open door was a sign they were inviting someone to join them.

A few men splashed in the water—very cool this time of the year—but the most popular activities seemed to be cruising and eating. Most groups had brought picnic baskets and coolers. Khalil had explained that it was customary to offer a piece of fruit or a Pepsi to a young man walking by in case he needed to fortify himself to continue his journey. An Arab offers food and drink to a stranger as readily as he offers his hand, a result of a desert culture where long journeys across the wilderness made travelers dependent on the kindness of strangers. An outstretched hand also showed he carried no weapons.

Dave drove to where the road ended at a large dune and then turned around, careful not to go off the road into the soft sand. He parked in a spot where he saw no other Westerners and spread a large towel on the beach, but still near the road. Then he took off his shorts and T-shirt self-consciously, feeling naked in his new Speedo. Three young Arabs to his left had taken notice of his arrival and were up on their elbows following his every movement with their quizzical brown eyes. One wore a *thobe* and the other two were in modest boxer-type swim trunks, showing their adolescent torsos and thin boyish legs. They looked to be the same age as his students. He quickly reached for his sunglasses, wondering if any of the men here were cadets from the base.

Dave stretched out on his towel, belly down, facing the road. There was a constant line of traffic going by, some of the cars circling from the big dune to the entrance and back. Khalil had said Majed normally went to the beach at around 1:00, after the big midday meal and before the mid-afternoon prayer time. Most people liked to nap during this hot part of the day, and a prince could slip away relatively unnoticed. His driver would bring him in a flat gray Mercedes with tinted windows. Dave just had to make sure that he was seen.

Looking at his watch, he saw it wasn't quite 12:30 and decided he could risk resting his head on his arms and closing his eyes for a few minutes. The smell of the sea and sand filled his nostrils and the constant rush of tires rolling by on the hard-packed sand had a lulling affect, making him lapse into a state of surprising calm. With a cool breeze off the sea, Dave imagined that Eddie was lying next to him and they were at Jenner-by-the-Sea back in California. He pictured the driftwood shelter they had built to block the wind the last time they were there. It was much like the forts they had built when they were kids, and it seemed that they had left a trail of nests, forts and shelters behind them, across time and places they'd been together. But there was something half-hearted about the construction of the one at Jenner. Dave had sensed it and knew that Eddie felt it, too, as he stared at their hastily constructed shelter.

"Do you think I'll die before you?" said Eddie when he fell down onto the sand as if he had been struck.

"Why are you thinking about that?" said Dave.

"I hope I do," said Eddie, a little too enthusiastically. Dave didn't want to pursue the conversation. He had a feeling where it was going and it made him uncomfortable

"Eddie. . ."

"That way," Eddie continued, "you'd still have somebody—Maura. You wouldn't be alone."

"Maura and I aren't hitched yet," he finally said. "Anyway, it might not work out."

"But you want it to, right?"

"Yeah."

"I thought so," said Eddie forlornly.

"Jesus, Eddie, don't sound so happy for me." Dave was getting irritated with the conversation. Eddie fell silent. The seagulls squawked overhead and the sound of the waves hitting the beach got louder as the tide came in.

"Don't be pissed," said Eddie.

"I'm not pissed."

"I think I know when you're pissed. Remember those days when we lived with Hazel?"

"Sure I do."

"We made a pact to stick together. I remember thinking, at the time, that other people come and go, even moms and dads, but brothers, that's for life."

"Nothing has changed. Sticking together doesn't mean excluding other people from our lives."

"I know. It's just that at certain times in your life, vulnerable times, you believe things and they stay with you, forever, even when you find out later they're not true."

Dave was riled. "What's not true? We promised to stick together and take care of each other. I still plan to do that. I don't know about you." Dave stood up and started walking down the beach. Eddie didn't try to call him back. He let him stew in the turmoil that he had always been good at stirring up in his brother.

A horn honked very close by, rudely shaking Dave out of his daydream. Spread out across his field of vision was a large white Oldsmobile with a traditionally dressed middle-aged Arab at the wheel. The round-faced man beckoned him to the car and Dave looked around to see if there was anyone else he could be motioning to. He only saw the three Arab boys, and they watched him intently, hanging on the moment as if something important were about to happen.

Dave got up and went over to the car window.

"Hey, *Sadiki,* you want oil change?" the man said eagerly. Dave looked at his car and then back at the man. "I just had one about three weeks ago." It seemed a strange place to drum up auto repair business.

The Arab laughed heartily. "Good joke," he said.

"Joke?"

"Come get in. We go for a ride."

Dave looked at his watch. It was 12:55. "I can't. I'm waiting for someone."

"Just five minute," the man said, moving his hand to his crotch. "I know a good place." He fondled an erection in the folds of white cloth beneath his overstuffed belly.

It hit Dave what "an oil change" was and he began to redden, embarrassed for this fat, unattractive man and his pressing needs. "Thanks, anyway," he said as he turned around and headed back to his towel. Out of the corner of his eye he saw the Arab boys smiling and chattering to each other like a group of excited monkeys. "Five minutes?" he said to himself, shaking his head. He sat down and faced the sea, but he hadn't heard the car pull away. Dave turned around, thinking to give the man a dirty look, but he appeared so pathetic sitting there, continuously motioning for Dave to come back to the car. He didn't have the heart to be nasty. He turned his attention back to the ocean and waited for the man to give up and go away. It was several minutes before he did, and by that time, the three Arab boys had already focused their attention on a brown pick-up, which had pulled into a space on the other side of them.

No longer the center of attention, Dave got up and took a walk down to the sea where he waded a few yards into the cold water and, bending over, washed his hands. Then he walked back to the edge of the road and did his first handstand of the day. He could only hold it a few seconds. He tried another one immediately, which also ended with a solid thud on the sand. He realized that one of his problems was a lack of concentration; one eye was always on the road. Then in the distance, he saw a gray car approaching slowly. Dave knelt at the side of the road, his heart racing while his mind came chugging to a halt, making everything appear slow and dreamlike. When the car finally reached him, he stared blank-faced into the tinted glass of the back seat. Then it was past him, creeping toward the big sand dune.

Taking a deep breath, Dave stood up and tried another handstand. His pointed toes reached up to the sky and stayed there a good ten seconds before he tucked his neck in and rolled forward. A smile spread across his face and he wallowed in the contentment a few seconds. Then he got up to look down the road toward the big dune that dwarfed the Mercedes coming back in his direction.

Dave went up again and started to falter, but was able to balance himself by scissoring his legs just as the car came abreast of him. The car stopped and the window went down. A square-faced man wearing a white *ghutra* leaned out the window and Dave, from his peculiar angle, had a view of his wide nostrils and the thick lashes that surrounded his dark brown eyes.

"You American?" the nice-looking Arab said.

"Yeah," Dave grunted.

"You Olympics?"

The question made Dave lose it and he fell over with a laugh. "No," he said over his shoulder.

"My country has a very good football team, you know. Maybe we go to the Olympics."

Dave was confused for a second. "Oh, you mean soccer," he said, turning around.

"Yes. We will show the world that we have more than oil money."

"I think it would be a good thing for Saudi Arabia."

"What state are you from?" the Prince asked.

"I grew up in Illinois, but I moved to California several years ago."

"Is wonderful place, California. I was there four years at Berkeley. I like it very much. You should come to visit me and we talk about California."

"Yes," Dave said in a voice that barely escaped from his tensed throat. "I would like that."

"How about tomorrow?"

"Tomorrow? Great. That's fine. What time?"

"My driver will pick you up at 5:00 in front of the Meridien Hotel. You know where is it?"

"But I don't even know your name."

The man stuck his hand out the window and Dave got up to take it. "You can call me Majed," he said.

"My name is Dave B. . . Barnes."

"Okay, Dave, I see you tomorrow, *insh'allah*." He took his hand back and the window went up. The car pulled away and Dave stared after it. Everything was going according to plan.

Maura flipped through the international edition of *Time* as she stood at the kitchen window, and at every few pages, looked out toward the street. In the name of censorship, several pages were missing near the beginning where liquor ads had been torn out. In the World News section, the page numbers jumped from twenty to twenty-five—probably excluding a story about Israel or an unfavorable article on the Kingdom.

Then she came to the People page where there was a picture of a newly slimmed-down Elizabeth Taylor sitting at a banquet table. A black Magic Marker had been slashed across her upper torso in the photograph. Every magazine seller was responsible for censoring anything that might be objectionable. Maura held the page up to the light of the kitchen window and saw that Liz wore a low-cut evening gown. How silly the photograph looked, like a child had gotten hold of the magazine and decided to scribble on the pictures. Maura looked out the window again and saw their silver Honda Accord pulling into the driveway. She ran with her magazine into the living room and curled up on the couch in what she hoped looked like a comfortable, unworried position.

"Back already?" she said, looking up from the Business page as he came in the room.

"Mission accomplished," he said excitedly. "I guess I should say phase one."

"What happened?" Maura tried to sound enthusiastic. "Did you meet him?"

"Of course. He took one look at my brilliant handstand on the beach and decided he had to meet me. He asked if I was in the Olympics."

"You must have improved since last night."

"I was able to hold one for about 30 seconds. I fell over when he asked me if I was in the Olympics."

"Did you have a conversation?"

"A short one. He said he was in California. He went to Berkeley."

"Small world."

"He invited me over to talk about California," Dave said quickly.

Maura was stunned even though she knew Dave wouldn't let up until he had succeeded in meeting the prince. Her facade of nonchalance melted away, laying bare her torment. "To the palace?" she shrieked. A foreboding began to pound in Maura's head, a voice telling her not to let him go. "So soon?" she said, her voice falling off.

Dave sat down beside her on the couch and glanced at the magazine. "I didn't know you were interested in Business." Maura looked down at the page and reddened slightly. She didn't say anything. "Maura, I'm not even going to mention Eddie this time. The Prince and I are going to have a nice little chat about California. I just want to get in good with him. Then I'm going to figure out a way to see him outside the palace, go for a drive or something. Maybe I'll meet him at the beach one afternoon. I won't do anything stupid."

Maura seemed relieved for the moment, and then a thought occurred to her. "What if he wants to have sex?"

"There's nothing in my contract, which says that just because I accept hospitality from a Saudi prince, I have to go to bed with him."

"Well, just don't do anything to insult him. I don't want you to come back with anything missing." Her mood had lightened some, but she still wasn't comfortable with the idea of his going to the palace, the place where it seemed Eddie had met his death.

11

DINNER AT THE PALACE

The French-managed Meridien Hotel was the newest and largest hotel in the area, a sandy-colored, twelve-story structure built with three wings providing sea views to as many rooms as possible. It stood aloof from the other buildings of Al-Khobar, hugging the Gulf with a wide beach extending out on either side. Across the street was a new mosque with a minaret towering high above the rest of the structure against the golden sky of late afternoon.

Dave arrived early at the hotel, parked his car in the perfectly landscaped lot and walked into the vast marbled lobby, a prime example of the garish opulence that had come to be the mode in Saudi Arabia. He had a half hour to kill, so he went into the cafe sectioned off from the main foyer of the lobby by plants and a large fountain. He sat at a small round table where he had a view of the driveway out the large windows, and ordered tea and a strawberry tart from the pastry cart.

At the next table, Dave pegged the Texan accent of the two casually dressed, cowboy-booted oilmen. They drank coffee from a silver service and munched croissants, which they held in their big hands like hot dogs. At the only other occupied table sat an attractive young couple in finely trimmed and tailored Arab garments, identifying them as non-Saudis. From their classy manner and dress, Dave guessed that they were from Abu Dhabi or Dubai. Only the lower half of the young woman's face was covered by a veil. She lifted her veil and, and with a nearly secretive gesture, raised her other hand from her lap and put a cigarette between her red lips. She took a drag, exhaled and then lowered her veil. Dave found it as shocking as if he was watching a nun smoke, yet she did it so gracefully, it looked, at the same time, very natural. The man talked, stabbed off big chunks of Black Forest cake with his fork—when he wasn't waving it about in the air—and drank coffee all at the same time. His attentive wife simply smoked her cigarette and occasionally made small comments.

The woman caught Dave staring at her, and instead of looking away immediately, as married women are supposed to do, she lifted her veil to take a drag of her cigarette and held him in her line of sight. Dave was the one who broke the stare and he didn't dare glance again in her direction for several minutes though he felt her eyes dart his way whenever her husband, whose back was to Dave, wasn't looking. Dave tried to focus on any number of other things, but she drew him back like a magnet, making him feel charged and at the same time guilty as their eyes met several times over the next fifteen minutes. Dave scoffed at the conservative Wahhabis, the religious leaders who insisted that Saudi women cover their faces, discouraging just such flirtations. But in the case of this foreign Arab woman and the more relaxed social atmosphere of the hotel, the half-veil only served to increase the attraction ten-fold. He squirmed in the realm of the forbidden. As Dave paid his bill, his eyes met hers one last time; they were like drops of tar floating on a white sea and they seemed to smile. Her mouth was hidden and he could not know what message it carried. He nodded to her very slightly, then walked back to the main part of the lobby and sat on a couch where he could see the cars coming up the driveway.

Majed's driver pulled up in front of the hotel at 5:10, a time that would be considered quite punctual in this part of the world where an hour wait for an appointment was not unusual. Dave took a deep breath and walked out the door while a bellman hurried down the steps to open the car door. Dave pointed to the front seat as he didn't want to feel chauffeured, plus he hoped to carry on a conversation with the driver who might, at the very least, be a source of information. If he was lucky, he might make a friend on the palace staff.

The driver's name was Tarik, a Pakistani, and he had been driving in Saudi Arabia for five years, the last four with the Prince. The job interfered with his marriage plans, he said, though he would soon be going back to his country to take a wife. But what he really wanted was to go to the States, and he asked Dave if he knew of any girls back home he could write to. They would want to meet him, he was sure, and would invite him to America. It had happened to a friend of his who now lived in Beverly Hills with an American wife, a swimming pool, and a Jaguar. And that guy wasn't even very good looking. He should be able to do better than that. Modesty was not one of Tarik's virtues, but his good looks and charm had obviously taken him a long way from his humble little village outside of Karachi. He also claimed to be a poet and dove into the glove compartment with one hand while he drove with the other. After much rummaging, he extracted a few rumpled papers—from a mass of tissues, cigarettes, matches and cassette tapes—and plopped them in Dave's lap. The poems were in Urdu.

"I'm afraid I can't read these," said Dave.

Tarik laughed and said, "No problem." Within seconds he began to spew out the English translations, memorized for that fantasized day when he would be in front of his American love.

After he finished the translations, he dug into the glove compartment again for a picture he wanted Dave to show to any single American girls he knew. In the picture, Tarik wore an intricately embroidered white shirt that hung down to the knees of his white baggy pants, Pakistani style. Next to him was a large colorful kite. He was a kite-flying champion, he explained, and then launched into a long description of kite flying. It was a very important sport in Pakistan and the object was to fly them high, and then try to cut the lines of the competitors with your own string, which had been coated with fiberglass. The last kite that remained in the sky was the champion.

While Dave listened to the Pakistani's stories, he paid close attention to the roads they were taking to the palace. He told Tarik that he knew a couple of nice girls who would probably be interested in a man like him and he would get their addresses from his wife. Tarik insisted he describe the girls and became very excited when Dave cupped his hands over his chest to indicate the size of their breasts. The descriptions also included blond hair and blue eyes. Tarik almost shouted with joy. By the time they got to the palace, Dave felt that he had made a friend he might need in the near future.

Majed was at prayer when they arrived and Tarik went off to pray as well, leaving Dave in an anteroom devoid of furniture, but with a large Persian carpet and velvet-covered pillows on the floor. A small fountain at one end of the room trickled down into a pool of goldfish, and there was a wall of arched floor to ceiling windows giving on to the garden. Dave stood at the window and tried to catch his reflection in the glass, checking to see how he looked in his white tuxedo shirt and blue cotton pleated pants. Maura had told him that he looked "almost enchanting" in an attempt to show her cool before he left. He had promised to be back as soon as he could.

A sparrow landed on an oleander bush just outside the window. It looked at him and chirped loudly, seemingly admonishing him for being there. Then he felt a presence in the room and turned around. Majed stood just inside the doorway. He was a tall man, a fact Dave hadn't appreciated as he had only seen him sitting in the car.

"Prince Majed, I'm sorry. I didn't realize you were here."

"Just call me Majed. How did you know I was a prince?"

"I'm afraid your driver let it slip."

"No matter. Anyway, sorry to disturb your meditation."

"Oh, I was only watching a bird in the garden."

"Some say that birds bring us messages from our loved ones." His voice had a deep resonant quality with a hint of a British accent. "I see that you are married. Is she here with you in Saudi Arabia?"

Dave had noticed that Arab men were astute about spotting wedding rings. "Uh, no," he answered, not wanting to make himself appear unavailable.

"Then this bird has truly come a long way."

"Yes," said Dave awkwardly.

"Please sit down. I've ordered some tea. Then we'll have something to eat."

"Thank you."

"So, tell me. How do you like my country?"

The question caught Dave off guard. "Oh, it's very, uh, interesting."

"Interesting? My first English teacher, trying to encourage me to improve my vocabulary, would fine me two pounds each time I used that word." Dave hung his head in mock embarrassment. "I'm sorry," Majed continued. "That was not a fair question. I know it is very difficult life for Americans here. It is too different. I would like to change that some, but I'm afraid I'm in the minority. It is happening anyway, but we pretend it is not. You can see the changes daily. And the more it changes, the more the fundamentalists want to send us back to where we were before. My family is bound to the Wahhabis by very old ties. They are conservative, but can be handled delicately. The danger is with those who are more right than the Wahhabis. These fanatics are never satisfied. We have the lesson of Iran." The door opened and a servant entered with a silver tea service on a large tray with a dizzying Arabic motif. Majed changed the subject. "But you didn't come here to discuss politics. Let us talk of California. Where do you live there?"

"In Santa Rosa."

"That's north of San Francisco, is it not?"

"Yes."

"Near Calistoga?"

"Not too far." Dave answered the Prince's questions, but his mind was still back on what he had said about the religious fanatics. He wondered if Majed had talked to Eddie about these things. Had Eddie learned too much? Though it was surprising to hear a Saudi prince speaking openly about his country, it hardly seemed a situation that could lead to murder.

The Prince repeated his question. "I said, have you ever been to the mud baths at Calistoga?"

"Excuse me. My mind keeps running away from me today. Yes, I went once. Did you go when you were at Berkeley?"

"Yes," he said gleefully. "It was my favorite thing. I went several times a month. It is strange for a Moslem whose religion stresses cleanliness to enjoy being buried in mud. I suppose the Western psychiatrists would have something to say about that. But it is the most wonderful feeling. I think of it still as I go to sleep at night. And the California wine is nice too. I loved to go to the wineries and see how it was made, to taste it and talk to the people who made it." The Prince paused and looked at Dave. "Don't be so shocked, my friend. A Saudi prince who talks of mud and wine is not so crazy, is he?"

"I guess I am a little surprised. You're not exactly what one might expect of a Saudi prince. And I hope you're not offended if I say that you don't seem typical of Saudis in general."

"What is typical? Typical is something the different search for but never find, and what the average try to run away from but are never successful. Despite what my religion and your constitution say, there is something unequal from the start. My very untypical beginning, born into a royal family, has at times, made me want to be more average. I tried to lose myself in the great mass of America's middle class, a group that is constantly trying to be something else, eating French food and driving German cars. But in the end I saw it was not possible. I couldn't run away from what I was. So now I am back in my country, praying to my God, dressing like a Saudi and eating my native food. And what about you? Are you a typical American?"

"I hope not," was Dave's automatic response. "I mean, it's not really a typical thing to come all the way over here and teach English."

"Ah, another English teacher." He pondered that a moment. "Yet, it is rather a typical thing to want more money than you are able to make in the States. I assume you didn't come over here for the adventure."

Dave felt on the spot, pressed to find something in his own character that proved the difference he had always felt from the average guy on the street. The Prince was right. Coming to Saudi Arabia to make money didn't make him unique. He looked at the other guys he worked with, most of them pretty average Americans who by some twist of fate had found themselves in a foreign culture that they knew very little about. Dave tried to distance himself from the majority of his co-workers, but maybe he was just one of the group that Majed had described, running away from his average American self.

The Prince watched Dave floundering in his pensive state. "Don't make too much of it. If it's any consolation, I don't find you typically American though I know very little about you. In Berkeley, I had a lot of practice determining who was really different and who was just trying to be. I developed a sort of sixth sense about it." Majed paused and sighed. "We have again strayed from our talk of California."

"California," Dave repeated, as if it were a magical word. "I miss it."

"Me too."

"You should go back for a visit."

"Yes," the Prince said, but it sounded like a remote possibility. He looked sadly down at his tea. Something in his memory troubled him. "I think it is time we eat," he announced.

The dinner was very much as Khalil had described it when he and Eddie had been there. Ten men sat on cushions around an oval table. Dave was not introduced to any of them and they ignored his presence for the most part. He thought he identified Majed's younger brother, Muhammad, by the evil eye the Arab occasionally cast his way. The man had many of the same facial features as Majed but was thinner and had a pinched expression that made him ugly.

The meal started with a watery soup in clear glass bowls and was followed by thick chunks of lamb, bones and ribs atop a platter of dark brown rice. Then there was lamb roast with gravy and very soft carrots, which they mashed into a paste to eat with the rice. The meal ended with a salad and then a large platter of fruit after which the men got up and left without ceremony in groups of two or three.

Majed didn't say much during the meal, only occasionally turning to Dave to ask him how he liked this or that. In truth, Dave had difficulty with the lamb, a taste he had never become accustomed to. Then without warning, Majed rose up and said he had to go to prayer.

As he hurried out, a servant was at his side pouring him coffee on the run. Dave was left alone at the table with a bunch of grapes in his hand. There was a tap on his shoulder and the Pakistani who had brought the tea earlier said, "Please come."

Dave dropped the grapes on his plate and followed him into another room which was furnished with French antiques—sofas, chairs, and tables whose legs had all been sawed off to make them sit lower to the ground. Beth had given him a quick lesson on the difference between Louis XV and Louis XVI furniture, and the legs, though chopped off, definitely had the less curvy style of Louis XVI. He assumed they were authentic and shuddered to think how they had been destroyed.

Dave sat on a sofa covered in burgundy velvet and was served coffee in tiny thimble cups, a thick murky liquid that tasted heavily of cardamom. He drank it quickly and winced at the taste only to have the servant rush over and fill up his cup again. He kicked back the second one, but shook his head and made a sign that he was finished when the man tried to pour him a third.

About twenty-five minutes later, Majed rushed into the room with his mishlah, a light gold-trimmed cloak, billowing out and his ghutra flapping back. "Sorry to keep you waiting," he said as he sat down heavily in one of the low chairs. And taking off his aghal and ghutra, he deposited them on a small table next to the chair. He had dark, wavy hair and his appearance was much improved by the uncovering of his head. "I think I'm ready for a drink," he announced as he stood up and motioned for Dave to follow.

They went out a door and along a covered walkway, which led to another part of the compound. A cool breeze blew through the arches and ground lighting brought the garden to life on either side. Spotlights were also focused on the minaret of the compound mosque rising high above the other buildings. They passed through a glass and oak door, then down some red marble steps, stopping outside of two large wooden doors. Majed opened a panel in the wall and pushed a button, making the doors slide in either direction into the wall. They stepped into the disco and sitting area that Khalil had described. Majed went straight to the bar, pushed another button and the doors closed behind them. He seemed anxious for a drink.

"You're not surprised at all this?" said the Prince, looking at Dave strangely.

"Oh, yeah," said Dave, letting his gaze float around the room. "Amazing." He wasn't very convincing.

"What would you like to drink? Vodka?"

"I'll have Scotch, please, if you have it."

"Of course. I'm getting bad at guessing. I used to always guess correctly what people liked to drink. On the rocks?"

"That would be fine." They took their drinks and sat down on the carpeted platform covering the length of one end of the room. Dave felt trapped, and yet unwilling to give up this chance to talk to the prince. It was still early, and he could excuse himself in a short time and get back to the base before Maura started to worry. Dave took sips of his drink to calm his anxiety and they fell into an uncomfortable silence as Majed stared off into a dark corner of the room.

"You know," he began, "every time I meet an American, it takes me back to those years in California. It has been almost eight years, but still the memories are strong."

"Do you meet many Americans here?" Dave ventured.

"A few. Not long ago. . ." The doors opened and Muhammad entered with three others. A servant carrying a tea tray followed them and they formed a little circle on the platform within earshot of Dave and Majed. Majed ignored them, but changed the subject. "Is your drink okay?"

"Yes, it's fine." Dave noticed that Majed had already finished his.

"In a few minutes we'll have music. I have a friend who is DJ in New York. He sends me tapes. Do you know this Grace Jones?"

"Yes, the strange-looking black woman." She had been a favorite of Eddie's, but Dave never understood the appeal.

"My friend took me to see her one time at a club in New York, The Flamingo. Her image is still stamped very clearly on my brain. I wasn't sure if she was a man or a woman until she showed us. She had this very short hair like flattop and a unisex suit. Then in the middle of her show, she unbuttoned her jacket and she had nothing on underneath.

My friends here wouldn't believe it." He nodded in the direction of his brother and friends, though he didn't look at them.

Then the Filipino boy-girls came in—four of them. The one leading the group Dave guessed was Rico from the description Khalil had given. He wore tight pink sweatpants and a Hawaiian shirt which was tied at the waist to expose a little of his flat tummy. He was short, slight, and dark-skinned, with pretty eyes that needed no make-up. His straight black hair was cut longer on one side so that it swept down half-covering one eye. When he entered the room and saw Dave, he pushed the hair back out of his eye and hesitated while a look of recognition spread over his thin face. He started walking toward the platform with quickened steps until he got close enough to see that he was mistaken. He stopped short, looking confused.

"Come here, Rico," said Majed. "Come meet my friend Dave."

"Hello, sir," Rico said in a soft sweet voice. He took Dave's hand limply, looked at him, then down at the floor, then at Dave again. "You make me think someone." Dave squeezed his hand tightly and looked hard into his eyes.

"No. You must be confused." Dave's reaction was a little too strong, his voice a little too loud. He felt that everyone was watching them and he began to laugh nervously. "No, no. I'm just another American."

"Yes, sir," said Rico, seeming to understand that something was amiss. "Let me fix you new drink." He took Dave's glass, bowed to Majed and took his glass as well. Muhammad and his companions went back to their conversation.

"You like this one?" Majed asked.

"He seems nice," said Dave, not sure what was expected of him.

"Would you like some music?"

"As long as I don't have to dance."

"I can't promise you that. Rico and his friends can be very persuasive." Majed slid open a small panel by his foot and pushed some buttons. In a few seconds, the music started with a heavy beat, unusual percussion, car horns and loose guitar riffs. Dave recognized it as Grace Jones' "Pull Up to the Bumper." It was a song that Eddie had liked a lot.

"I think you know this one," Majed said.

"Yes." Dave realized that he was wiggling his foot to the music. The three boy-girls had taken to the dance floor and undulated their bodies in a manner that seemed unconsciously sexual, as if the music itself prescribed it, drew it out of the dancers.

Rico came back with the drinks, served them, and then took his place on the dance floor splattered with little specs of light from the mirrored ball. As Dave watched the dancers, he began to relax and leaned back against a pile of pillows. Unconsciously he glanced at his watch and Majed noticed.

"Is it late?"

"No. It's just that I have to work tomorrow, very early."

"When you are tired, tell me. I will have Tarik drive you back. Did you have to drive far to the hotel?"

"Not too far."

"Where do you work?"

"At the Navy base," said Dave hesitantly.

"Oh, yes." Majed nodded his head. "I have met others from there. Recently there was one, but I can't remember his name. Blond like you." Dave froze, clutching the edge of the large pillow. Was it possible that Majed didn't know?

The Prince called Rico over. Dave caught Rico's eye and stared at him fiercely, shaking his head slightly.

"Rico, what was the other American's name from the Navy base?"

Rico looked at Dave, then back at Majed. "Which one?"

"Just a few weeks ago with Khalil."

"I don't know," he said, shrugging his narrow shoulders.

"Come now, my little rabbit. You always remember their names. And that one I think you had a special liking for."

"Well, I can't remember," and he skipped back to his partners.

"Anyway, I think he was from the Navy base. I haven't seen him again and Khalil left the country because of an illness in his family, I understand." Dave bit his tongue, wondering if anything showed on his face. All indications were that Majed spoke the truth and really didn't know what had happened to Eddie and Khalil. Dave felt a sense of relief. He didn't want to believe that Majed had anything to do with

Eddie's death. The finger then was pointing more and more clearly toward Muhammad and his companions, making him feel very uncomfortable in their presence. He took a big gulp of his drink, and finishing off the Scotch, he put the glass down. Muhammad's servant immediately snatched it up and went over to the bar to replenish it. Majed looked a bit surprised, but he seemed more concerned with Dave's nervous behavior. "Is everything okay?" he asked.

"Yes," said Dave distantly. "These songs just remind me of someone in California." He listened to the lyrics of the new song: "Sweet dreams are made of this. . ." and the fresh drink was set down in front of him.

"I hope the music isn't bothering you," said Majed. He downed his drink and motioned for the servant to refill his glass too. The servant looked at Muhammad and Muhammad nodded. "I can turn it off."

"No. I'm okay, really." The alcohol was taking its toll as he kept losing touch with what he was doing, why he was there. The music shook him with memories of Eddie. It almost seemed that Eddie himself was hidden in the DJ booth spinning the records, Eddie with a scar across his throat, his face a livid gray.

Dave stared at his glass, almost empty again. Had he drunk it? His head felt like a bowling ball rolling around on his shoulders and the tips of his fingers were numb. This had never happened to him before when he drank. He felt very, very relaxed, but he still had enough awareness to tell that something wasn't right. He needed to reach out for something to hold on to, but everything around him seemed fluid, like they were in an underwater world. Majed talked to him in words that he couldn't understand, meaningless sounds floating through the close air. He felt himself trying to get up, though without good control of his functions, he slumped back against the pillow. He tried again and was almost standing up when his legs buckled under him. The Filipinos stopped dancing and watched him with alarm on their faces. He waved at them to keep dancing. Why had they stopped?

"I'm sorry," Dave said, turning to Majed, though he wasn't conscious of what he apologized for. He wanted to cry while all he could do was grin hopelessly.

Majed said something to the servant and Muhammad jumped into the conversation. An argument ensued in harsh guttural tones, as if the flesh were being ripped off each word before it was sent out.

Majed leaned close to Dave. His face was wide and distorted. He tried to talk over the music, which to Dave sounded like a 45 being played at 33. "My brother says you should not be on the highway in this condition. It is dangerous for you. Perhaps he is right. Tarik could take you very early in the morning."

Dave could barely keep his eyes open and didn't understand how he could have gotten so drunk. But he knew he had to call Maura. "Telephone?" he said groggily.

"Mubarak, take him to the telephone," Majed ordered. The servant helped Dave up, and with the man holding on to his arm, Dave was able to stagger out of the room. The Filipinos were huddled on the dance floor, hanging on to each other as if they were watching an execution.

12

THE PRISON WITHIN

It was 10:30 in the evening and Maura was folded up on the couch, hugging a pillow while she watched the movie *Frances*. Frances Farmer was about to get an ice pick stuck in the corner of her eye and be lobotomized forever. Dave should have been home by now. The psychiatrist described this innovative new surgery, transorbital lobotomy, a miracle of modern medicine. Why hadn't he called? Probably couldn't get to a phone. The patient would be freed of her torturous mental disorders. Maybe he had car trouble. Car trouble? Dave had just mentioned a few days before how good Saudis were about stopping to help people stranded on the side of the road. They brought Frances in. The doctor put the pick into position. And the phone rang. Maura flew off the couch. It was a long ring, meaning it was a call from outside the compound.

"Dave?" Maura answered anxiously.

"No, Maura. This is your mother. Isn't Dave there? Is anything wrong?" Maura heard the satellite transmission a split second after it was being said. When two people started talking at the same time their words met somewhere over the Atlantic Ocean and cancelled each other out.

"Oh, Mom! No, nothing's wrong. Dave just went to the store. He..."

"He what?"

"He. . .uh. . .forgot the grocery list."

"The what?"

"He forgot the grocery list. I thought he. . ."

"Are stores. . ."

". . .was calling to find out what we needed. Mother, please don't start talking until I'm finished. It's too confusing, this long distance."

"Can I talk now? I said, 'Are the stores open this late?' What time is it there?"

"About 10:30."

"I thought so. I had to get Herb to figure out the time difference for me."

"Dave's at Safeway. You know they always stay open late wherever they are."

"I would think Dave would be in bed by now if he has to get up at 4:30."

"Were you afraid you'd have to talk to him?"

"Why should I be afraid to talk to him? We're perfectly capable of carrying on a conversation. But of course I called to talk to you, dear. Herb and I have been thinking and we've decided that we're just going to insist you come to your little brother's graduation in June."

"Oh, you've decided, have you? What about Max? Does he have a say in this?" Maura carried the phone into the living room and put the VCR on pause. She didn't want to miss the part where Frances had a reunion with her old boyfriend.

"Of course he wants you to come. You are still coming back to California for your vacation, aren't you?"

"Well, I don't know. We. . ."

"You don't know! Maura, don't tell me you've changed your plans."

"No. I mean maybe. I don't know. Mother, I don't want to stay on the phone too long because Dave might be trying to call."

"Well, if it's just a matter of a shopping list, I'm sure it can wait a few minutes. Are you sure nothing is wrong? You seem upset."

"It's just this movie I was watching, *Frances*. . .yes. . .but listen, Mother, I'm afraid if Dave can't get through, he'll come back home and forget some things we really need. He's so forgetful sometimes."

"All right, Maura, I get the message. But promise me you'll call within the next couple of days, some time when you feel like talking."

"Okay. I promise. Give everybody a hug for me."

"Call us collect, soon. Goodnight, dear."

Maura set the phone down on the coffee table and slumped onto the couch. Why did mothers always have a knack for calling in times of crisis, especially when you can't tell them what the crisis is? How did they know, even from thousands of miles away? "Dave, where are you?" she screamed. And picking up the remote control, she zapped the screen and there was the new Frances. All her rough edges had been smoothed out, the fire in her eyes doused. Her old boyfriend watched her walk by. Although he still thought she was beautiful, when he came up along side her and tried to talk to her, he realized that it was too late. They'd gotten her.

For a short while Maura was lifted out of her own fears by wallowing in the tragic story of Francis Farmer, a Hollywood beauty who had everything but the ability to play the game. But when the movie ended, Maura was overcome with a tremendous hopelessness, for now she was sure that something had happened to Dave and there was nowhere to turn for help. She thought of calling Beth, but the possibility of her not being home so depressed her that she didn't even want to risk the call. It was not until the tape ended and the screen turned to snow that she got up and went into the bedroom. She sat down on the bed and started to plan her future. She could work she guessed, but how would she be able to tell her mother that she would be coming home alone, a little earlier than expected, and worst of all, tolerate their not completely disguised sense of relief. She imagined the pick going into the corner of her eye and then into her brain, piercing the lobe of her cerebrum.

When the phone rang at 6:00 the next morning, Maura didn't even have to guess who it was. They were short rings. "That'll be Jerry," a voice in her head said. Her eyes were wide open as they had been all night and she leaned against the headboard with her feet stretched out in front of her. Her arms were wrapped around a pillow. She had heard the birds and then the early morning prayer call. She had watched the window behind her go from black to gray in the mirror above the dresser. She had cried and screamed and pounded the pillow, none of which had brought him back.

There was no point in answering the phone as she knew how the conversation would go, unless Jerry had something definite to say, and then she didn't want to hear that either. Still, she would have new duties now and answering the phone would be her first in a long string of unpleasant events. She swung her legs onto the floor and stood up. She fluffed up the pillow and dropped it into place by the headboard before walking in to pick up the phone.

"Hello."

"Hello, Maura. This is Jerry. It's already 6:00 and I noticed that Dave didn't sign in. No one's seen him, so I just wondered if he overslept or something."

"No."

"Oh. Well, could I talk to him? Is he there?"

"No." Maura's voice sounded as if it was computer-generated.

"Where is he?"

"I don't know."

Jerry paused as if he didn't want to proceed. She was sure he wanted to hang up and forget about it right then and there. But he, too, had his duties. "Maura, could you tell me what's going on? Was he gone all night?"

"Yes."

"When did he leave?"

"Yesterday afternoon about 5:00."

"Do you know where he went?"

Now Maura hesitated. Then she figured it didn't matter anymore who knew what

"To meet a prince."

Jerry let out a choking sound. "I knew it. He wouldn't listen. I told him. Maura, just hold on. Don't do anything. I'll be right over." She didn't know what he thought she was going to do in the next few minutes that she couldn't have done during the long, torturous night.

Jerry must have run over as soon as he dropped the phone, as there was a knock on the door within a few minutes. When she opened it, Jerry got his first glimpse of the defeated Maura, in extra large T-shirt and cut-offs. Her hair was a rat's nest and strands of it stuck to the perspiration on her forehead. The dark circles under her eyes and her white face made her look ghoulish.

He looked shocked to see her in this condition. "Maura, I'm going to take you to the U.S. Consulate," he announced as if it were a decision that he had struggled with, but was surely capable of providing results.

"For what?"

"Maybe they can help."

"Even if they could, they probably wouldn't."

"I can't stand to see you like this. It's not like you. We're going to the Consulate whether you like it or not. We're going to explain the situation and they'll have to do something. Why wouldn't they?"

Maura didn't want to try and explain her pessimism or argue with someone who still believed. "So, let's go," she said.

"Like that?"

"Is there something wrong with the way I look?" she said vacantly.

"You look like. . .like. . .shit!" Maura was so startled to hear him use the word, she cracked a smile. Jerry's face was a blooming red and Maura headed for the bedroom to save him further embarrassment.

While Maura changed her clothes, Jerry stood in the hallway shouting, "He could have run a red light and landed in jail. They do that, you know. . .I mean put people in jail for running red lights. Maybe he couldn't get his car started or. . .uh, the Prince insisted he spend. . .the night." His voice trailed off as he found himself in uncomfortable territory.

Maura reappeared with a skeptical look on her face. She wore a midi-length blue jumper over a plain white blouse. Her thick, dark hair was pulled back on both sides and held with small combs of carved teak from Africa. She had even put on a little make-up, just a little.

"When my grandmother gave me this," referring to the jumper, "I never thought I'd wear it." She cocked her head to one side, looking like a cynical girl reluctant to go off to private school.

"Well, let's go. You know, no news is good news."

Nothing was worse than someone trying to play Pollyanna in the face of grim reality. Maura felt the sudden urge to strike back. "Are you sure you guys didn't receive another accident report?" Jerry didn't answer and Maura closed the door behind them.

A narrow shaft of light from a high rectangular window struck the wall just above Dave's head, making him feel hot. The lotion that the Filipino boy-girls used to color his hair burned his scalp and seeped down into his brain where it stirred up a terrific headache. He opened his mouth to tell them to stop, but his voice wouldn't work because everything was all gummed up. His arms too were paralyzed. The dying lotion, as it turned out, was actually glue and it had jammed every process in his head except consciousness; he was aware of it all happening, but he couldn't do anything about it. He began to experience panic without any of the physical manifestations. His mouth screamed and his limbs flailed though the Filipinos couldn't see it. They still hadn't realized their mistake and kept pouring the lotion into Dave's scalp.

Dave woke up in a sweat with the smell of vomit in his nose and his head feeling like it had petrified and been severed from his body. There seemed no connection between what he thought and what he felt. Without moving his head, he sensed that he was alone, and then his eyes took a brief survey of the small room with the one high window and a heavy wooden door. And looking down, with blurred vision, he could detect little splotches of last night's dinner covering the front of his clothes. He wondered when that had happened; he remembered very little after leaving the Prince in the disco. Very slowly he started to get up, causing a dull pain to creep up the back of his head while the room took a few spins. There was a dense fog in his brain that made every move and thought a chore and led him to the obvious conclusion that this was no ordinary hangover. With great effort, he gained a sitting position, and then tried to stand up on his rubbery legs. They didn't want to work at first, though he was eventually able to get them going and shuffled to the door. It was locked, but there was a small opening in its center with three vertical bars through which he shouted. A uniformed Saudi stood up from his chair and stuck his face up to the little window. Dave pulled back.

"Could I have some water, please?" Dave said. He was so parched that the words stuck to the inside of his mouth and were barely intelligible. The guard only sneered and started to sit back down. It appeared he didn't speak English. Dave tried to think of the Arabic word for water, but all he could come up with was *wadi* from the students' textbook. Though *wadis* were actually riverbeds, which in Saudi Arabia were dry most of the year, he decided to give it a try. "*Wadi. Wadi,*" he said, making a drinking motion with his hand. The guard laughed and started down the hall.

A few minutes later, one of Muhammad's companions from the night before came in, followed by a servant carrying a pitcher of water and a glass. The servant poured a glass of water and Dave took it and started to drink. Then he stopped and looked at it suspiciously. "Don't worry, there's nothing in it," the man said with a sly smile on his face. He waited for Dave to gulp down the water, and then motioned for him to sit down.

"Mr. Bates. . ." he began in a strong British accent.

"No. . .Barnes," Dave interjected. His mind began to click and survival was at the forefront.

The Arab smiled at him as one does at a child caught in a lie. "Mr. Bates, we know who you are. We weren't in fact very surprised to see you. And now that you are here, we must decide what to do with you. I'm a little disappointed at your government's lack of success in keeping things under control. They can cause rulers and whole governments to rise and fall around the world, but they can't keep one man from following the trail of his brother. I admire you for that. I never thought the familial bonds in your culture were very strong."

Dave didn't see any reason to try and continue the charade. "I just want to know why my brother was killed," he said bluntly.

"It was unfortunate. Some of Muhammad's followers are as zealous as Majed's friends are decadent, excuse me for saying so. I have never seen two brothers so different."

"That doesn't tell me why my brother was killed."

"You are a big enough problem now. The more you know, the bigger problem you become."

"Are you saying that Eddie was killed because he knew too much?"

"Yes and no. We did not plan to kill him for his intended crime. But one of our number acted independently. He comes from a long line of *Ikhwan*, soldiers of Allah who take quite literally the *Hadith*, a book of our Prophet's doings and sayings. They feel it is their duty to cleanse and purify our country. Though I don't support his methods, I admire his dedication to the Prophet." Dave had a worried look on his face. "In case you're wondering, he is no longer here at the palace."

Dave relaxed a bit and thought over what this man had been saying. He had walked right into their hands. "Have you been in touch with officials of my government all along, since my brother's death?"

"I think it better that I not tell you any more at this time. You will be treated well. You will eat well. I will have some new clothes sent to you. If you need anything, ask for me. My name is Ahmad."

"I would like to see Majed."

"No, I am sorry. Your first request and I deny you. We have been too free with Majed because he is a high-ranking Prince whose father gave this palace to the two brothers. He is the oldest here and their father is very sick in Jeddah. We must respect him. But only the younger, Muhammad, has remained loyal to his people and the Qur'an. Majed was too much infected with America. I say too much. You must forgive me. I have to go. *As salaam alaykum.*" He swept out the door with the servant close behind.

"Wa alaykum as salaam," Dave mumbled after him. It felt absurd to be wishing peace on someone who kept him a prisoner.

13

BEHIND CONSULATE DOORS

On the ride to the consulate with Jerry, Maura trotted out the agonizing thoughts that had plagued her throughout the night. She talked about how she shouldn't have let Dave go, though at the same time realized there was no stopping him. She talked about how close the brothers were, how obsessed Dave was to find out the truth about Eddie's death, and how Eddie's gayness had gotten him involved with a guy named Khalil. Jerry proved to be a surprisingly good listener, in spite of some of the details, which must have disturbed his Mormon sensitivities. But when Maura fell silent, Jerry changed the subject.

"All this," Jerry said, pointing to the development around them as they got near the American Consulate, "including you and I being here is because of one thing."

"What's that?"

Jerry wiggled in his seat and brought out his teacher voice. "The Dammam Dome!"

"And?" said Maura.

"It's like a super well. They knew the stuff was down there, in the 1930's. They drilled six times without success. Then one magic day in 1938, they struck what they were looking for. And since that day, the oil has gushed from that well and a bunch of others. It changed the country overnight."

Jerry also pointed out Aramco, the Arabian American Oil Company, a sprawling suburban township that had the look of Anywhere, U.S.A. Sprinklers arced across green lawns on tree-lined streets of ranch style homes. "Most of it was built in the 1950's and 60's. It sort of looks like 'Leave it to Beaver,' doesn't it?"

"I guess the only things missing are a church steeple and a neon sign pointing out the local bar," said Maura.

"And there's the consulate right over there," Jerry said.

"Funny how it is so close to Aramco. Guess they have to protect those billions Aramco generates for U.S. oil companies."

"Guess so." Jerry looked distracted as he tried to find the visitor parking lot. "I've never actually been here."

Jerry and Maura passed through the tight security of the main entrance, which included metal detectors and guards who scrutinized the visitors with a hard stare. Once past the security, they came upon a middle-aged receptionist in thick-framed glasses whose nametag read, "Margaret Talbot." Jerry started to speak, but Maura stopped him. "I'll do it," she said. The woman looked up from her work and took off her glasses, attached to a thin gold chain around her neck, and dropped them to her large matronly breasts.

"May I help you?" she asked in a disinterested way.

"I would like to report a missing American, my husband." Maura's voice was calm and clear.

"How long has he been missing?"

"How long? I don't know. About 14 hours?"

"I see," said Ms. Talbot, pursing her lips. She held the right temple of her glasses as if she were about to put them back on and be done with these people who had interrupted her. "We don't actually consider a person missing until they've been gone for twenty-four hours."

"Look," Maura began, leaning over the counter. The woman's attitude had provided the challenge she needed to snap out of her self-pitying state. "You and I know damn well that if someone is missing more than five hours in Saudi Arabia, they're missing. It's not like they've gone off on a fishing trip or something." Ms. Talbot looked at Jerry accusingly, as if he were responsible for reining in this difficult woman.

"I understand that you are upset, but this is an office of the United States Government and we do have our regulations."

"Well, my husband and I happen to be citizens of the United Sates and I would like a little cooperation from an agency of the government thereof. So, if you would please get on the phone there and call the consul, I would like to speak to him. I'd even take an assistant consul."

"I'm afraid picking up the phone wouldn't do much good right now as none of them will be in until 8:00. But if you'd like to make an appointment for later on in the day, you could call back after eight and talk to the consul's secretary." She smiled a victorious smile.

"I don't know if you are a hard of hearing or just a heartless bitch, but my husband is missing and I'd like to talk to somebody. There must be somebody here I can talk to. This is an emergency." Jerry stared at Maura, his face taut as if he were trying to think of a way to cool her down.

Ms. Talbot hardly seemed fazed by Maura's remark. She was a trooper and had heard a lot worse. "Young lady, and I use the term loosely, you won't get anywhere by insulting the personnel of the U.S. Consulate. Now, if you'd like to sit down and wait, perhaps someone will be able to see you after eight."

Jerry looked at his watch. "That's only half an hour, Maura. I'll sit and wait with you if you like." He steered her away from the reception desk to some benches with green vinyl cushions on them. The receptionist put on her glasses and went back to work as if nothing had happened.

Dave sat on the edge of the small metal-frame cot and surveyed his surroundings. The interior of the room had never been finished—the concrete walls were unpainted and the floor was rough cement, making it seem that it was intended to be a small storeroom. Daylight and the sound of birds came in from the small window so high up he could only see a patch of blue sky from where he sat. He was worried about Maura, knowing she must be hysterical without news from him.

The door swung open and two guards motioned for him to come with them. Dave panicked for a moment, wondering if this was the end, the long march down the hall to the electric chair. . .no, how did they do it here? Of course, they cut your head off. But he saw that one of the guards carried a bundle of clothes and they looked too nice to get all bloodied.

They escorted him along the corridor to a new, clean bathroom equipped with a shower, sink, toilet and even a bidet. There he took a shower and changed into the clothes they had given him—a gold silk shirt and white linen pants, which still had the Wilkes-Bashford of San Francisco tags on them. Majed must have bought them years ago and never worn them, a time when he was thinner as they fit Dave perfectly. He took a look at himself in the mirror. His face still lacked color and the clothes were not quite his style, but he was glad to be rid of the vomit-encrusted heap of laundry on the floor.

They then took him back to his room and told him he would be served breakfast. A few minutes later, the door opened and Dave was surprised to see Rico enter with a tray.

"Rico!" he said.

"Ssh. Ssh. Ssh," Rico hissed. "American style," he said loudly, setting the tray down on a wobbly little table. Then, in a low voice, "Majed say he sorry. Can do nothing. But don't worry."

"I have to get a message to my wife."

Rico looked surprised. "In America?"

"No. She's here. I'll give you her number and you can call her and tell her I'm okay. Bring a pen and paper next time." The guard stepped into the room and barked something in Arabic.

"Okay. I'm coming out," Rico said to the guard. "I try," he whispered to Dave.

The guard leaned on one side of the doorframe with his arm stretched out across the exit. He leered at Rico. Rico stopped in front of him, and when he didn't move, ducked under his arm. The rough-looking Arab turned and watched Rico's ass roll from side to side in his gauzy white slacks as he moved down the hall. The guard turned back to Dave, gazed at him for a second with a cruel grin, then closed the door.

Dave sat down to inspect his American breakfast—scrambled eggs, beef sausage, toast and coffee. It didn't look very appetizing, but his stomach was empty. They had forgotten one thing—silverware.

"Maybe if you tried to control your temper, Maura, you'd get more accomplished," Jerry said. It was difficult for him to be so direct, but he sounded genuine in trying to help her.

"But they're all such idiots. They're supposed to be here to serve American interests and they act like they're doing you a favor to give you the time of day. It seems like American interests translates into American dollars, not people. And we have a pretty good idea that they were involved in a cover-up of Eddie's death."

"You have no proof of that," Jerry reminded her in a fatherly manner. "Plus, what good is it going to do if you let them know you think that? Try gaining their sympathy. If Dave is in jail or kidnapped or something, you'll need their help." Maura looked at Jerry's watch. It was a little after 8:00. She stood up, swallowed hard and walked back up to the receptionist.

"I'm. . .I'm sorry I blew up at you before. I guess I'm feeling a lot of tension with my husband missing." She was all smiles and charm. "Perhaps I could speak to someone now. If you tell them I'm Mrs. Bates, like in Eddie Bates and Dave Bates, I think they might see me."

Ms. Talbot stared at Maura suspiciously as she picked up the phone. Her shoulders were thrust back in a manner befitting the power of her position. "Sir, I have a Mrs. Bates down here, like in Eddie Bates and Dave Bates. She says that her husband is missing. . .No, there's a gentleman with her. . .I don't know. He's wearing some kind of company uniform. . ."

"Tanley Arabia," Maura interjected.

"Tanley Arabia, Mrs. Bates says. . .yes, sir. I'll send her right up."

Maura gave her a big smile.

"Take the stairs over there. At the top, turn right and go to the end of the hall. Consular agent McVee will speak to you." There was a pouty edge to her businesslike manner. Maura turned and gave Jerry the thumbs-up sign, then headed for the stairs.

Consular agent McVee shook her hand warmly and looked very serious. He was a handsome young man and had the smooth air of a recent graduate of an Ivy League school. He led her to a sitting area of a large plush office where she gracefully set herself down on a modern leather sofa while McVee took a matching armchair on the other side of an oak and glass coffee table.

"Now, how can I help you, Mrs. Bates?" It was as if he had just asked how the weather was outside, but she controlled herself from saying the first thing that came to mind.

"My husband, David Bates, left yesterday evening to have a meeting with a Saudi prince. He didn't return last night and he didn't show up for work this morning. I don't know what to do. This is all especially distressing because just a few weeks ago his brother, Eddie, was killed.

"Was killed?" McVee appeared shocked.

"In a car accident here in Saudi Arabia," Maura said hurriedly. She was trying very hard to play the distraught, helpless wife, talking in deliberate hushed tones.

"And where was this meeting supposed to take place?"

"I don't know exactly. At the prince's palace, I believe."

"Did he mention the prince's name?"

"Yes. It was Prince Majed."

"Okay. You make yourself comfortable here and I'm going into another office and make a few phone calls."

"Oh, I hope you can find out something." She smiled, and when he was almost to the door, said, "Mr. McVee, please don't come back and tell me he's been in an accident. I just don't think I could bear it." The sardonic tone in her voice took him by surprise.

"I won't. I mean, not unless that's what's happened." He joined his hands in front of him and then brought them up to his mouth, partially covering a nervous twitch. With reddening cheeks, he turned and walked out of the room.

When he came back about 10 minutes later, Maura looked at him with soulful eyes

"Did you find out anything?"

"No, actually I didn't. The police don't have any information, so he probably wasn't in an accident. We have someone trying to get a hold of our contact with the royal family in the area." He stopped, realizing that Maura wasn't listening to him. She stared over his shoulder out into the hall. She had seen a man walk from one office into another, a man who looked very familiar though he wasn't wearing sunglasses. "What's the matter?" said McVee.

"Who was that man?"

McVee turned around and looked at the empty hallway. "What man?"

Maura got up and started walking out of the room. "Mrs. Bates, where are you going?"

She stepped into the hall without answering, and then into the office where she had seen the man disappear. There was a secretary at a desk in the room and a closed door. Maura headed at full speed for the door.

"I'm sorry. You can't go in there," the secretary announced, but it was too late. Maura opened the door and stepped into a conference room. Standing a few feet away were Mr. Sunglasses and a distinguished middle-aged man, the gray in his sideburns matching the wan color of his suit.

"So, we meet again," said Maura to Mr. Sunglasses. The two men stared at her and said nothing.

McVee came in behind her. "I'm sorry. I couldn't stop her."

"That's all right, son. We'll take care of it," said the older gentleman. The young McVee backed out of the room and closed the door.

"Won't you sit down, Mrs. Bates?" There was a large oval conference table with twelve chairs. Maura remained standing. "My name is Frank DeVito and this is the Consul General James McVee, senior."

"Father and son team, huh?" Maura was through playing games. She was ready for battle.

McVee nodded.

"And Frank, I didn't quite catch your title."

"Mister. Mr. DeVito."

"But why so formal? We're practically old friends. We've been around the world together."

"Mrs. Bates," said McVee, "we have reason to believe that your husband is still in Prince Majed's palace. I assume that's the matter you came here to discuss."

"Well, are you going to get him out?"

"It's not that easy. There's not really much we can do at this point. It's an internal matter that's especially delicate because the royal family is involved. It's in their hands."

"Like with Eddie."

"The Edward Bates affair was an unfortunate accident."

"Accident, my ass. He was murdered and you know it. You covered up for them."

"I don't know where you get these paranoid—" DeVito put up his hand to stop McVee.

"Mrs. Bates, do you have any idea how important good relations are with the royal family in light of American interests in Saudi Arabia?" DeVito said.

"You mean financial interests?"

"I mean world peace and stability. We're talking a very touchy situation here. The Russians or Iranians would love to see a break between us and the Saudis, so they could jump in here and claim the world's richest oil fields. Your brother-in-law and now your husband have gotten involved with a very controversial man in the royal family. We can't risk an international incident."

"What is this? Some kind of ends justifies the means? A sacrifice of one, or two for the good of many? I think you could have Dave out of there in five minutes if you wanted to."

"What do you expect us to do? Storm the palace? There are something like ten royal palaces in this area. We don't even know which one he's in."

"So you're just going to sit back and do nothing?"

"There's really nothing we can do right now except keep you posted through our contacts."

"No. You're not going to do anything because you don't want to do anything. You don't care. In your eyes, we're just a bunch of troublemakers." Maura started toward the door. "Well, I'm not going to sit back and do nothing. That's my husband they've got in there." She exited violently from the room with DeVito following close behind.

"May I remind you, Mrs. Bates," he called after her, but she didn't stop walking, "that you are a guest in this country and you could be asked to leave at any time." She disappeared down the stairs, her thick hair bouncing on her shoulders. She went straight past the receptionist and Jerry sitting on the bench.

"Let's get out of here," she said without stopping.

"Maura, what happened?" He caught up with her on the front steps.

"They refuse to do anything. They don't give a shit about Dave Bates. Well, I do. If they won't help me, I'll find someone who will." It rang of an idle threat despite the determination in her gait. There was little recourse for a woman, much less a foreign woman in Saudi Arabia, especially when she was up against the royal family.

"Help you do what? Do they know where he is?"

"Yes. They're quite informed. He's in the palace, but they won't do anything to get him out." Maura stopped at the bottom of the steps and turned to face him. "I don't suppose I can count on any help from Tanley on this?" Jerry looked away, trying to think of what to say. "Just as I thought." She whirled around and headed for the parking lot.

"Wait, Maura," he said, running after her. "I can't speak for Tanley. I'm just on the academic side. I'll talk to Bud and Tom and maybe they can work through Mansour, our liaison with the Family."

"Oh, great. Bud and Tom."

"They're all we've got, Maura. We have to work with them." Maura was shocked to hear Jerry show the tiniest sign of disloyalty to Tanley. It made her feel somehow proud. "As soon as we get back, I'll set up a meeting." They arrived at the car and Maura waited for him to unlock the door, drumming her fingers on the roof and looking off into the distance."

"I don't mean to be a bitch."

"I don't think you're a. . .I think you're being strong. I hope Peg would have the same strength if anything happened to me."

"I'm sure she would, and I'm sure she would handle herself better than I have."

"You don't have to apologize. I'll do what I can. I really want to help."

"Thanks, Jerry."

By the time Maura arrived home, she had resolved to be diplomatic in her meeting with Bud and Tom. Though she had little faith in their willingness to help on the basis of their benevolence, she knew they'd like to avoid a scandal as much as anyone. The air in the house seemed close as she opened the door and noticed that the flowers in the hall had wilted. She went into the living room and flipped on the radio. They were playing Cindi Lauper singing "Money Changes Everything," and she shook her head at how inappropriate it was for the moment. She and Dave and Eddie used to joke how that was their theme song in Saudi Arabia. It was a time filled with so much hope for a better life after they made their money and left the Middle East. It had all turned into a nightmare. She switched on the central air-conditioning and the air began to clear. Then she went into the bedroom and took off her clothes. Just as she was about to step into the shower, the phone rang.

"Hello," Maura gasped, out of breath from running for the phone. She clutched a towel around her.

"This Maur-ra?" The voice pronounced her name like a child.

"Yes. Who is this?"

"This Rico. I have message from Dave."

Maura collapsed on the couch. "Oh my God! Is he all right?"

"Yes. He okay, but like prisoner."

"Where is he? Can I talk to him?"

"No. This secret call. He in room at palace. Palace of Majed."

"Did they hurt him?"

"No. He okay."

"What are they going to do with him?"

"I don't know. I can't talk more. I must go."

"Wait, Rico. Call me again, please, when it's safe."

"Okay. I try."

14

ON THE BEACH

Maura sat in a dreary office with her arms crossed in front of her. Her meeting with Jerry, Bud and Tom was pretty much as expected and she pressed her lips together, trying not to say what she was thinking. They asked her not to contact anyone in the States for fear that it would get into the press. If that happened, there was no telling what the Saudis might do. Or their supervisors back at Tanley headquarters in the States, thought Maura. Then Tom, who had been silent throughout the meeting, leaned forward in his chair and tightened the lines on his forehead. He got the nod from Bud. "Just before our meeting, I talked to Mr. DeVito at the Consulate. He says that the Saudis now deny having Dave at all. They won't even discuss the matter. So there's a chance we're barking up the wrong tree."

Maura half jumped out of her chair. "Bullshit!" she shouted. "I happen to know that he is in the palace and he's alive. He also has a very specific request. He'd like to get out of there as soon as possible." The men looked stunned, and then quickly returned to a posture of disinterest.

"How do you know that?" asked Bud.

"I got a call from someone on the prince's staff."

"You've talked to someone inside the palace?" Bud's tone was incredulous. "What did he say?"

"Only that Dave was a prisoner and that he was okay."

"How do you know this person was reliable?" Tom asked.

"He sounded like he was making the call at great risk. He could only talk a couple of minutes. And he's someone that Khalil, the man who first took Eddie to the palace, told us about. Apparently, he's very close to Prince Majed."

"Why didn't you tell us this before?"

"I'm telling you now. I only got the call a little before coming over here." Maura stood up. "I think this conversation is over. You obviously have nothing important to tell me."

"Wait, Maura," said Jerry. "Of course, we want Dave back safe and sound, but we're getting resistance." Tom and Bud looked at Jerry like he was out of line.

"Just let us know if this guy calls again," said Tom. "We'll keep working on it."

"And if you hear anything," Maura said on her way out the door, "you'll let me know, won't you?" Her words were glazed in a coat of sarcasm.

"Of course, Maura," said Bud. "We'll keep you posted."

Maura went home to sit by the phone. She imagined that if anyone called, she wouldn't be the only person on the line.

Rico was smiling when he brought Dave's dinner that evening.

"Did you talk to her?"

"Yes. I tell her you okay."

"Good."

"Majed has plan. Don't worry."

"What? I thought. . ." The guard coughed. He stood in the doorway, handling his crotch.

"I must go."

After the door closed, Dave could hear them talking in the hall. The guard spoke in Arabic and Rico answered in English.

"Yes, I like," Dave heard Rico say coyly. "No, I can't now. . .because the Prince is waiting me. I come again, tonight maybe."

The phone sat like a pouting child that refused to speak on the coffee table while Maura stretched out next to it on the couch. Exhausted from losing a night's rest, she soon fell asleep. From deep in a dream she heard a ring. She reached out and grabbed the phone, but heard only the drone of the dial tone as she put it to her ear. The doorbell sounded again, slicing through the complete darkness of the house. Maura got up, turned on a light and went to the door. Through the peephole, she could see a Saudi in thobe and ghutra. She put the chain lock on and opened the door as far as the chain would allow.

"Yes. What is it?" she said.

"Don't be alarmed. I am a friend." From the sleeve of his thobe, he pulled out a small stone shaped like a rose and handed it to her through the crack in the door.

"What's this?"

"It's a sign from my Prince."

"Prince Majed?"

"Yes. May I come in?" Though he appeared friendly, his eyes kept darting behind him. Maura hesitated.

"I'm sorry to disturb you at this hour, but I didn't want to be seen." Maura stared him in the eye and after a short time her intuition led her to remove the chain and let him in. The Arab stepped into the hall and Maura closed the door behind him.

"What time is it?" she said, looking at the hall clock. "Eleven o'clock! I thought I had slept about five minutes. Please, come into the living room." The visitor sat down on the edge of the couch as if he were afraid of sinking into it while Maura went about the room turning on lights. She still held the desert rose in her hand. It was smaller than the one she had seen in Khalil's room. "Why do you have my husband?"

"It is not Majed. It is his brother Muhammad and his *Wahhabi* brothers who hold him. Majed is very sorry about this. He doesn't have very much influence in his family right now, so we must, shall we say, work outside the system. He very much wants to see your husband safely out of the palace."

"What do you mean by 'outside the system'?"

"Majed does have friends who will help you. It will be dangerous. But if your husband stays in the palace, it will also be dangerous. I don't know what they will do. Maybe arrange an 'accident' or keep him in prison until everyone has forgotten about him. If we help him escape, we can only hope everything goes well. *Insh'allah*."

Maura was reticent about trying to negotiate with the Saudis. She also didn't know whether she should trust the man in front of her. Recent history had made her mistrustful of everyone, though she wanted to believe he was a friend. "What's your plan?"

"You will come with me tonight. We go to a tent on the beach. Your husband will join you there. At the time of the first prayer call, just before dawn, a boat will come to take you to Bahrain. Friends there will help you." It sounded so simple.

"But how will Dave get out of the palace?"

"Rico will take care of that."

"Rico?"

"Yes. He has a way with the guards." The man spoke flatly and Maura didn't give it much thought.

"I see. But will it be safe for my husband?"

"*Insh'allah,*" was all he had to say.

"Is there another choice?"

The man shook his head. "I think this is the best plan. Please get what you want to take with you. I must go to my car for something."

Maura sat in shock as the man walked out of the room. He wasn't giving her time to think about it. On the other hand, she didn't like the thought of Muhammad's men arranging an accident for her husband. She jumped up and went into the bedroom where she located her large shoulder bag and stuffed it with some clothes, their passports and what was left of their traveler's checks. She looked around the room one last time and saw two Bedouin bracelets that Dave had given her, made of hand-pounded silver. She threw them in her bag and walked out into the hall. The man stood there with a black *abaya* and veil draped over his arm.

"You should put these on." Sadness came over his face. "They were my wife's."

"Were?"

"Yes. She died last year in childbirth."

"I'm sorry," said Maura, taking the black garments respectfully. She wrapped the *abaya* around her and put the veil over her head, shivering at the thought of wearing a dead woman's clothes. Then she experienced for the first time what it was like to see the world through black gauze. Though she could still see, reality was a step farther away, especially in the low light of the hallway. She ducked into the hall bathroom to look in the mirror and saw herself indistinguishable from any Saudi woman on the street; it was a perfect disguise. The beige canvas shoulder bag, however, was not a good match.

"Come. Let's go." The man seemed anxious to get moving.

As they drove along the coast road, the man, who finally introduced himself as Ibrahim, talked about his first trip to England as a young boy and how he had been charmed by the green rolling hills outside of London. He loved the dairy cows and the little villages of stone houses, but arriving in the city, he became frightened. When they took him down into the Underground, he never thought he would see the sky and his desert homeland again. Maura sensed that he was trying to say something about fear, but she wasn't afraid.

His soothing voice calmed her and his impressions of English life were at the same time naive and keen, childhood memories lodged deep in his psyche. In her world under the veil, she could have listened to him indefinitely, feeling no pressure to respond and safe from any reading of her facial expressions. She was in a private domain, and in spite of all the times she railed against the social imprisonment of Saudi women, she had to admit she felt protected from the outside world.

When they finally pulled off onto a rough rode that led down to the beach, the man fell silent and switched off the lights. There was a crescent moon hanging above the Gulf and way down at the far end of the beach was a black spot that gradually took the shape of a tent.

The shelter, large enough to stand up in, was made of dark, heavy canvas and had an old, musty smell mixed with the aroma of camel dung fires. On the floor was a colorful plastic woven mat and several pillows. Ibrahim left her with a blanket and a Coleman lamp, saying he had to return to the palace.

The lamp was bright and made her feel conspicuous, so she turned it off and stepped outside the tent, a black figure by a dark shelter on a mid-winter night. There was a good breeze off the gulf which caught her *abaya* and veil, making them flap in the wind, and looking up at the stars and the sliver of a moon, she felt timeless, transformed by her disguise into a character with no past and no future, bound to the desert and its eternal shifting of sand.

Dave lay awake on his cot, his hands behind his head, with the notion that something was going to happen soon. He knew that what Rico had whispered to him before had to be done quickly, while Muhammad and his men were still confused about what to do with him. On the way out, Rico had flirted with the guard and hinted at a date. Dave imagined that while Rico distracted the guard, someone else would come and open the door. It could be very simple. But the palace was so quiet, no noise at all in the hallway. He began to lose hope, though Rico's words kept echoing through his mind, "Majed has plan. Don't worry."

Some time after midnight, Dave thought he heard Rico's voice outside the door. It was soft and cooing like a pigeon calling to its lover. Dave got up and tried to peer through the little window in the door, but he could see almost nothing. Gradually his eyes adjusted to the low light and spotted a small shadow leading a large one through an open door across the hall. The man jerked Rico's arm, and then pushed his face down to his crotch. There was a rustle of khaki uniform and low grunts, followed by the sound of a belt clanging to the stone floor.

From Dave's angle all he could see was the man's tensed back, his legs spread, everything still in soft shadow. Then the guard growled, yanked Rico up and turned him around. There was a tiny shriek and a sound of ripped clothing. Dave had a hollow feeling in his gut and wanted to pull away from the door, but couldn't. Just then, the man kicked the door and it slammed shut.

Dave stayed at the window with his head against the bars. There were muffled groans from the Arab, but not a sound from Rico. His stomach churned as he expected someone to leap from the shadows at any moment to free him. He strained to look down the hall, but there was no movement.

A short time later a painful cry rang out, and Dave feared that the guard had broken the delicate Rico, snapped his neck, or done him some horrible violence beyond the violation. But when the door swung open, it was Rico who rushed out with a large key ring in his hand. He quickly inserted the key and unlocked the door.

"Come quick," Rico said.

"What have you done?" Dave looked at the dark stains on Rico's hands and the place on his pants where he had tried to wipe them off.

"Come," said Rico, leading him down the hall. Dave stopped at the doorway of the room across the hall and saw the guard writhing in pain in a pool of blood. There was a knife beside him on the floor. The room reeked of sour sweat and sex. The man looked up at Dave and reached out his hand.

"Rico, we can't just leave him like this." Rico ran back and slammed the door in front of Dave's face.

"You crazy? Come on." He took Dave's arm and pulled him. They ran down the hall and through a door that led to the outside where they went along the side of the building, crossed the street, and passed behind the mosque to the outer wall. Following the wall, they could hear the waves hitting the beach on the other side. Finally they reached a gate and climbed over it. A dog barked in the distance. "I thought dogs were unclean, forbidden by the Qur'an," he said. Or maybe he just thought it. He wasn't sure. His heart pounded so violently as they ran that his head, still recovering from the drugs they had given him, became filled with distorted images and each foot hitting the ground echoed through his brain. He felt the bloodied guard just behind him, reaching out to grab him. The single dog had turned into a pack and they were coming after them. They weren't going to make it. They weren't going to make it.

"The dogs," Dave shouted. Rico slowed down a little so that Dave could catch up with him.

"What?"

"The dogs."

Rico turned around and looked back toward the palace. "No dogs," he said, slowing down to a fast walk. Dave turned around too and saw only the long distance they had run. He felt foolish and changed the subject.

"Where are we going?"

"There is a tent. Not too far."

"Then what?"

"A boat to Bahrain."

"What about Maura? We have to get Maura. If she stays here they might do something to her."

"Don't worry. You will see."

"What do you mean? Will she meet us there?"

"Don't worry. Majed take care of everything." Rico started running again and pulled Dave after him. Dave resisted.

"Don't worry. Don't worry. Don't worry. Is that all you can say? What makes you so damn sure Majed's going to take care of everything? They don't seem to pay much attention to him around the palace."

"Majed help me many times before when I am in trouble and he will help again. I do anything he ask me. That's why I'm here, and you, too, out of palace."

"I know. I'm sorry you had to do that. Now you're in as much trouble as me. What are you going to do?"

"I go to Bahrain. Majed has friends there. They will take care of me. I will miss him very much, but he will come visit me. Now, we must hurry." They had slowed the pace again while talking. As they speeded up, they saw a dark figure running toward them and they stopped.

"Rico, why is that Saudi woman running toward us? This is not good. We should go another way."

"Wait. I don't know. Maybe she has message." When she got closer, Rico called out something in Arabic to her, but she didn't answer. She continued toward them, and then stopped a few feet away.

Maura lifted her veil. "Well, don't you recognize me?"

"Maura!" Dave shouted and rushed toward her. He took her in his arms and hugged her tightly. "God, am I glad to see you!" The wind snatched her veil and took it away, though in the commotion she didn't realize what had happened, feeling only a sense of loss thrown in with the joy of reunion. She was free again. . .and exposed.

Maura looked over Dave's shoulder and smiled at Rico. "Thank you," she said.

Rico returned her smile. "Come. Let's go." They all three started running again and soon reached the tent where Dave lifted the flap and they passed inside, falling to the tent floor in the darkness.

"I don't believe this," Maura said as she rolled over and found Dave, hugging him again.

"I thought you'd be mad at me," said Dave.

"I am. I'm furious."

"I guess it was pretty stupid. I walked right into a trap. They seemed to know I was coming."

"I'm not surprised. I ran into a friend of ours at the Consulate this morning?"

"You went to the Consulate?"

"It was Jerry's idea. He came over when he realized you hadn't signed in for work."

"Jerry? I'm surprised."

"He really cares, Dave. He was in a very difficult position. I'm glad he was around. I was desperate."

"Sometimes I think you'd be better off without me."

"Don't even joke about it. You wouldn't have believed what a mess I was last night when you didn't come home. But I don't want to talk about that. At the Consulate, you can probably guess who I saw."

"Sunglasses?"

"Mr. Frank DeVito to you, bub. No official title, at least none that he cared to reveal."

"Gotta be CIA. Did you talk to him?

"Oh, yeah. We had a wonderful little chat about world peace and whatnot during which they explained that their hands were tied because of the touchy situation with the royal family and all that crap. In the end, I'm afraid I wasn't very diplomatic."

"I can imagine. Who else was there?"

"The consul general and his son, the assistant consul. If I ever see any of them again, it'll be too soon. How did you escape?"

Dave didn't answer.

Rico broke the dark silence. "Where is lamp? We need lamp."

"It's here. Why?"

"We make signal when we hear *Allahu Akbar*."

Maura felt around the pitch-dark tent. "Here it is. Should we light it?"

"Yes, we need it soon."

When they had it lit, the first thing Maura noticed was the dried blood on Rico's pants. She looked at Dave, but his gaze fell to the ground.

"What do we do until the boat comes?" Maura said. She kept looking at the spot on Rico's pants.

Dave reached over and put his hand on Maura's leg. "I hope Majed knows what he's doing."

"Majed has many friends," said Rico.

Dave looked at him like he was tired of hearing that. "It seems that Muhammad has a lot more. Look where I ended up. Rico, do you understand why they drugged me and kept me prisoner?"

"I think so. You Eddie's brother. I know that right away. Even at first, I think you Eddie. I was surprise."

"I realized that. But you really didn't know that Eddie was killed?"

"Not other day. Majed don't know too. Now he know and tell me. When they take you, Majed argue much with Muhammad. Muhammad tell him about Eddie and cassette."

"Cassette?"

"You know, cassette." He made a demonstration with his hands of little wheels turning, and then hummed a song.

"I know cassette, but what does that have to do with Eddie?" Even as he asked the question he had a pretty good idea, though the details were missing. "Why don't you tell us what you know about that evening that Eddie came to the palace?"

"Okay, but you know my English is. . ."

"That's okay. Just tell us as best you can."

"Eddie come with Khalil that night and. . ."

"Yes, we know that part. Begin with after Khalil went to bed."

"Okay. Majed is getting drunk and he want no more to be with his brother and those guys. He ask Eddie to come to his rooms. Eddie start to bring drink and Majed say no. It is agree only drink in disco. Eddie go with Majed and Muhammad don't try stop him. One of Muhammad friend is very angry. I follow Majed and Eddie, but Majed tell me go to bed. I go and then enter the rooms of Majed through other door and sit by door to room where are they. They don't see me.

"Majed ask Eddie how he meet Khalil in desert and Eddie say he looking for desert rose. Majed laugh and say, 'And you find me. I am Desert Rose.' He say that under sand there is more than oil. The Desert Rose will rise from the sand and bloom. Saudi will be modern country not like desert camels with lot of money. You see, when Majed drunk he talk crazy, like want to be king and give country back to people and all this.

"Then Eddie say, 'Wait a minute.' He must go to Khalil's truck for some eye drops. He has problem with eyes. They hurt. I follow him. He don't see me. He go outside to truck, but no for eye drops. He get very small cassette and put in his pocket. When he come back, he ask Majed many question political. Majed say when he come back from States, he find many people who like him, have same ideas. He want to make more modern not just roads and houses, but thinkings. Saudi can't just buy technology and not thinkings that go behind it. Of course conservatives don't want even technology, but Majed say they are stupid. But he really angry at people who want make country like Iran. He also say the Al-Saud should begin think about democracy. He laugh when he say this because he know this make family very mad. Then he look sad and say Eddie he drink too much, every night, no good.

"They talk a little more and then Majed fall asleep on pillows. Eddie get up and go in hall and look around. I go around other way and he surprise to see me. I take him to room where he can sleep and he say he want be alone. When he close door, I listen. He turn on cassette and I hear Majed's voice. Then I see Muhammad and others coming. I run to Majed's room because I am afraid. Later I think I hear something, but I don't know."

"Like what, Rico?" Dave asked in a low voice.

"Like scream. I try forget. I think is dream. I like Eddie very much. They tell Majed next day that Eddie go with Khalil early in morning."

Dave lay back, folded his arms across his chest and closed his eyes. He appeared calm, but his insides were twisted in knots as if every fiber and cell was pulled taught at the information he had long searched for. His mind, however, came quickly to the present. He hadn't counted on a little knowledge being such a costly venture, endangering not only his own life, but now Maura's and Rico's. He was in no better position than if he had set out for simple revenge, a bullet in the head of Eddie's killer. Perhaps he would at least have felt a crude satisfaction from that.

Maura sensed Dave's troubled thoughts and they fed her own fears. And hugging her knees, she found herself praying to a God that she had long before abandoned, who had helped her once when she was a little girl and had gotten lost in the woods on a family camping trip.

Rico jerked his head up. "What's that?"

"What?" said Maura.

Rico went outside the tent and then came back in. "It's the *Allahu Akbar* of first prayer call. We must watch for signal." He and Maura went out and looked toward the sea. A light flashed three times from out in the water. Rico opened the flap of the tent three times in response.

"Look," said Maura, pointing down the beach. There were headlights a long way in the distance. Rico stuck his head inside the tent.

"Dave, quick. Somebody coming," he shouted. Dave jumped up and went outside where Rico pointed toward the fast approaching headlights. "Let's go," Rico said, heading for the water. Maura grabbed her bag and she and Dave ran after him. By the time they got to the water, the speedboat had pulled in within a few yards of the beach. A dark hulk sat at the controls wearing Western clothes and a menacing expression as he looked over his shoulder. They waded out and climbed in the boat while the driver offered no help nor said anything.

The car reached the tent and an Arab jumped out and started waving his arms frantically. "Wait. It's Majed. He come to say goodbye."

The boat lurched forward and sped off toward the pale light of dawn while the figure on the beach continued to wave as he became smaller and smaller. "Why you don't wait?" said Rico. The driver said nothing.

"I guess he doesn't speak English," said Maura. The boat was going so fast she could hardly catch her breath, and her heart pounded with a sickening feeling.

About two miles out the boat started to slow down, and then stopped.

"What's he doing?" said Dave.

"I find out," answered Rico. He said a few words to the man in Arabic to which the man responded by turning around and pointing a gun at them.

"Because it's the end of the road, Jack." He spoke with an American accent. The three of them stared at the gruff character in white-eyed wonder while the boat rocked, and all that could be heard were the waves lapping at the side of it.

"What's going on? Who are you?" Dave asked.

"Don't worry about that," said the raspy voice. "Just step outside the boat and I'll be saying my goodbyes."

"But you're supposed to take us to Bahrain," Maura said with desperation in her voice. The man turned to her, his mouth twisted into a cruel grin, and then started to laugh.

"I guess Majed not come say goodbye. He want to warn us. Who tell you come?" Rico asked the man.

"Shut up, Squirt. None of your fucking business. Just get your asses out of this boat, all of you."

"I can't swim," said Rico.

"Then that means I won't even have to bother shooting you."

Without hesitation, Rico lunged for the man's gun arm and bit into it. The man cried out in pain and the gun went off at the same time. Maura screamed and Dave jumped up and slammed his fist across the thug's face. Rico slumped to the floor and the gun along with him.

"Get the gun," Dave shouted, trying to hold the man down. Maura was stunned, unable to move. "Maura, the gun." She reached down and picked up the pistol from next to Rico's moaning body, then knelt next to him and took his head in her left arm. "Rico," she said. "Are you hurt bad?" Just then, the man brought his knee up hard against Dave's chest and knocked him back to the edge of the boat. "Stop it," Maura screamed, pointing the gun at him. Everyone froze.

The man let out his cruel laugh again. "So, the little lady's got the gun. Ever fire a gun before? Ever kill a man before?"

Maura's hand started to shake.

"Give me the gun, Maura," said Dave.

"No," she said in a trembling voice. "I've got it."

"All right, but if he moves, shoot him. I mean it, Maura. Shoot him."

"Listen to the big man talk. Easy for him to say."

"Maura," Dave said in a firm voice. "Put both hands on the gun."

Maura took her arm out from under Rico's head and aimed the gun with both hands. "Now, tough guy," said Maura. Her voice was more controlled. "You get out of the boat and *we'll* say goodbye."

The man thought a minute. "Okay. I'll take my chances out there." He got up and moved to the side of the boat while Maura followed him with the gun.

"Watch out," Rico shouted weakly. The man's leg swung up and caught Maura on the side of the head, knocking her to the floor. She was dazed for a second, but she still had the gun. In a second, he was on top of her and the gun went off. Once. Twice. Three times. Dave grabbed the man from behind, pulled him off Maura and threw him to the other side of the boat with more strength than he knew he had. His head bounced against the edge and he landed in a heap. He remained still. Then Dave was down on his knees next to Maura.

"Maura! Shit! Maura, are you all right?" She let the gun slip from her hand and rolled over facing the deck. She groaned and her body began to shake.

"Oh, God, Maura, are you hurt?" He turned her over and saw the blood all down the front of her clothes. He took her in his arms, but she kept trying to cover her face.

"Maura, say something, please."

Maura gasped for breath and tried to wiggle out of his arms. She thought she was going to get sick, but Dave just squeezed her tightly. After a couple of minutes she was able to say, "I. . .I'm not hurt." And then she whispered, "Did I kill him?"

"I don't think so," said Dave, looking over at the man who started to show signs of life. Maura pulled away and wiped her face with her hands, not realizing that she was smearing blood on one cheek. She crawled over to Rico and avoided looking at the man who was curled up, cradling his guts as he groaned.

"Rico," Maura said tenderly.

"You. . .got. . .him?"

"That was a very brave thing you did, Rico. You saved our lives."

"I am happy then. Majed will like that. I can die happy."

"No," said Dave, standing over them. "We're going to get you to a hospital. You'll be all right." Dave went to the driver's seat and started up the boat. "Hey, buddy, which way's Bahrain?" he said to the man on the floor.

"Fuck you," the guy growled.

"Toward the sun," said Maura. An orange light rose above the haze on the water and a few clouds reflected pink and orange light while the last stars faded from the sky.

Dave pulled back the throttle and the boat leapt forward toward the little island sheikhdom. How he was going to explain their presence when they got there, he didn't know.

Maura took Rico's head in her lap. He winced with pain at the movement and said, "Maur-ra, I die now."

"No, you're not." His frail body already seemed light and lifeless. A few seconds later she felt him go. She let out a long shaky breath and continued to hold him.

Dave turned around and said, "How's he doing?" Maura shook her head and Dave looked down at Rico's ashen face. "Oh," he said and slowed the boat down. There was no rush now.

"Why are you slowing down?" Maura shouted above the din of the motor.

"What? I can't hear you." Maura took Rico's head and rested it carefully on her bag. She went up beside her husband.

"Why are you slowing down?"

"We have to think about what we're going to do. We can't just pull up to the dock in Bahrain and say howdy do. We've got a gun, one dead body and another half-dead on board."

The wounded man was able to growl another, "Fuck you," this one a little weaker than the last. Maura picked up the gun off the bench as if it was a dead rat, and threw it overboard.

"Are we going to do that with Rico and the other one?" Dave asked.

Maura glanced at Rico and shook her head.

"I think we should go back," said Dave.

"Are you crazy?"

"I was thinking we could leave them on the beach where Majed was. Maybe he's still there. Without them we might have a chance of sneaking into Bahrain. And even if we got caught, we might be able to talk the Bahrainis into just taking us to the American Embassy. Like this, who knows what they would do. Probably ship us right back to Saudi Arabia."

"I don't want to go near that place again. I'd rather take my chances on the open sea."

Dave turned the wheel sharply, starting a wide arc. "We're going back," he said.

"No," screamed Maura, grabbing the wheel. Dave pushed her away hard and she tripped over the man on the floor and fell back into a seat. "You don't know what you're doing. You've completely lost your senses." She started to get up.

"I'm warning you, Maura. Stay away from this wheel." Dave finished the arc and let out the throttle toward Saudi Arabia. "It's probably too soon after prayer for there to be any patrols. Maura shook her head and fell back into the seat where she folded her arms across her chest and glared at Dave in anger and disbelief. Dave opened up the glove compartment and found a pair of binoculars. He tossed them to Maura. "Help me look."

After a few minutes, he thought he saw the palace. "Look to the left of that." He pointed to a place on the beach. Maura picked up the glasses, though her eyes still burned with rage. "If Majed's not there, we'll just put them on the beach and then take our chances in Bahrain."

They were less than a mile out now. "I see the tent," said Maura. "There is a car by it."

"Just one car?"

"Yes."

"Okay. Let's go in. Do you see Majed?"

"I guess it's him. There's an Arab watching us through binoculars."

"Oh, shit!" said Dave. A boat sped toward them from the south. Dave let the throttle out as far as it would go and it looked like they could gain the beach before the boat caught up with them.

Majed was in the water when they got to shore, his thobe soaked from the waist down. He eased the boat forward and stared into the boat as if he was looking into a tomb. "Give me Rico," he said. "Hurry."

"He's dead, Majed," Dave whispered.

"I was afraid of this. Come quickly." The other boat had stopped offshore a ways.

"What about the other one?" asked Dave.

"Leave him. Let Muhammad and his friends take care of him. Come with me. No one will bother you when you are with me." Maura looked at him with raised eyebrows. Majed cradled Rico's limp body in his arms. "So it has come to this. I am sorry. Someone betrayed my plan. I found out too late. I don't know who are my friends and who are not." Tears formed in his eyes as they hurried up the beach.

"Where will we go?" Maura whined.

"I will take you to the Consulate."

"We don't exactly have friends there. I think they'd as soon see us out of the way as anybody," said Dave.

"But you are Americans. They represent your country, a country that has everything—riches, power, freedom."

"A country that has everything doesn't need individual people," Dave said with a bitter grin. "At least not people like us."

"I will go with you. I will talk to them. I am still a prince. I am still Al-Saud." Majed got in the back seat with Rico and motioned for Dave and Maura to get in the front with the driver. It was Tarik and he looked Maura over carefully before nodding to Dave, though he didn't say anything. He appeared to be enjoying the excitement.

A black car came down the beach toward them and Majed told Tarik to go fast, not to stop for anything. The Mercedes bumped along the rough road and the black car, another Mercedes, stopped, turned around and fell in behind them. When they got on the main road and passed the palace, a second black Mercedes started following them as well.

Maura stared straight ahead with a scowl on her face.

Dave turned to look at her. "Don't be angry, Maura. I'm sorry if I hurt you in the boat."

"I'm not angry. I'm scared and tired and my head hurts. It all seems so hopeless."

"I think we're going to get out of this. I don't know how. I just feel it."

"How do you figure?"

"We've got something to bargain with."

"What's that?"

"Our silence."

"I'm sure that's what they have in mind, permanent silence."

"I don't think they'll try to kill us now that Majed is involved. We can at least try saying that we'll keep our mouths shut."

"Are you willing to trade that for freedom? I mean, now that you know what happened, don't you want to tell somebody? The world should know."

"I figure we just have to convince them that we aren't interested in pursuing any investigation or selling a story."

"It's you that has to be satisfied with that."

"For the time being. I set out to find out why it happened. No amount of exposé or justice can bring Eddie back."

"Or Rico."

"Or Rico," Dave echoed.

15

BACK TO THE CONSULATE

It was an uncommon delegation that emerged from the gray Mercedes and proceeded up the steps to the United States Consulate in Dhahran that Sunday morning. The other cars in the spontaneous motorcade, the black ones, had stopped outside the Consulate compound. Majed's thobe was bloodstained and still wet with sand clinging like a border around the bottom edges. Maura's clothes were bloody as well and her hair was windblown and wild about her pale and weary, blood-streaked face. Dave's silk shirt was torn and smudged, and his gait showed the fatigue of a long night.

When Ms. Talbot spotted them coming in the front door, she was on the phone immediately. They didn't even stop at her desk, but continued past her with Maura leading the way toward the stairs. "There's no one here yet," Ms. Talbot sang out as they went by.

"That's all right. We'll wait," Maura sang back. The three of them went up the stairs and took seats on a bench outside the consul general's office. A few minutes later, a young man came by with a silver coffee service. He apologized to the Prince.

"I'm sorry, your highness," he said. "We have only American coffee."

"That's fine." They sat silently, drinking the weak coffee from Wedgwood cups with the saucers cradled in their hands.

Dave broke the silence. "Once you're rid of us, what will you do? I'm afraid we've caused you a lot of trouble."

"No, it is I who have caused you much trouble. I feel responsible for your brother's death and Rico's. I am feeling great pain for this, for everything." He paused and looked at the shaky hand with which he held the cup. "There is a hospital in Jeddah for people with drinking problems, for my people who go on long binges outside the country and need a place to dry out when they get back. It is very quiet, of course, but it has seen its share of my family."

"There are some good programs in the States. Maybe it would be a good idea for you to go there," Maura suggested, thinking he might be better off outside his country when the word got out about the things he had done.

"No. This is my country. These are my people. I must accept it and find a way to work for what I believe in a Saudi way. If I went to the States again, it would only make me confused. I have been playing a child's game, thinking I could change my country by talking about it and living as I pleased. But sometimes people get hurt in child's games and it makes you grow up. Have you not wondered why I have not been back to the States in almost eight years? I tell you.

"When I went to Berkeley, to the University of California, I tried to get lost, as I told you earlier, in the society of America. I studied English very hard and especially to lose my accent which, as you can see, was not a great success. I enrolled in a few psychology courses to show that I was normal and gave myself up to the fashions and behavior of the time. I spent less and less time with the other Saudi students and more and more time trying to meet Americans. Still, I thought of myself as Saudi, my country as Saudi Arabia, my religion as Islam and Allah as my god.

"Then one night, after I had been there several months, I went out to a jazz club with some American friends who convinced me that I should try one time alcohol. Thus I proceeded to get drunk very quickly. That was the night my life fell apart and I realized how fragile my reality had been. That was the night I met Fernando. Up until that time I could resolve my flirtations with American society as just that, a phase of youth which would pass when I went back to Saudi Arabia to take my place as a mature man. Fernando, with his innocent look and lingering stare, stole, in a matter of seconds, not only my heart, but my youth and cast me into a limbo from which I could never escape. I was caught between denying family, country and culture, and denying my heart. I could no longer be the frivolous youth, and yet I didn't see how it would be possible to take my place as a mature man in my culture, to marry and have a family as I was expected. Many similar to me do it, but I felt like I couldn't. What happened when I met Fernando was very serious though it seemed anything but that at the time. We laughed a lot. I must have been very funny as a first drunk.

"It is strange that I should meet Fernando that first night I drank alcohol as it seemed that I came down with the disease and discovered its palliative at the same time. Whenever a conflict arose between what I was and what my heart wanted me to be, I took to the bottle, as you say. It is a habit that I have found hard to break.

"Fernando was a beautiful boy, with smooth white skin, bashful blue eyes, and light brown hair streaked with gold. He was Argentinean, but his parents emigrated there from Italy. He was in the States studying political science. Though shy, he was very athletic and very much a man, not like the boy-girls here. With him, my lust and my love had a chance to breath together and that is a beautiful thing. Soon we were lovers and as long as I had enough to drink and he was patient, we were happy together. We would go to all night parties in San Francisco and weekend trips to New York and Los Angeles.

"Each year I would come back here for Ramadan and try to hide the change that had happened to me, while at the same time watching the change that was happening to my brother, Muhammad, in a different way. From an unpopular and awkward youth, he was becoming a self-righteous religious scholar, a source of pride to my father while I was becoming more a source of confusion to him. He began to regret that he had ever sent me to study there. By the end of Ramadan I would be so miserable that I would decide I must break off with Fernando when I went back to the States. I knew it had to end some day, so I thought it better to do it sooner than later. But as soon as I would see Fernando again, I would forget all about that. He really had me and I loved and hated him for it.

"One afternoon I came home to my apartment. Fernando had gone to visit his parents for the holidays. In my living room were sitting my father and bother, Muhammad. I felt a great shame. They had already packed up all my things and they had a ticket for me back to Saudi Arabia that afternoon. There was no choice for me but to go. You see, in the States I was two people, but in the presence of my father the Saudi one strangled the other. I had no chance to say goodbye to Fernando and I have had no communication with him since that day. To speak of it still makes my heart heavy."

Majed's words lingered for a moment in the hall air, then a cool draft blew through and dissipated them. The coffee, too, in the bottoms of their cups had gone cold. And then the draft brought two sets of steps beginning a slow but determined climb up the stairs that were out of sight down the corridor. The approaching feet created an ominous drum roll that echoed along the walls, then their figures emerged, hesitating slightly at the top of the stairs in postures that suggested a recent routing from sleep. But as they came closer, a transformation occurred, making them taller, their walk surer and their chests more pronounced.

As McVee and DeVito passed, Majed, Dave and Maura stood up and followed them into the office. DeVito stepped aside, allowing them to pass and then closed the door. Majed took command of the situation immediately. "My name is Majed bin Hassan bin Abdul Aziz."

"We're pleased to meet you, your highness. I'm Consul General James McVee and this is Mr. Frank DeVito."

"I assume you know Mr. and Mrs. Bates," said Majed. He turned to Dave and winked. "She is your wife, isn't she?" Dave blushed slightly at the lie he had told earlier.

"We've met Mrs. Bates, but I'm afraid this is the first time we've had a chance to meet Mr. Bates," said McVee.

"Yes, well, now that everyone has been introduced, I would like to explain my purpose here. I am assuming that you have been informed of the situation as it now stands. So just let me say, that I will arrange for safe conduct of these people out of the country and I would like your cooperation."

"We will be happy of course to cooperate with you in any way we can, your highness. But have you discussed this with other family members, for example, your uncles?"

"I will take care of it. And I will personally escort them to the plane to make sure they get on it. I'm sure you are interested, as I am, to see that your fellow Americans are safely out of the country."

"We appreciate your concern, but we don't expect you to risk your own safety."

"Are you implying that a Saudi prince might be in danger in his own country?" Majed thundered.

McVee looked at DeVito. "Your highness, we only—"

"All I'm asking is that you make the arrangements and take care of their safety until I return to take them to the airport. When is the next military flight?"

"Not until tomorrow night."

"Then it will have to be commercial. As soon as possible."

"We'd like a stopover in Germany," said Maura, taking them all by surprise.

"Germany?" Dave said, almost inaudibly.

Majed had confidence that Maura knew what she was doing. "A stopover in Germany," he said.

"First class," Maura added.

"First class," Majed repeated.

"Yes, well, there are a few things we'd like to clear up with the Bates. Would you mind, your highness, if we spoke to them alone?" McVee said. Majed sensed the hardness of these officials behind their polite exteriors, their ruthless dedication to their country and all it represented.

"Make the arrangements first," said Majed. "It is vital that these people leave the country as soon as possible. I will come back to pick them up one and a half hours before the flight." DeVito got on the phone and made a first class reservation for two on Lufthansa to Frankfurt. The flight was at 11:30 that morning and Majed promised to be back for them at 10:00.

When Majed had gone, McVee sat down and folded his hands on the desktop. Dave and Maura sat on a couch against the wall and DeVito remained standing next to McVee's desk. "Well, this is a fine mess you've gotten yourselves into. You're lucky to have a prince on your side though it still remains to be seen whether he'll get you out of the country without any interference from the rest of the family. We understand that there were two deaths in this little incident this morning." He shook his head like a scolding grade school principal.

"Two?" said Maura, stunned by the news. She felt sick to her stomach. The dead man's blood was still on her clothes.

"Yes. We received confirmation of the second on our way in this morning.

"He was an American, wasn't he?" said Dave.

"He was carrying an American passport, but he was a man for hire, working for any government, any cause."

"It's a wonder you learned so much about him in such a short time."

"Yes," said McVee, ignoring Dave's insinuation. "It is, isn't it? In any case, speaking as a representative of the United States Government, I must remind you of the seriousness of your actions. Moreover, this could have easily turned into a nasty international incident had things gotten more out of hand. Your actions in Saudi Arabia have been an embarrassment to the United States."

"Wait a minute—" shouted Dave, standing up, but DeVito cut him off.

"Shut up and sit down. Listen to what the consul has to say."

"We are willing," McVee continued, "to comply with the Prince. But before we do that, we would like something from you." McVee paused and Dave took advantage of the lull to put in what he had to say. He had sat back down and was a little calmer now.

"I won't be so naive as to say I'm disappointed at your behavior as representatives of Americans in Saudi Arabia. I can't even say that I'm shocked by your participation in the cover-up of my brother's murder. But I will say that just because you are government officials doesn't make it right. And I suppose you're asking us to give up the only small satisfaction we might have from the whole mess—the telling of the story and some hope of an investigation. But for a promise of safe conduct out of the country and no further interference in our lives, we'll keep our mouths shut."

"That's precisely what we're asking, for the sake of everyone involved. Of course, you're accusations are entirely without proof and with little chance of being proven. If you had ever tried conducting an investigation in Saudi Arabia, you'd know what I was talking about."

"I don't need proof," Dave affirmed. "I know." There was a dangerous electricity in the air. DeVito stood hunched over like an animal ready to pounce.

"I would like to say something," Maura began. Dave looked at her, anxious about what her mouth might produce. "Not that we don't trust you, of course, but I talked to my sister in Paris last night. She has the whole story—an alcoholic Saudi prince who wants to overthrow the family rule and establish a democracy, his involvement with an American employee, the employee's murder and cover-up with the compliance of the U.S. Government, the kidnapping of his brother by members of the royal family, etc. If we don't call her by 8:00 this evening to tell her we're safe, she's going to *Le Monde* with the story. The French press would have a heyday with it before it spread across the ocean."

"And who would believe it?" sneered DeVito. "It sounds like a plot for a cheap novel."

"Something that juicy would at least be worth an investigation by some crack reporters, wouldn't you think?" Maura stared at them with a poker face. Dave tried not to smile. The only sound in the room was DeVito scratching his hoof on the floor.

"I'm sure we'd all like to avoid any negative publicity, including your friend the Prince. So, let's just leave it at that. You're free to go and we will trust you to keep your word of silence." DeVito gave him a disappointed look like an attack dog held in check. McVee's face slowly became drained of seriousness and miraculously produced a smile.

"I imagine you'd like to get cleaned up before your trip. I'll get someone to show you where you can do that." With that, McVee got up and walked out of the room and DeVito followed close behind.

A quick call to Tanley brought Jerry to the consulate with a change of clothes. "We really appreciate this," said Maura as she hugged him. She smiled to herself as she imagined him going through her underwear and choosing some for her to wear. "You thought I looked like shit yesterday. Look at me now." Jerry reddened and began pulling away.

"Believe it or not, I think I'm going to miss you." He smiled shyly and turned to Dave. "If you give me an address, Dave, we'll ship the rest of your stuff. I'll send your last check and put in a letter of recommendation if you like."

Dave stuck out his hand. "Thanks, Jerry. It's hard to imagine what the future holds right now, but it sure wouldn't hurt to have the letter."

"Have a good trip and good luck." Jerry waved and walked out the door.

"I'm glad he didn't try to say anything heavy," said Dave.

"I'm going to write him a letter of thanks when we get settled somewhere. He was really there when I needed someone."

At 10:00, Dave and Maura were at the front door of the Consulate. Majed wasn't. Ms. Talbot pretended to ignore them while a black Mercedes sat outside the compound gate. By 10:30 their giddy excitement had turned into a gnawing anxiety. The junior McVee kept coming halfway down the stairs, checking to see if they'd left yet.

"Should I ask McVee if there's a consulate car available?" Dave said. Maura shrugged her shoulders and continued twisting the strap of her bag around her finger. "I think he'll come," Dave concluded. "Saudis are always late."

At 10:45, Dave started up the stairs to talk to McVee. Then he heard the sound of screeching tires followed by Maura yelling, "He's here." Ms. Talbot looked up so fast her glasses slid off her nose. Maura and Dave ran out to the car and threw themselves in the back seat.

"Sorry," said Majed. "Always I must fight with my family. I say I want to send Rico back to the Philippines. His mother is there. My brother says, 'Bury him in the desert,' which is not so bad as all Saudis are buried there, even the kings. But I want to send him back to his mother." As they pulled out of the compound gate, the black car fell in behind them. "I see we have an escort again," Dave mentioned.

"Don't worry. They won't do anything."

The car sped along the road to the airport, which was just a short distance from the Consulate. Tarik dropped them off at the front entrance and Majed whisked them through customs to the waiting area. They had just called for the boarding of the Lufthansa flight.

"See, this way no waiting in lines," Majed said with smile.

"And no long goodbyes," Maura added.

Dave took a deep breath and began, "Majed, we. . ."

Majed held up his hand. "You don't have to say anything." He took Dave's hand and held it warmly while he looked deeply into Dave's eyes, as if he were still unsure exactly what an American was. "My American friends used to tell me that in English 'Peace be with you,' sounds like something from a bible movie. So, I say it in my language: *As salaam alaykum."*

"Wa alaykum as salaam," answered Dave. It was the first time he really meant it. "I hope we meet again someday."

"Insh'allah." Then Majed took Maura's hand. "I wish you a happy life together and many children. . .if you want them." Maura had a lump in her throat that wouldn't let her speak. "Go now," he said.

They handed their tickets to the man at the gate and boarded the buses, which took them out to the plane while Majed waited at the window until they were off the ground.

"Here we go again," Maura said as they took their seats on the 747. "I wish we could go directly to Paris. I guess it's too risky, huh?"

"I don't know. You're the one that got us going to Germany. I think it's a good idea. Frankfurt isn't that far from Paris and hopefully Beth will be able to drive over with Khalil. By the way, you didn't really talk to her last night, did you?"

"No. I guess I was taking a chance with that one about her going to *Le Monde.* I just get so sick and tired of them thinking they have all the leverage."

Dave shook his head and looked at his wife. "You are so strong."

She put her hand over her mouth and looked out the window. "I killed a man, Dave." Her body shivered.

He put his arm around her. "You saved us. It was him or us. You did what you had to do."

16

Frankfurt am Main

The Lufthansa jet touched down at its home airport, the super-modern Rhein-Main outside of Frankfurt, in the early afternoon. Dave and Maura were relieved to be back in the West, despite its brisk pace and stark winter reality, a reality that had no bearing on the moods of the people in the airport who were quite friendly. And when they asked about hotel reservations, they were cheerfully referred to "Hot Resy" a machine on the other side of a parade of passersby. Though at first put off by the idea of this impersonal service, they consulted the computerized system and were amazed at its efficiency.

They punched in the type of accommodations they were looking for—they decided to go for the deluxe—and the machine gave them a typed confirmation for a small fee. They were booked in a room on the tenth floor of the Frankfurt Intercontinental with a view of the Main River. As they stepped out of the taxi in front of the 21-story modern hotel with hundreds of windows staring down at them, they felt the lack of intimacy they might have at a bed and breakfast. But then a little anonymity after their recent experiences seemed a better idea.

From their tenth floor room Dave and Maura watched the barges and tour boats on the gentle river that hardly seemed to move at all.

Around the hotel were other modern towers, but along the river were old church spires and low, solid stone buildings from past centuries.

Dave stood behind Maura with his arms around her waist and his chin resting on her head. "Do you like it?"

"The room? I feel like I'm on top of the world, the most wonderful sense of deliverance."

"I'm glad then that we didn't pay for the penthouse. This is expensive enough."

"David Bates, I don't want to hear one word about the cost of this hotel. Just let me enjoy this beautiful moment, and then I have to go call Beth."

"It's hard to believe that the whole city was almost entirely leveled during the war." It took someone like Dave, thought Maura, to bring up wartime destruction at a time when they should be soaking in the gratification of being alive and out of Saudi Arabia.

"But all those old buildings along the quay," Maura protested.

"Reconstructed."

"Oh," said Maura in a tone somewhat closer to earth.

"I wasn't trying to bring you down. I was just thinking how incredible it was that they've bounced back, what you can do when you have to start all over again."

Maura could see that she wasn't going to be allowed to drift on her newfound cloud of security without thinking about the future. "I think I'll call Beth now."

"Where are you?" said Beth, her voice bordering on hysteria. "I've been worried sick about you. I didn't hear anything. What was I supposed to think?"

"We're alive and well in Frankfurt," said Maura, "but we damn near ended up on the bottom of the Arabian Gulf."

"Frankfurt? Why did you go there? What happened?"

"I can't explain it all now. I'll tell you the whole story when I see you. I hope it will be soon. We figured it wouldn't be a good idea to come to Paris right now."

"That was smart. They've had me in a couple of times for questioning, something about my relatives on rooftops, running away from police. You would be amazed how poor my French becomes when I have to talk to the police. I also have a good friend who is a lawyer. So, are you guys okay?"

"Yeah, considering. What about Khalil?"

"Not good news. He's at the police station."

"Oh, no."

"Yeah. You almost missed me. My lawyer friend Jacques and I were just getting ready to head down to Tonnerre to get him out."

"What happened?"

"The old bitty who lives next door to my place down there, above the horsemeat butcher, in fact she might be the horsemeat butcher...anyway she thought there was something strange going on, so she called the cops. I guess in her mind, an Arab in Tonnerre was something strange. When the police came and questioned him, he refused to say anything for fear of getting me in trouble. That was sweet, but they took him in. We're just hoping they don't connect him with the incident in Paris."

"When does it all stop?" she mumbled.

"What?"

"Oh, nothing. It's just one thing after another."

"You sound tired Maura. Why don't you two just relax and I'll call you back tonight when I know more what's going on. What hotel are you in?"

Maura hung up the phone saying, "You're not going to believe this. The police took Khalil in." Dave didn't answer. She turned around and saw that his eyes were closed and his breathing was deep and regular. He looked more peaceful than she'd seen him in weeks, an innocent child curled up on a giant white bed under a painting of a panther in a cubist jungle.

She watched him sleep for a while, uncurl and lie flat on his stomach. Her gaze swept up the wall to the crouched panther and back down to her unsuspecting husband. He jerked a couple of times, then moved to his other side and very slowly rolled on to his back where his breathing nasalized into a snore. Now he was an unshaven, disheveled gypsy whose home was where he laid his head and the harsh sounds coming from his throat proclaimed his right to be there.

Maura approached the bed like a cat and as soon as she touched it, his snoring stopped. She slid in beside him and draped her arm across his chest. He took hold of it. The light was fading and the traffic down in the street increased as the people of Frankfurt left their Sunday afternoon gatherings and headed for their homes to get ready for the workweek.

Dave opened his eyes at the first low-pitched flutter of the phone. The room was dark and he sensed immediately that Maura wasn't there.

"Hello," said Dave.

"Hi, Dave. Did I wake you?" It took Dave a minute to realize that it was Beth he was talking to and not Maura, their voices so similar.

"No. . .I mean, well. . .yes, as a matter of fact."

"Maybe you should put Maura on if you're still groggy."

"I don't think she's here." There was worry in his voice. "I don't know where she is."

"She probably just stepped out for a walk or something."

"I wish she wouldn't do that."

"Why? She can take care of herself."

"We've made too many enemies lately."

"In Germany?"

"Well, no, but these enemies are well-connected."

"This is all sounding a little cryptic since I don't know what the hell has been going on for the past couple of weeks."

"Don't worry. You'll hear the whole story. I guess I'm being paranoid. What's happening over there?"

"We got your friend out of jail and—"

"Friend? Jail? What are you talking about?"

"Didn't Maura tell you?"

"I guess I fell asleep."

"Khalil was taken into the police station, but he's out now and we're planning a trip to Frankfurt. I'm looking forward to it. I've never been there."

"When are you coming?"

"As soon as possible. We want to get him out of the country before someone connects him with the Paris rooftop chase. We'll leave in an hour or so. That should put us there early in the morning. Jacques is coming with me."

"Who?"

"My lawyer."

"That's good. You won't have to drive back alone."

"And don't worry about Maura. I'm sure she's all right."

When Maura walked out the front door of the hotel, she noticed a sinister-looking man in a dark suit and overcoat standing across the street. He looked so much like a caricature of a stakeout man that she thought she was walking onto a spy movie set. There was also something about his face that looked vaguely familiar. She thought she must be imagining things and headed up the street in the direction the desk clerk had sent her. There was supposed to be an American-style drugstore a few blocks up and she wanted to replace some of the toiletries they had left in a trail behind them every time they had had to pick up and run—tubes of toothpaste, bottles of shampoo, hairbrushes, and unopened packages of disposable razors.

As Maura walked, she caught, out of the corner of her eye, the man crossing the street. She pulled up the collar of the camelhair coat she had bought at the airport, and buttoned the top button. Having come from the warm desert of Saudi Arabia, the cold penetrated straight to her bones and made her shake. She stopped to look in a store window and noticed that the man followed at a casual distance behind her. He ducked into a doorway. Maybe she should go back to the hotel, she thought. Or to the police. They would never believe her far-fetched story. The ordeal was over, she kept saying to herself. They would be going home in a day or two. He was probably just some horny guy who thought she looked like an easy American lay. As a group of people passed, she fell in just ahead of them and quickened her pace. He quickened his pace as well.

She turned around and saw that he was just fifteen yards behind. She stepped into a crowded cafe where she was hit with steamy warmth emanating from the noisy crowd. Unbuttoning her coat, she weaved through the tables and touched a waitress on the arm. "*Wo ist die Toilette*?"

"Back there," she answered in English and pointed with her pencil.

"Thank you."

On her way to the restrooms, she noticed that there was a side entrance, which gave on to an alley of small shops. She exited quickly and regained the street where she peeked around the corner and saw that the man was waiting outside the cafe. When he wasn't looking, she stepped out onto the sidewalk and headed briskly in the direction of the drugstore. In the next block, she found it, an island of fluorescent light with countless aisles of multi-colored products. As the store was relatively uncrowded, it didn't take her long to collect all the things she needed.

At the checkout counter, she was a little thrown when the woman said the total in German. "*Wieviel kostet es*?" She squinted at the digital numbers on the modern cash register.

"Twenty-six marks," the woman said in English.

"It seems that everyone here speaks English," Maura said with a little laugh.

"My father's American. U.S. Army," the checkout girl said dryly.

"Oh," said Maura, gathering up her plastic shopping bag. "Well, thank you." The girl was already ringing up the next customer.

The street was filled with Sunday evening strollers, but there was no sign of the mysterious man. Figuring she had lost him, Maura decided to go straight back to the hotel the way she had come. About a block from the Intercontinental, a car door swung open almost directly in front of her and a man stepped out and took her arm.

"Would you come with me please?"

"What is this?" She resisted and his fingers dug into her arm. "Ouch! You're hurting me." She said it loud that the people on the street might hear her. Now it seemed no one spoke English.

"If you want to see your husband alive again, you must cooperate." He had an Arab accent and dark fierce eyes.

"What do you mean? Where is he?"

"Please get into the car." He pushed her toward the opening.

"Not until you tell me where my husband is. I just left him. . ." She didn't see the man emerge from a group of people crossing the street and hit the Arab with a hard object from behind. He slumped forward against the car door and her arm was passed from one man's hand to another. The new one ran and pulled her along.

"Wait!" she shouted, still clinging to her shopping bag. "My husband. . .they have him." It dawned on Maura who this man was. It was Ibrahim who had taken her to the tent on the beach, Ibrahim in a dark suit and overcoat.

"No. They're lying. Keep running."

They heard a car door slam and an engine start. The BMW pulled out of the space and came after them. When it was alongside them, the rear window went down and a gun gripped by a dark hand was thrust out the opening.

"Down," Ibrahim yelled and threw her to the ground. Two shots whizzed by them into a store window. A woman nearby screamed. The BMW tires squealed and they took off down the street. Maura looked at the man on the ground beside her. He had a gun in his hand, but quickly put it back under his coat and got up.

"Let's go." He pulled her up and they started running again. They didn't slow down until they were a few yards from the hotel entrance, then they walked in as calmly as they could.

When they got in the elevator, Maura surveyed the damage. She still had her bag from the drugstore, but her jeans were soiled and she felt the raw flesh of a skinned knee underneath.

"Sorry," Ibrahim said.

"That's okay, believe me. Better dirty slacks than a bullet in the head. I just hope my husband is still in the hotel room." Maura paused and became pensive. "I guess I was foolish to think it was all over."

"Some people are still worried about what you might say to the world. I also found out some other information recently. The cassette tape that Eddie made is missing, or so the friends of Muhammad claim. They say that Dave stole it from the palace."

"But how could he have?"

"They don't always think logically."

"Are they really trying to kill us?"

"Maybe just trying to scare you. I didn't want to take that chance."

"Did Majed send you?"

"He was afraid something like this might happen. He sent me to protect you."

"I'm really grateful. Why didn't you identify yourself when you first started following me?"

"You didn't really give me a chance. You did quite well in losing me."

"Are you sure they didn't get to Dave?"

"They decided to go after you." The elevator door opened and Maura hurried out, running down the hall to their room. Ibrahim followed close behind her. When she knocked on the door, Dave answered it almost immediately.

"You're here," she shouted, falling into his arms.

"Of course. What's happened? Who's this?"

"Our guardian angel sent by Majed. He just saved my life." She turned to Ibrahim.

"Come in and close the door. Dave, this is Ibrahim. He's the man who brought me to the tent on the beach."

Dave shook the man's hand and turning to Maura said, "What do you mean 'saved your life'?"

"Some guys tried to kidnap me. Then when Ibrahim got me away from them, they started shooting at us. Jesus!" Maura shivered. "I almost got killed again."

Dave threw his arms up in exasperation. "What do they want from us?"

"Ibrahim thinks they might just want to scare us. But then there is the other possibility. . ."

"Well, as soon as Beth gets here with Khalil, we're leaving."

"Did you talk to her?"

"Yes. Khalil's out of jail and they should be here early in the morning."

"Great. I think there's a flight around 10:00 or so."

"Dave turned to Ibrahim. "How far do you think they'll go? Would they follow us to the States?"

Ibrahim tugged on his chin. "I don't know. I don't think they would go to the States, but maybe. Anyway, I am with you until you leave for America." Dave glanced around the room. "Don't worry, I have my own room next to yours. If you need to go out, call me. If someone comes to the door, call me before you answer it." Ibrahim got up to go. He seemed shy and uncomfortable in their presence.

When he had gone, Maura started to tremble. "I can't believe it, you know. . .it hits you afterward. . .so much has happened. . .these men said you were in danger. . .that I had to go with them. I thought they had kidnapped you again. . .I. . .I. . ." Dave put his arms around her and she burst into tears. The impact of the incident had just now reached her and made her unstable on her feet. It was hard to believe that this was the same woman who had shaken up McVee and DeVito at the consulate with her toughness, shot the guy in the boat. He liked that she could break down in the intimacy of his arms. He was in love with both of her characters.

Dave and Maura lay back and stretched out on the bed, holding each other tightly. "I'm really scared now, Dave. They could follow us anywhere, just pop up in the middle of dinner someplace and nab us or blow us away. I thought it would be over when we got out of there, but right now our lives aren't worth a hill of beans." The image made Dave chuckle. "Why are you laughing? It isn't funny?"

"It just sounded funny. And I'd rather laugh than cry right now. I guess being held a prisoner and then narrowly escaping death really woke me up, gave me a strong urge to live. Life seems very precious now. I don't think they'll follow us to the States. It'll all blow over in a while and then we can get back to some kind of normal life. And we can't live in fear when we have money to spend," he said sarcastically. "We can do all kinds of things like put a down payment on a house, buy a new car. Or fuck the security and get around-the-world air tickets and pick up things on the way to start our import store. We can't let a few crazy Saudis, or whoever they are, get the better of us." Dave stroked the nape of her neck and she was much calmer now.

"Don't stop," she said. "Keep talking. I like the sound of your voice close to my ear."

"I want to go visit Mom and Albert for a while. . .and Eddie. That'll give us time to think about what we want to do. They probably will try and talk us into not going back to Santa Rosa, but I don't think I could stomach living in Greenbrier. Anyway, we have enough money to keep us going for a while."

"And we have another mouth to feed," said Maura dreamily.

"What? You're kidding. You mean. . ."

"No. I mean Khalil. I feel kind of responsible for him."

"Oh." His face showed both disappointment and relief. "I guess I'm not quite ready for the other."

Maura laughed. "Yeah. I think getting settled would be a good idea first. But what about Khalil?"

"He should still have plenty of money left from Saudi Arabia. And if we did go through with the store idea, he'd be a good partner. He could do our buying in Arabic-speaking countries."

When Beth, Khalil and Jacques arrived at about 5:00 in the morning, Dave and Maura were still awake discussing plans for their future. . .and Khalil's if he was interested. The weary travelers knocked on the door. "It's us," called Beth, and Maura let them in. After hugging her sister, she went out into the hall to see if Ibrahim was at his post. She made a sign that everything was okay, and he ducked back into his room.

Khalil looked even more attractive than Maura remembered despite some dark circles under his eyes. He probably hadn't sleep much at the police station. Beth, on the other hand, was lively, wired from the trip and wanting to know the story of what had happened in Saudi Arabia immediately. She didn't seem the least bit uneasy that she might be in danger, too.

"Your own bodyguard and everything," she said wide-eyed after the long story was finished.

Jacques, who had been lost in the reunion melee, seemed to take the situation more seriously and wore a concerned look on his face throughout the telling of the story. "Have you contacted the authorities?" he asked.

"No," said Dave. "We figured the best thing for us to do was to leave the country as soon as possible and hope they don't follow."

As the men got into a discussion, Beth grabbed Maura, dragged her into the bathroom and closed the door. "Well, what do you think of him?"

"Who?"

"Jacques. Who do you think?"

"Well, he's. . .we haven't gotten to talk to him much. He's. . .nice looking. I thought he was your lawyer."

"It's all happened so fast. I've known him for a while, but nothing started until I began having trouble with the police. He's been wonderful and he seems to know all the right people, I mean in the police department and everything."

"That's great, Beth, if you're headed for a life of crime."

Beth laughed. "You're the one that got me started, remember that. Anyway, he's so kind. You don't meet many like him, especially at my age."

"What do you mean, at your age? You sound like an old woman. You're still young."

"Not for marriage."

Maura was shocked. "Is this Beth I hear talking? You want to get married?"

"Maybe not a formal one, but long-term companionship might be nice. I think I could stand having someone like him around full time."

"It's really easy to get used to. For a while there, I thought Dave was gone and I started thinking about what it would be like to be alone. . ." Maura was cut off by the sound of Dave shouting in the other room.

"Don't open it," he said. Khalil had started for the door when he heard the knock. Dave went for the phone, then gunfire sprayed into the wood around the lock and the door crashed open. The gunman hesitated, seeming surprised to see three men sitting in the room, but in his confusion he started shooting anyway. Ibrahim burst from his room and surprised the second gunman in the hall, firing two shots and knocking him to the floor. He then backed up against the wall and tried to peer around the corner into the room.

Dave, Khalil and Jacques had all fallen to the floor with bullet wounds. Dave took one in the arm. The gunman, surprised by the sound of firing in the hall, turned to point his Uzzi at the doorway. There was a momentary silence while the gunman started backing up toward the bathroom. Dave, who was lying on the floor between the man and the bathroom, reached out and grabbed his leg, throwing him off balance and sending him to the floor alongside him. The action caused an agonizing pain in his arm and he almost blacked out, but when he could see again, he found himself staring into the Arab's eyes, glazed with hatred. It was the third eye, however, the muzzle of the Uzzi pointed right at him, which caused his life to flash in front of him. At the same time he heard Maura scream his name through the bathroom door. Ibrahim rushed in the room, shouted in Arabic to the gunman on the floor and then fired two shots into his prone body. It all happened in a matter of seconds.

When the shooting started, Maura had lunged for the bathroom door, but Beth stopped her. "No, Maura, don't." Beth held her as tight as she could while Maura struggled and screamed, "Dave! Dave!" The shooting stopped and after a minute of the cruelest silence, Beth let her go. Maura rushed into the room and saw Dave standing next to Ibrahim, holding his bloody arm. They looked down at the man on the floor.

Maura stared at Dave's arm. "Oh, God, you've been shot!"

"Yeah. It's not that bad. Better get some help." Maura heard a woman out in the hall start screaming as she stepped over Jacques and Khalil to get to the telephone. While she called the hotel operator, she looked down on Khalil's white face and her stomach turned. He appeared dead. Then suddenly, his eyes opened and he tried to smile which quickly turned into a grimace as the bullet lodged in his hip sent out a surge of pain.

Beth emerged from the bathroom slowly, holding on to the molding of the doorframe, a petrified expression etched into the heavy make-up of her face. She edged around the bed and knelt down next to Jacques. He opened his eyes when she took his hand. "Jacques. Jacques. I'm so sorry." The front of his shirt was all bloody where a bullet had gone into his abdomen. He mumbled something. *"Ne parles pas, mon cher,"* she urged. *"Je m'occuperai de toi."*

On the other side of the bed, Ibrahim turned the gunman over on his back. "Is he dead?" Dave asked.

"Yes, very. An eye for an eye; a tooth for a tooth."

"What do you mean?"

"There is your brother's murderer."

Dave made no response, but the information hit its mark. Revenge, he thought, had come to him after all. Though it wasn't exactly sweet, there was a balance in it that appealed to him.

When Dave looked up from his thoughts, Ibrahim had slipped out of the room. He went after him, but a curious crowd had gathered in the hall and he couldn't tell which way the Arab had gone. The door to his room stood open and the room was empty, the bed made as if no one had occupied the room. Dave pushed through a bunch of onlookers to get back into his room and found Maura trying to comfort Khalil.

"Ibrahim's gone," said Dave. "Disappeared." Maura raised her head and nodded.

The police arrived in a few minutes, soon followed by the medics from the ambulance service. Dave and Maura spent the rest of the day between the hospital and the police station where they were questioned at length.

The German detective summarized the situation with a certain disgust. "Now let me see. We got you, an American couple working in Saudi Arabia and on your way back to the States. We got your sister, living in France, on 'holiday' here with her French boyfriend. We got a Lebanese, formerly worked in Saudi Arabia, now living in France and wants to go to the States. We got two dead Saudis, *mein Gott,* and we don't got another Lone Ranger-type who saved the day and now has disappeared. What does any of this have to do with Germany? I ask you. It's like the Jews and the Arabs who come here to do their dirty work and leave us with a mess. Why is that?"

Dave and Maura didn't know how to respond, not that the detective really expected them to. They both sat like zombies, staring at the German. Dave's newly bandaged arm throbbed. "Can we leave?" he asked.

"You mean my office or the country?"

"We want to go home."

"And what about your friends?"

"We will arrange a visa for Khalil to come to the States as soon as he can travel. Beth and Jacques will, I'm sure, return to France as soon as they can."

"And the mystery man?"

"I imagine he's on his way back to Saudi Arabia by now. We have no other information on him."

"All right, I let you go. Is better you leave before we are having more trouble." The remark broke through their numbness. More trouble? Could there be other assassins on the way? "Please leave an address where I can contact you," said the detective as he dismissed them.

That evening they were on a flight to New York where they would have to spend the night before going on to Greenbrier the next day.

17

Spring in Greenbrier

Dave sat in Joan and Albert's breakfast nook with his bandaged arm resting on the table. Maura stood behind him, leaning against the wall. Her right hand was placed lightly on his shoulder. Joan and Albert were across the table wrapped in expressions of confusion and disbelief as Dave told the story of how Eddie died and their terrifying adventures to find out why it had happened. Dave paused, and Maura went into the kitchen for the coffee pot to refill their cups. He kept getting distracted by the yellow roses and birds in the wallpaper surrounding them on three sides. He imagined Eddie coming around the corner with his sleepy eyes and crooked smile, making him realize it was all a bad dream. With his mind drifting, he went in and out of the story; some of his lapses were from lack of sleep and others deliberate as he edited out parts that would upset his parents more than need be. And when he got to the shoot out in Frankfurt, he watched Joan's face show every bit of the pain he had experienced in taking the bullet.

Albert put his hand on Joan's and squeezed. He spoke with an uneven, faltering voice. "I'm sorry you kids had to go through this. I just wish you had come to us sooner. We could have gone to the authorities, or somebody."

"Don't you see, Albert? Nobody was interested in truth or justice. Everybody wanted to sweep it under the carpet and be done with it. I knew something strange was going on when I saw Eddie's body in the funeral home, but if I had made a big stink about it, they would have come down hard on all of us then, and I never would have found out the truth."

"But you might have been killed," wailed Joan.

"I opened up a wound that was embarrassing to them. My only regret is that other people had to get hurt. I had to find out why it had happened. And very often, you don't get answers by going to the authorities, especially when they are the very ones who have a vested interest in keeping the why a secret. I just couldn't stand to have any more secrets in my life."

Albert blinked a couple of times and looked down at their joined hands. Dave felt Maura's fingers tense up on his shoulder. Joan, who had just taken a sip of coffee, resettled the Canonsbury Wild Clover cup into the exact center of the saucer with the tiniest clink, and then looked at her son as if she didn't quite understand the silence in the room. Dave's breathing stopped as he looked into his mother's eyes, holding her with his stare, not letting her go as he had a thousand times before.

Her upper lip began to twitch and her eyelids fluttered. The green overpowered the gray of her irises as if emerging from behind a cloud, and for one brief moment shined like polished jade. And in that moment, Dave saw that she knew everything, as a mother knows everything, the memories flooding her with pain and abomination, the guilt she had tucked away so long ago. And just when the wave threatened to turn her under, Dave softened his gaze, relaxed his jaw, and released her. He wasn't looking for confessions or apologies; it was too late for that. He only wanted to know if she knew what his father had done to him, the abuse he had suffered in the years before the man, who was now little more than a ghost, abandoned them.

Through the open window, spring floated in, riding on a wisp of daffodil. Dave breathed deeply and reached up, taking Maura's hand in his. "Anyway, we're home safe and sound."

"Thank God," said Albert in an exaggerated boom that cracked the tension in the air.

Dave got up and lifted his coat off the back of the chair.

"Where are you going?" asked Joan, her voice breaking with emotion.

"Just for a drive." Maura helped him put his coat on.

"Now? Don't you want Maura to go with you?" Maura looked at Joan and shook her head.

"I can drive as long as it's automatic."

"Well, be careful." Joan's eyes filled with tears again. She looked away. He kissed her on the forehead and then went out the door.

It was cold, but the sky was clear as Dave backed out of the driveway. He saw, under the trees with their new spring foliage, an orange-breasted robin hopping across the brown, flat grass of the yard. "Ah, spring," he said out loud.

Albert's Buick LeSabre Black Beauty floated along the roads, absorbing every bump, drifting around every curve, rolling up and down the gentle hills of Greenbrier and finally down to the road that snaked along the river. After a series of bends in the road, the muddy river came up against a dam, and on the other side of the dam was a lake that had been declared contaminated even before Lake Erie. The wooded river road climbed up to the main highway thick with traffic and he took it across a bridge to where the nice lakefront homes were. Then it narrowed and became less traveled as it passed through the old subdivisions and the new ones beyond them.

The car seemed to go by instinct while Dave's mind wandered through the many years he had ridden as a child, and then later as an adult, driven the road himself. And when he arrived at the sign for Meadows, where the family cemetery was, he remarked how close it was to Greenbrier, in contrast to the childhood memories, which had it so far. Just past the sign was a new shopping center with a supermarket where he stopped and bought some roses, all they had, about two dozen. They were red.

He threw them in the back seat and continued on to the cemetery, which sat between two old dilapidated farmhouses with wide porches sporting empty rockers. The farms attached to the houses had been eaten up by the developing town of Meadows. Across the road were new tract homes with cemetery views if they ever bothered to look out their closed and curtained windows with the heat on all winter and the air conditioning on all summer. On the back side of the cemetery a woods had survived, offering the mourners a direction to look during the burial when they wanted to think of their loved ones being in a peaceful place.

The Buick glided into the deserted, rundown graveyard, which look like a place where they didn't bury people anymore. Then Dave spotted Eddie's burnished new stone that stood out among the old weathered ones. He got out of the car and approached it timidly, his arms laden with roses, and crouching down, he laid the flowers on the grave next to a bouquet of daisies and irises that Joan must have brought that morning. He sat down and started picking off the yellow leaves from the rose stems.

"Hi, Eddie. I brought you some flowers. . .a bunch of them. . .roses. That seemed appropriate. They smell real nice." He stretched out alongside the grave and leaned on his good arm. The sun had gone down behind the trees and enriched everything from its hiding place with a golden light. The air was very still, but he could smell a wood fire coming from one of the farmhouses.

"I miss you, Eddie. I miss you a lot. It's kind of hard to put into words, like an empty space inside me, an empty pain. It's strange to think of emptiness causing pain. Remember how we always used to wonder what a bullet felt like every time we saw those people on TV and in the movies getting shot up? Now I know and it's nothing like the pain you feel when someone is taken away unexpectedly. Of course, I just got it in the arm and maybe it's not fair to compare. I never imagined it would be you. I thought about Mom dying someday, but never you. You were so much a part of me that I assumed you'd always be there. I don't know if any of this makes sense. Things have been all jumbled up in my head since you went away. I nearly got Maura and me killed a couple of times trying to find out what happened to you. But while I was doing it, I felt closer to you. I talked to and touched people who were the last to talk to and touch you. I guess what I'm trying to say is I love you. . . and I never knew how much until you were gone. And when I got pissed off at you for the dumb things you did, it didn't matter. That time we made a crummy shelter at the beach, it didn't matter. None of the fights or arguments we had matters now.

"So don't get mad at me. I have to tell you something, something I should have told you a long time ago. I planned to, but there was always an excuse, and then it was too late. Our father, our real father, didn't die in a car accident on a business trip. He killed himself right there in our garage. Everybody hushed it up to protect you, and so mom could recuperate from her breakdown without being reminded of what a disaster her marriage had been. As time went on, it became easier to perpetuate a myth rather than deal with the truth. So the guilt I felt never had a chance to get out. You see, he had feelings that he didn't know what to do with, a sickness. He brought it to me. That night when you and I got drunk, I didn't hit you because you were trying to crawl in bed with me. I opened my eyes and in my drunkenness saw, not you, but him standing over me. It brought back things that I had tried so hard to forget. I lashed out. But I could never tell you why without telling the whole story.

"He made me promise not to tell the things that he was doing to me, that people wouldn't understand. And I didn't tell for a long time. The day before he sailed out into the great unknown in his beloved T-bird, Miss Johnson—remember the evil Miss J.?—got angry with me for not paying attention in school, said I had been staring out the window for weeks and she was tired of it. I was sent to a counselor who somehow got me to spill the beans. Stan, that was his name in case you don't remember, must have got wind of it, or they contacted him. I don't know. Maybe he just woke up that day and decided he couldn't take the family life anymore. Who knows? In my nine-year-old head and for years after that, it was all my fault.

"Until today I never knew if mom was aware what was going on. We're all pretty good at ignoring things we can't deal with. Cover-ups. The world is full of cover-ups. I've been pretty good at it myself. But you know what? When I saw him that day in his car with the garage full of exhaust, I was glad, glad that he wouldn't do anything that would hurt you, that you were safe. Even back then I wanted to protect you. In the end, I guess I didn't do a very good job. When you were killed, the guilt came back all over again, that I had failed you in some way. It seems all my life I have felt guilty about one thing or another. And then a few days ago, when the gunman burst into the hotel room and started shooting...well, I survived. The second time in a couple of days when I should have been a dead man. Why? Why are you and our father in the ground, and I'm still here? There's no rhyme or reason to it. It's not fair. It just is. No amount of guilt is going to change it. The living must go on living."

His lips almost touched the brown dead grass that surrounded Eddie's grave. It gave off a scent of the world getting ready to spring to life. He grabbed a hunk of it, pulled it up by its roots, and then tossed it aside. "Okay, enough of that. I'm not going to cry. It's too fucking cold out here."

He touched the bare spot he had created, and whispered, "I'm sorry, Eddie, if I hurt you. I'm sorry I never told you things I should have."

Dave fished from his coat pocket the now torn and tattered pages of Eddie's journal he had been carrying around for weeks. "I wanted to read something of yours here, so I think I'd better do it now while there's still some light." He unfolded the pages, pressed them flat in front of him. He also took out the dessert rose that Khalil had given him in Frankfurt, the one he had found in his truck the day after he met Eddie. Dave used it as a paperweight to hold the pages from being taken away by the wind.

There are two sunsets in this land: one false, one true. One when the sun drops behind the layer of haze which perpetually lounges on the horizon, and the second when the sun edges over the horizon itself, throwing Arabia into true dusk.

Islam has a method for determining true dusk as it's the time of day for the Maghreb (Sunset) prayer call. Before the modern system of scientifically determined prayer times, the caller at each mosque would lay a black thread and a white thread across his wrist and at the point, in natural light, when he could no longer distinguish the difference, he would call out for prayer to begin.

On the streets in Saudi Arabia, men traditionally wear white and women black. But in the failing light of nightfall, Arab men sometimes have a difficulty telling the difference between black and white and find themselves in the intimate embrace of a brother or friend.

There is also a tradition in Arabia to think of after sunset as the time of day for life to really begin. This is especially true during the religious month of Ramadan when no food or drink including water may pass the lips between dawn and sunset.

I remember one night, beginning a search for a brother or friend while the shops were closing for prayer. The screeching metal doors slid down the tight tracks cutting through the heavy night air, sounding like a scream until it was drowned by the sudden shotlike explosion of the fully extended doors striking the pavement. From across the street came the clang of gates brought together and the eerie rattle of a chain joining them in a clumsy embrace. These sounds echoed up and down the street as a car sped by honking at each intersection sending shadowy figures scurrying, gripping more tightly the plastic shopping bags which dangled from their wrists. Men ducked into cars and alleys as the rags on their heads flapped with the sudden haste.

The Filipinos, Thais and Indians gathered in groups in front of the secured shops, holding on to each other, unsmiling, waiting for what was coming next. And then it began, the low wail fanning out over the dirty desert town on the thick air, sending a shiver through the infidels. Allahu Akbar. The doleful sound grew, crackling and sputtering, trying the limit of the speakers until it had penetrated everything. And just as the shock wore off, another call began from the opposite direction, rolling over the minglers from a more distant tower. We, the imported workers, caught between the two calls, stared straight ahead, blank-faced, and quickly touched our back pockets to remind ourselves that the fat wallets were real. For we are the lost, the seekers who have brought our plight to the Arabian sands, and some of us will be delivered; the rest will be buried under the sand like the desert roses which cannot bloom by day and must flower in the darkness.

Dave pulled his coat tight around him and rested his head on his arm. He closed his eyes. "I'm so tired," he said. His hand stretched out and knocked the desert rose off the pages. A breeze rose up, peeling the papers off one by one, carrying them away. He dreamed of an old, empty house where he walked from room to room in the darkness. He curled up on a Bukhara rug in the corner of a large room and fell asleep. Then a warm hand began to stroke his head and for a moment he thought. . .

"Dave, are you okay? I was worried about you. I guess you fell asleep." It was dark and his joints were stiff from the cold ground. He rolled over and saw Maura crouched over him.

"Hi," he said. "Help me up?" Maura took his good arm and helped hoist him to his feet. He stared at the disorderly and crumpled pile of journal pages stuck under her arm, and then his gaze moved past her to one of the old farmhouses across the way. It was all lit up now, and from its chimney gray smoke curled against the black starry sky.

"On the way out here," Maura began, "I reached into my pocket, and look what I found." She pulled out the desert rose that Ibrahim had given her as a sign from Majed. She crouched down and placed it by Eddie's headstone, next to the one Dave had brought.

"I'm glad you came to get me," said Dave, kneeling down next to her. He broke a rose off its stem and gave it to her. "It's from Eddie."

They started for the car and Maura cradled the cool petals of the rose under her nose. Then she looked back over her shoulder and said, "Thanks, Eddie."

ABOUT THE AUTHOR

Vincent Meis grew up in Decatur, Illinois. From there he went south, and then east, and then west. Eventually he would cross the great oceans. For the last twenty years he has lived in San Francisco and taught English as a Second Language at the City College of San Francisco. He has also taught English in Saudi Arabia, Spain, and Mexico.

Made in the USA
Charleston, SC
14 August 2011